Promise Her

Military Men of Lexington

Her

D1636796

andrea johnston

For everyone that suffers in silence.
Find the light in each day and keep fighting.

Promise Her

Military Men of Lexington

Andrea Johnston

Prologue

Taylor, 18 years old

When I was a kid my grandpa would tell me one day I would stand at a crossroads in life. The path I chose would determine the type of man I would become. As a ten-year-old, I didn't have a damn clue what he meant. A crossroads? Like a fork in the road? A four-way stop that always made my dad cuss up a storm at the "damn fools who won't move their ass"? I was never really sure, but Grandpa seemed confident the day would come, and I idolized my Grandpa, so I waited. And waited. For years.

As I stand before the white brick building with posters hanging in the windows, a different branch of the military depicted in each one, I'm at that crossroads Grandpa mentioned. This was not my plan in the slightest. I've busted my ass on the football field since I was six years old with one goal in mind—play college ball. Not just any college ball but for a D-I school.

I've shattered every record in state and my goal is within reach, I just have to choose it. The offer is sitting there, waiting for me to sign on the dotted line, to commit to the program and my future. My dad thinks I'll go all the way to the pros and doesn't understand my hesitation. Joining the military was never something I considered. Sure, I have friends who've known this was the only answer for them. That on their eighteenth birthday, they'd stand here, in front of this building, the benefits of joining the service more than they could pass up. Stepping through these doors doesn't mean I'm giving up on my dreams, it only means I'm choosing a different fork in the road. I'm at my crossroads.

"Ya ready to do this, man?"

I stumble forward as my best friend, Henry Gilbert, smacks me on the shoulder. Henry has always known the military was his way out. His way out of this city, out of his family's downward spiral, and mostly his way to a better life. Education, travel, and a skill set that doesn't compare to anything else, he's been talking about enlisting since we were fifteen years old.

When our country was attacked on our own soil, his determination to enlist only grew. What he didn't think would ever happen is me standing here with him, my hand poised to open the door and change the course of my life. But, that day, watching as our nation mourned tremendous loss, I felt compelled to do something. Playing ball is great, and it's always been part of who I am. Yet, as I sat staring at the television and watching the news coverage, I knew, in that moment, there was a different path for me. I was at my crossroads.

"I don't know that we'll ever be ready for this," I reply, taking in a deep breath as I ready myself for this next step.

"Don't be a fucking pussy, Taylor. Speaking of, imagine all the pussy we're going to get once we wear that uniform. The ladies love a man in uniform."

"Jesus, Lyle. Do you always have to be so crass?" I ask our buddy. This decision is his only choice unless he wants to end up in prison. His reputation alone has him on a first-name basis with the police, but it's the crew he runs with when he isn't hanging with us that will be his demise. Bad news doesn't begin to cover it.

Henry high fives Lyle after his comment, and I roll my eyes at both of them. Henry tries to play it tough but, the reality is he isn't that guy. Besides, you'd think by now he would have taken a cue from me—you catch more flies with honey than vinegar. If he did, he wouldn't still be carrying his "V" card around with him, right next to his driver's license.

"Look guys, I've waited for this day for a long time. You know my only plan for my eighteenth birthday was to enlist and then go find some whiskey and a hot little number to celebrate with," Henry reminds us.

I look to Lyle who only shrugs. I want to point out that none of us are old enough to buy booze, but Henry cuts me off before I can. "Don't be such a fucking baby about it, Taylor. Man up. Or do you think you can't handle it, pretty boy? That's what this is about, isn't it? You're scared. That's fine. I'm not. I'll fight for my country with pride while you crack the books and live the high life like your mommy and daddy want you to."

Glaring at Henry, I release the handle of the door and turn to face him fully. I'm taller and bigger than both these guys. I could beat his ass here in front of the recruiters' office. I won't. This is how *he* gets when he's nervous and feels alone.

I've known him my entire life and am used to his bullshit. His outbursts and jabs at me and my family aren't anything new. He doesn't complain when my parents embrace him as one of their own, but then he goes home to the squalor and the fighting, and the green-eyed monster appears. If his parents are deep in their boozing, he lashes out with a shove or offer to kick my ass. I take the brunt of his frustration because I know he is hurting and not because he doesn't care. Our childhoods were polar opposites, but we've always been there for each other. Even when he pulls this kind of shit.

"Have no doubt, I am not scared. This is our life, Henry, and I don't take mine or yours lightly. I can't wait for basic and see how much the drill sergeants make you cry when you mouth off to one of them like you just did to me." Without another word, I open the door to the recruitment office. Ushering in Henry and Lyle, I take another deep breath before slowly exhaling and sending up a little prayer that we aren't making the biggest mistake of our lives. And that my dad doesn't kill me for choosing a life in the military over playing football.

Scarlett, 16 years old

Your sixteenth birthday is supposed to be special. It isn't called a "Sweet Sixteen" for nothing. Except, my parents don't believe in huge celebrations to mark milestones like a birthday. No, their idea of a special birthday is a new car with a big bow and photographic evidence to include in the family Christmas card. The sole purpose is not to reward their child for hard work and dedication to their education. No, it is simply to show the world how perfect their lives are.

Perfection.

A level I've worked my entire sixteen years to reach only to come up short each time. My brother, Maxwell, is my father's doppelganger in appearance but my mother's in drive and ambition. At twenty, he's set himself up to graduate from college a year early and if he follows the *perfect* plan he's established, he'll be sitting for the state bar and taking his place as one of the youngest associates at my mother's law firm by the time I finish my first year of college. Maxwell, never Max, only ever his full name, is an overachiever to the max. Ha! I love saying things like that because it pisses him off.

Looking at my reflection in the full-length mirror, I assess my appearance, finding every physical flaw and wishing I had it in me to conform to what my parents want. Just for once I wish I didn't feel an overwhelming need to stand up for myself, to argue what I think is best for me over what my parents tell me I should do. Why can't I be more like my sister?

Eliza lucked out not only in the looks department but she also won the genetics lottery when it comes to book smarts and a sense of humor. She's a master at working my parents' expectations. Fall in line. Don't argue. Play the game until you are on your own.

While I'm smart enough, it's not "Hamilton Smart" as my parents like to call it. Living in a home with four intellectuals is exhausting, and the fact that they label everything with our last name is embarrassing. "Hamilton Smart," "Hamilton Humor," and the ever popular "Hamilton Way" is beyond pretentious.

Pulling a cardigan from my closet, I take one final look at my appearance in the mirror. My auburn hair is pulled back in a low ponytail and I have on just the right amount of makeup to feel confident, but my mother won't know there is any on. Because Hamilton women don't use their looks to get ahead in life. I look like the average teenager ready to spend her Saturday studying in the library, working hard to raise my GPA. What they don't know is I'll be spending the day like I do two Saturdays a month. Volunteering at the local senior center. Caring for others is my passion. Being around people and making them smile is what makes me happy and something I have vowed to pursue after high school.

Slinging my purse across my body and picking up my backpack, I quickly close my bedroom door and take the stairs two at a time as I rush out the front door. The best way to avoid the looks of disappointment in my parents' eyes and the annoyance of my siblings is to not allow an opportunity for engagement.

College can't get here soon enough and if I'm lucky, not only will it bring me freedom, but I'll also find my path in life. Friendship, happiness, and love. I don't want a big career or need professional accolades to feel complete. I only want to find happiness with a man who will love me for who I am. True all-consuming love that makes a person believe happily ever after exists. Some may call me a hopeless romantic and, well, those people would be right.

"It takes a minute to find a special person, an hour to appreciate them, and a day to love them, but it takes an entire lifetime to forget them." – *Author Unknown*

Chapter 1

Taylor

"Baby, I don't know why you're playin' hard to get. You know you like what I'm offerin'." This guy has been throwing lines at every woman who has stepped up to my bar tonight, and I'm about done listening to him. Own a bar they said. It'll be fun they said. Actually nobody said that and if they had, they'd be sorely mistaken. Being a bar owner is not only hard work but when you continue to schedule yourself for shifts behind the bar, it's frustrating.

Normally I have a high tolerance for the shit some of these guys say. If there was a category for pick-up lines and come-ons on a game show, I'd win every round. And, it isn't just the men. The flirtatious women who push the limits with their plunging necklines, come hither smiles, and breathy voices are nearly as bad.

Mr. Hard-to-Get has turned this sweet young woman into a sudden mute. Eyes blinking rapidly and mouth wide open like a fish on a hook, I'm giving her ten seconds before I step in. While I wait for her to put him in his place,

I quickly replace a few of the empty beer bottles for the group to my left, barely taking my eyes off the scene before me.

The sounds of the bar are like white noise to me now. It wasn't always that way. I relished in the excitement and fed off the energy of a bustling bar. Clanking of beer bottles as they're thrown in the garbage, the laughter and high fives amongst the patrons. Every sound fueled me. Now, I don't hear it. I'm more focused on the next customer in front of me, needing to anticipate their need, recognize when they need to slow down, and in a case like this, possibly intervene and escort one of them out the door.

Country Road is my baby, and I'm proud of what I've done with the place. The traces of the old honky tonk it once was still linger around the edges but the space has morphed into more of a local watering hole with a hint of sports bar that has an occasional live music night. Everyone is welcome, and that's why we're the most popular bar in the area.

Six years ago when I left my military life behind me, I found myself on the back of my bike, traveling across the state of Texas toward the Gulf. Exhausted and starving, I stopped in the small town of Lexington. A cold beer and a burger was my plan, but when I stepped into the loud bar with too many pool tables and not enough tables, I found a frazzled bar owner and his side kick getting their asses handed to them. As I waited to order my beer, people were getting rowdy and a few customers started mouthing off. I stepped in and played the role of bouncer to settle things down. It's something I'd been doing for years with my unit, so it wasn't a stretch for me. The owner thanked me and, when things calmed down, bought me a beer. We spent the last hours the bar was open talking and when I was still in town three days later, he asked if I was looking for a job.

Even in those early days, I knew being behind the bar wasn't going to be forever. Tonight, as I stand here counting down from ten, waiting for the petite blonde to put this guy in his place, I know my nights slinging beers are coming to an end. I'll stick to paperwork and lunch crowds to avoid this shit.

"Can I get you another cranberry juice, sweetheart?" I ask the girl, breaking up their conversation. She visibly relaxes at my interruption and nods her head. As I pick up her empty glass and replace it with a fresh drink, I turn to the guy.

"Looking to close out?"

Scowling, he barely glances. "Nah man, we're good."

I wait a beat to see if he gives me his full attention. When he doesn't, I turn around and pull his card from the counter. "I meant I'm closing you out. Tonight's on me. Do you need a rideshare or cab?"

Glaring, he looks down at my hand where his card sits between my fingers. Looking from the card and up to me and then the girl, he growls and snaps the card from my hand. Stomping away, I watch his group of friends follow him. Once they're out the door, I turn my attention back to the young girl in front of me.

"You okay?"

"Yeah, thanks for that."

"No worries. Where are your friends?"

"At our table. I just needed a break from"—she waves her hand around behind her— "that. It's a lot. So loud and so drunk. Being the designated driver is nice when I have an early class tomorrow but sucks when everyone is so annoying."

Laughing, I nod in understanding and top off her juice

as my name is called from the far end of the bar. One of the servers is holding the phone up like I have a call. I sent in an order for liquor earlier, and it's a little heavier than usual. I'm sure it's my rep confirming I haven't lost my mind in the amount of whiskey I ordered. I motion I'll be right there and turn back to the customer.

"You try to enjoy yourself, and if anyone else gives you trouble, just let someone on staff know. Okay?"

"I will. Thank you again." Her shoulders have dropped, and her smile is genuine. This is how my customers should be, not feeling blocked in and pressured by some asshat with an attitude.

I knock on the bar twice and walk away. Taking the cordless phone, I hold it to my chest and say, "Thanks. I'll take this in the office."

In a few steps, I'm out of the main area of the bar where it's a little quieter and bring the phone to my ear while pulling my keys from my pocket and unlocking the office door.

"This is Taylor."

"Sugar." I don't recognize the voice but the only people who still call me by my bootcamp nickname are guys I served with. Or, of course, my sister when she's a pain in my ass.

"Who is this?"

"It's Connor. Uh, Twig."

Wow, Connor Hall. Talk about a blast from the past. It's been at least a year since I've seen or heard from him. Only a few years younger than I am, Connor joined the military later in life and discharged early for medical reasons. It's such a crazy coincidence how many of us former military, men who served together or have met through the years, are living in Texas.

"Hey man, what's up?"

"It's Wolf, man. He's . . . he . . . there was an accident. He's gone."

Pausing just inches from my desk chair, I shake my head. It's an instant reaction when you think you've heard something wrong.

"What? What did you say?"

Maybe if he repeats it, I'll understand. Maybe he'll say something different and not what I heard.

"It was an accident. He was just getting ice cream, man. One more deployment. That's all. How could he survive it all only to have this happen?"

My friend's sobs fill the line, and I'm stunned. Blown away and confused.

Henry Gilbert is dead. My best friend for most of my life died.

Pulling the chair out, I settle behind my desk. Needing to understand, I cut him off. "Are you sure? I mean, maybe he'll pull through. How's Scarlett? She wasn't with him, was she? The baby? Oh shit, Connor . . . man, tell me they're okay."

"It's not a mistake. Red was at home. She's in shock, I think. Hell, we all are. Cap is with her now. The doctor gave her something to relax and get some rest. I have seen some fucked-up shit, Taylor, but this was an accident. He was just getting his wife ice cream. His *pregnant* wife."

I try to keep up with what he's saying, but it's more than I can handle. "Twig, I have to go. I'll call you back." Hanging up, I sit for a few minutes. My eyes focus on the calendar hanging on the wall. It's still showing January, and I think for just a minute I should get up and change it.

Yet, I can't move. I've lost a lot of people in my life. Men in my unit, guys I grew up with. My parents.

This is different. Henry was more than my friend. He was my brother in every way that mattered. His life was just beginning. Wiping the tears that have fallen from my eyes, I take in a deep breath, pull my cell phone from my pocket, and call my sister, Addison.

"Little brother."

"Addy . . ." My voice breaks, and I suck back a new batch of emotion. "It's Henry. There was an accident. He didn't make it."

The line is quiet for a few minutes, her sniffles the only sound. "Are you sure?" Her voice is quiet like she's afraid to speak the words.

"Yeah." It's one word but all I can give her right now.

I let her cry, wishing I could hold her and comfort her. Wishing we could comfort each other. For Addison, Henry and I were more than her annoying little brother and his friend. Sometimes we were her allies and others her defenders. She loved him as much as I did.

"Addy, are you okay?"

"I'm just numb, Tay. I don't understand."

"I know, sis. I know. I'm going to settle things here and call Connor and Grant. I'll keep you posted."

She whispers, "Okay" before ending the call.

Not prepared to deal with this just yet, I set the phone down and rest my head in my hands. I don't bother to hold in the emotions boiling inside of me; letting them pour from me like a faucet. I learned years ago it's better to let the pain out. When you don't, it will eat you up inside. What's left is a shell filled with a new kind of pain.

Chapter 2

Scarlett

When I was young, I hated washing dishes. I thought it was gross and didn't understand how you could use the same water that dirty plates and cups sat in to make those same things clean. It made no sense to me. Looking into a sink full of lemon scented suds, I see a piece of food float to the top and cringe.

Gross. It turns out I still don't like washing dishes. But, putting them in the dishwasher gave me nothing to do. And I need to stay busy. If I stop then everyone sitting in my living room will want to talk to me. Or ask me questions I don't want to answer. Again. Am I okay? Do I feel okay? Do I want to rest for a bit?

Until last night, I never realized how little I like being the center of attention. I appreciate the concern, but I don't have answers for their questions. So instead, I keep washing dishes and hope they leave me alone.

Staring out my kitchen window, I watch a pair of small birds land on a branch. Their little wings flutter as they settle. I wonder if they're a couple or just friends. Do they know each other, or are they strangers who happened upon the same tree branch?

Random questions like that have been running through my head all day. When you stop talking and just listen, your mind wanders. Sometimes it ventures into a dark corner and other times it's the bright sunlight. Looking at these birds is part of the sunlight. Maybe their story is just beginning. A hope for a new life together.

"Scarlett, honey?" A large warm hand grips my shoulder, pulling my attention from the window.

Turning my head but not moving my hands from the dishwater, I turn to my friend. Grant Ellison has been a great friend to both Henry and me over the years and was the first person I called when the police arrived at my house following the accident. A former captain in the U.S. Army, he's a strong presence with an absolute no-bullshit aura about him. He's tried to be strong for me and I appreciate that. Grant is a good man. Kind and giving, it makes me sad he doesn't have a partner in life. A woman to be cared for and loved by him. Children to be raised by a man with more integrity than most will ever know.

"Hmm?" I ask, looking back at the dishes as I dip them in the clear water and place them in the dish rack.

"Honey, you have been washing these dishes for over an hour."

"Oh." I look into the sink and notice the suds are almost gone. The water is no longer warm, and my fingers have started to prune.

Taking the offered dishtowel, I dry my hands and watch as Grant reaches into the sink and releases the plug. Water swirls down the drain, a strange gulping sound as the last bit leaves the sink. I feel like my life is just like that water, spinning and slowly draining until the last gurgle. Not the greatest metaphor but it's the best I can do right now.

"I spoke to Taylor, and he'll be here in a couple of days. Mercy and Shane have left, but I'm worried about you. I know you haven't eaten much today. Why don't I make you something, and if you're really nice, I'll sit through one of those saccharine sweet movies you like so much."

Smiling, I lift my hand to his cheek and pat it once. "You're too good to me. I do have a bit of a headache, so I'll give you a pass on the movie." Placing my hand on my baby bump, I sigh and close my eyes.

"Have a seat and I'll heat something up for you. We have like six casseroles and three pies. Any requests?"

"Nothing too spicy. I feel a little sick."

"So no pie either?"

"Let's not get carried away. I know those are Vera's pies, so don't even think of holding out on me." I point my finger at him to drive home my seriousness.

Laughing, he rummages in the refrigerator and appears with a blue casserole dish. If memory serves, that's from Mrs. Abbott. Shane's mother is an amazing cook, and I sit up a little in my seat at the prospect of her food. While the microwave ticks, Grant pulls one of my fizzy waters from the refrigerator and flips the tab before placing the can in front of me.

Taking a sip, I let the little bubbles pop on my tongue and a small smile appears on my lips. With just Grant and me here, I feel like I can finally relax a little. It's been an overwhelming and horrifying twenty-four hours. Henry and I were settling into our new normal. Making plans for co-parenting and how we'd announce to our friends, who are actually our family, we were ending our marriage. Only, we didn't have an opportunity. Instead, just weeks before he was set to deploy for the last time, he was struck by a drunk driver.

And didn't come home. The tears fall freely from my eyes, dropping on to my black shirt. Looking down, I see the bump and the tears turn to sobs instantly. Our son will never know his father. Henry will never see our child grow and learn to walk or swing a bat. Gone are his opportunities to share his knack for a good knock-knock joke and his love for fishing. Missed opportunities for us to find our new version of family.

"Oh Red," Grant says as he squats to eye level. His hand rests atop mine, and I smile through the tears.

"I think I'm just going to lie down."

Rising from the table, I take my water and head for my bedroom. Not bothering to change, I simply kick off my shoes and crawl on top of the covers. Settling onto my left side, I run my hand along the opposite side of the bed. Henry's side. It's been months since he's slept there, but tonight I wish I could reach out and touch him. To know he's okay.

I've loved Henry Gilbert for ten years and for each of those years, I prepared myself for his deployments and the possibility he may not return. What I didn't know was that one senseless act would completely change everything I had prepared for.

Chapter 3

Taylor

I always imagined bad news would come in the middle of the night. At least, that's how it happens in the movies. Unfortunately, this isn't a movie, and it isn't often that life works out as you imagined.

I'm still reeling from the news I received two days ago. It's been five years since I've felt the damn devastation that runs through my veins. The last time came in the form of an IED. It was a split-second swerve that changed the lives of so many. I lost a lot of my brothers that day, not even sure if I would make it home in one piece. Losing men in combat, saying my own goodbye to them, was something I learned to accept and work through over the years. That last deployment was when I knew I was done. Done facing mortality daily.

This loss is different, more personal. Henry Gilbert has been my best friend since we were old enough to ride our bikes without training wheels. We grew up together, we became soldiers together, and somewhere along the way, we grew apart. No longer as close as siblings, our bond would never falter. Regardless of how much time we spent out of contact, he remained my brother by choice.

And now he's gone.

Dead.

It doesn't seem possible. Yet, I know it is. I'll never forget my pain as Connor's words filled the line with the news. Memories of our life growing up together consumed my mind and kept me from sleeping all night. When you're young, you never think of death. It's something that happens to other people, never to you. Your best friend is supposed to be with you for life. Through good times and bad. Henry and I grew up in completely different homes, our home lives polar opposites. But it was through those differences that we bonded, and through it all we were always there for each other.

When I enlisted, I was forced to alter the way I viewed death. It was no longer an unattainable notion but a reality. And still, I can't believe this has happened to him. To us. At a time when he was venturing into a new phase of life as a father, all of it was stolen from him.

Once, under the stars as we camped in my backyard, I promised I'd always be there for him. My family was a safe place for him to fall. I'll keep that promise for his own family. For his wife and child, a safe place for them to escape if necessary.

Pulling back on the throttle of my bike, I let the engine roar, the vibrations in my hands an anchor to the moment. I approach the sign in the distance at a rapid speed. A rest stop is in a few miles. Looking to the vast road ahead of me with nothing but my thoughts and the crisp air to keep me company, I have to stop and check in with my sister. Addy hated the day I bought my bike, and before I left this morning, she sent me a text making me promise I would check in through my drive. I'm sure the fact that Henry was out on a road similar to this when he had his accident is fresh in her mind.

She hates this bike and everything it stands for. That's likely attributed to the fact that the first time my nephew saw it, he thought it was cool as hell and told her when he was old enough, he'd have one just like it. Mason may look at this bike like it's a cool piece of machinery, a means to get from point A to point B while looking badass, but it's more for me.

My bike and the open road have always been how I've dealt with the demons that lurk deep in my subconscious. A lot of men I served with, those who made it home, have found their solace in many forms. I've watched men self-destruct after suffering horrific injuries or were unable to let go of the memories. If I've learned anything in my dozen years in the Army, it's that not all scars lie on the surface. Some of the worst scars rest below the surface and only those who bare them can fully understand their depth.

I worked hard after each deployment to seek the help I needed to process through my feelings. To work the demons that haunted me each night as I closed my eyes. They may never completely go away, but if I can keep them to a dull whisper and not the roaring storm they once were, I'll be okay. I'll survive.

The same can't be said for others. Henry was one of those who refused to seek guidance and support when he needed it most. He needed that intervention long before he enlisted. Long before he was faced with some of the darkest days of his life.

Our friendship was tested over the years, but nothing caused a rift between us, brothers by choice at a young age, until Scarlett. Henry's inability to appreciate the gift he had at home pissed me off. The chip on his shoulder grew and festered with each deployment. By the time I accepted my discharge, he was bitter and angry. Angry at the world, at himself, and oddly enough, at me.

And I was angry at him. Unlike me, or some of the other soldiers we were close to, Henry had someone waiting for him at home. A beautiful, loving, and patient woman who loved him with all her heart. A smile, the first I've allowed in days, appears at the thought of Scarlett.

I've always admired a woman who wears her confidence and independence like a badge of honor. The night Henry and Scarlett met, I knew she was that kind of woman. Strong, independent, and confident, Scarlett Gilbert is every man's dream come true, and Henry was the lucky bastard she loved.

As more memories of Henry flood my mind, I let off the throttle, slowing to pull into the rest stop. The stop is relatively deserted but there are a few families standing around talking and an older man walking a dog on the grass. Wanting a little privacy for my call, I drive to the far end of the parking lot near a large tree. Once I park and dismount, I pull off my gloves and helmet. Secured, I pull my phone from my saddle bag and press my sister's number.

"Hey," she says quietly. This loss is hitting her hard, and I imagine it's bringing with it the memories of losing our parents years ago.

"Checking in as ordered."

"Thank you. How far out are you?"

"Not too long. Couple of hours. You holding up okay?"

Sniffling, she doesn't say anything for a few minutes. I give her time and walk around a little. I'm not as young as I once was and not too proud to admit I'm a little stiff from the long drive.

"Yeah. Landon has been great. Apparently, we're going camping."

Barking out a laugh, I welcome the sound of her soft chuckles on the other side. "Do not laugh. It's true. Be safe and I'll see you in a few days."

"I'll let you know when I get there."

We say our goodbyes, and I end the call. Before putting the phone away, I pull up Grant's contact information and send off a quick text. When I first met Grant Ellison, he was a mean sonofabitch. Or at least I thought he was. I was a punk kid a little too arrogant and confident, certain I knew more than I really did. He not only put me in my place but saw something in me I never knew was there. Taking me under his wing, I learned a lot about being a soldier and leader from this man.

Moving to Fayhill a few years after his retirement, he found a small community of like-minded ex-military men and women and easily transitioned to civilian life. It's also how Henry and Scarlett found themselves settling there. Grant opened his life to them and I'm grateful he's been the one to be there these last few days.

Me: I'm about 2 hours out.

The three dots jump and stop before jumping again with a response to follow.

Grant: See you then. We're at my house.

Me: 10-4

Slipping the phone in my pocket, I head for the large

building housing the bathrooms before I head toward what I'm sure is going to be an exhausting and intense few days.

As I approach the town of Fayhill, I slow my bike to a reasonable speed and sit back a little, letting myself relax. A small diner catches my attention, and I contemplate stopping. Convenience store snacks don't offer nearly enough nutritional value for the drive I just made. But a shower and a beer sound a lot more enticing. When I approach the end of Main Street, I spy a gas station and pull in to top off before heading to my destination. While I wait for the pump to click the tank is full, I tap out a quick text to Grant that I should be at his place in less than ten minutes.

Placing my phone in my saddlebag, I cross my arms and wait. Taking in the town around me, I can see the draw. In the few minutes I've been standing here, I've only seen one or two cars, and only a handful of people roam the streets. It isn't hard to imagine why so many ex-military settle in Fayhill and the surrounding towns. This town is the polar opposite of every aspect of deployment. There's no shouting, gunfire, or explosions to be found.

Once the pump clicks its completion, I return the nozzle to the cradle and strap on my helmet. Sliding on the bike, I cringe as the engine roars to life. Normally, the loud sound is more like white noise to me, but here it sounds ten times louder. "Sorry," I mumble to myself as I exit the station and am back on the road to Cap's house.

Fayhill is the epitome of small town, so it only takes a few minutes to make it across town and to the neighborhood my friends live in. I've been here once or twice before and appreciate his home for what it is—small and temporary. The term "cookie cutter" comes to mind as I spy people gardening and mowing lawns, and kids shooting baskets in their driveways.

The fact that a neighborhood like this exists in Fayhill is a surprise. The houses, while all very similar in appearance, are great starter homes. A lot of guys we know from our military days are looking for towns like this to start their families or to reconnect with civilian life without the overwhelming obstacles city life brings.

This isn't the type of place Cap talked about when he'd fill the quiet nights with his plans after retirement. Rolling hills, a place to fish, and neighbors far enough away you could go days without seeing them. Those were his requirements for life after the military. Truthfully, I never expected him to retire. I figured he'd spend his senior years barking orders at the newest recruits and enjoying every minute of it.

I pull into his driveway, parking behind a large truck. The grass is cut with precision, and the front porch is adorned by a single hanging basket of flowers. Somehow, I doubt these flowers are Grant's doing. Laughing to myself, I kill the engine and sit for a few minutes, gathering my thoughts. It's important to be strong for Scarlett. That I'm here for her like Henry would want. Like I always promised him I'd be.

Chapter 4

Scarlett

To say the last few days have been a blur would be an understatement. My heart is broken. Shattered into a million jagged shards over my kitchen floor, in the spot I stood when I heard the words that would forever change my life. My husband, the father of my unborn child, is gone. Dead.

Thinking the word "dead" makes my stomach flip, and a shiver skirts my spine. This wasn't supposed to happen to us. Henry was going to see this final deployment through and seek the help he needed to be here for our son. To be the best father possible, even if we were no longer together.

Losing him is awful, a part of me is missing, but it isn't only the loss that hurts. Keeping the secret of our failed marriage from everyone in our life hurts as much, if not more. I understand his reasoning and, knowing the decision to end our marriage was mine, I owe him the respect of keeping that information to myself.

Henry was so worried about appearances. What people

would think of him. He believed people would look at him like he had abandoned his pregnant wife and he was less of a man because he couldn't make his marriage work.

As I watch Grant thumb through his mail, I know in my heart there would have been no judgment. Our friends, especially the three men who loved Henry the most—Grant, Connor, and Taylor—would have supported our decision.

"You hungry?" Grant asks as he tosses the mail on the table. Standing before me with his hands on his hips, I giggle a little at his stance. It's so rigid and official. Intimidating.

"Relax there, soldier."

Cocking his head, he scrunches his brows like he doesn't understand the words I've spoken, triggering a string of giggles. Laughing feels good in this moment. It feels like all I've done is cry or sleep for days.

"Shut it. Food?"

"Nah. I could go for some ice cream, though." I don't realize what I've said until I see the sympathy on Grant's face. Offering a small smile, he relaxes and simply nods before leaving me on his couch and making his way to the small kitchen.

My thoughts return to Henry and our marriage. The reality is, our marriage was over long before I found out I was pregnant. We were just too sad and so far into our own denial we couldn't see it. Not long ago, we were trying to conceive a child, mistakenly assuming a child would fix the cracks in our marriage. It was a desperate attempt to heal what was so clearly broken.

Then Henry received news of his impending deployment, and instead of dreading the inevitable, we chose to share a bottle of wine and reminisce over the best years of our life together. Those memories led us to find solace in each other's arms, a reminder of who we once were. Without protection. I knew within a few short weeks we had created a new life. An innocent child who would bond us together forever, in a way that our faltering marriage couldn't.

Because we wouldn't know when his deployment orders would come, I insisted on a blood test to confirm my pregnancy. The test confirmed what the home tests said: we were pregnant. When we were given the opportunity to know the sex at that time, I vetoed Henry's wish to wait until the baby was born. I had an overwhelming need for him to know this child. To start building the special bond a father has with his son.

We were both excited at the prospect of having a son. We spent hours talking over all the things we'd do with our child, and in those moments, I vowed to do everything I could to save our marriage. To put my feelings and needs aside so our son would never know anything but how much his parents loved him and each other. Our love may have changed, but there was no doubt I still loved Henry even if I wasn't necessarily in love with him.

Like he knows I'm thinking of him, the small waves I feel when he moves begin in my stomach. They're light and at first freaked me out, but now I welcome them. Resting my hands on my stomach, I lean my head back, my feet propped on the table in front of the couch and close my eyes. These flutters center me and remind me of the amazing things yet to come.

And like they often do, my thoughts jump to Henry and the day I changed everything.

Seeing a small pea-sized blip on a little screen while his rapid heartbeat filled the tiny room, overwhelmed us both. I was filled with hope and happiness. Then I looked at my husband, tears falling freely from his eyes, and I knew. We had to put our own pride aside for our child. I needed to give him the life he deserves, and the life Henry never had. Telling Henry my thoughts was difficult and, until this week, the single most heartbreaking moment of my life. I wanted us to be the best parents possible to our baby. In order to do that, we couldn't be together. We no longer brought the best out in one another, and our child deserves more than two parents settling. Going through the motions.

"Sugar just sent me a text. Should be here soon."

Startled, I look at Grant standing before me, a large yellow bowl extended to me. Sitting up, I take the bowl from his hands and peer inside. Yes! Three flavors of ice cream. Taking the spoon resting in the bowl, I scoop a sampling of each flavor into my mouth and smile.

"Mankwhoo," I mumble with my mouth full.

"I think that was thank you. You're welcome."

Grant leaves me alone, and I'm left with thoughts of Taylor arriving. Taylor Cain is the type of man women dream of meeting, one who is unattainable and almost fictitious. His eyes change like an old school mood ring, and I've seen many women over the years try to figure out what makes them change colors.

That's something that has always bothered Henry about his childhood best friend. The way women flocked to Taylor. Wanting to know everything about him just from his looks. But they didn't know the man beyond the mysterious eyes and brooding demeanor. His heart and selflessness oozes from every pore, making him the man he is. Taylor would give his life for his friends and family, and he almost did just that, for his country.

I never truly understood the competitiveness and underlying jealousy Henry felt toward Taylor. They'd known each other most of their lives and were as close as two people could be, but still, over the years, I saw a shift in their relationship. Anytime Taylor was around, Henry's demeanor changed. Last year when we moved to Fayhill, the rift between them was obvious to everyone, especially me.

I have known Taylor as long as I've known Henry. When I didn't know how to handle Henry's moods or what to say after a deployment, I would turn to Taylor. The conversations were short, but he was always there for me. For us. Like he is now.

The loud rumbling of a motorcycle's engine signals his arrival outside. Grant walks to the front door and opens it as two heavy footsteps sound on the front porch. With one more bite of my ice cream, I wipe my mouth and set the bowl on the table. Rising from the couch, I move toward where they're standing, using hushed voices. When they hear me approach, Taylor offers a tiny smile. Sympathy is written all over his face, and I rush to him.

His body is warm against mine and offers nothing but comfort as he holds me. I absorb it all, selfishly holding on to him like a lifeline. Quickly my emotions overwhelm me, and I don't stop them. A flood of everything I've held inside releases one tear at a time.

When my sobs slow to more of a hiccup, and I've sufficiently soaked his shirt, I step away from Taylor and wipe my face with my hand. Normally, I'd fiddle with the ends of my long red hair, but since I'm on day three of dry shampoo, it's sufficiently tied on top of my head in a messy bun. Without my security blanket, I awkwardly bite my bottom lip and whisper, "Sorry."

"Scarlett, honey, don't be sorry. I'm the one who is sorry. How are you holding up?" His hands grab onto my biceps, rubbing up and down. What a loaded question.

How am I holding up? How do I feel?

Numb. Confused. Sad. Hurt. Pissed off. Guilty.

Mostly, I'm consumed with guilt. For years I've prepared myself for Henry's death, assuming it would come with him a world away, fighting for freedom. Never did I assume an argument would lead to his death. That's the real story. We were fighting. I was exhausted, my hormones in hyper-drive and his patience thin.

"I don't know why it's so fucking hard, Henry. I'm just asking for a little respect. If you aren't going to come home at night, please tell me. I was worried. I'm sick of you being so goddamn selfish." My hands are gripped so tight into a fist my knuckles are white. In the past, when he's pulled this kind of behavior, I've cried. I've begged him to tell me where he's been and who he's been with. As strange as it sounds, I know he's not with another woman. Henry hasn't broken that vow. He's battling his demons and reliving his experiences overseas as he prepares for yet another battle. It's also why I asked for a divorce. Why I need this to end, I can't watch him self-destruct.

"That's right, Scarlett. I'm the big fuck up. Why are you still living here with me if I'm such a loser? Why did you marry me? You knew what kind of piece of shit I was destined to be. I warned you, but you didn't listen. You thought you knew best. I know who I am to the core, baby. I'm the loser whose parents chose the bottle over him. I'm the guy who busts his ass just to get by and it's still not enough." His eyes fill with tears and I hate myself for pushing him. He's vulnerable, I know that. Thankfully he hasn't been drinking. He's argumentative and self-loathing

on a good day, but with alcohol, it's a completely different level. Regardless, there's always the possibility he'll say something, something I'll never forget and something he'll never be able to take back.

Stepping toward him, I reach my hand out, but he cringes, pulling away from my reach. "I'm sorry, Henry. Please don't put yourself down. You are not a loser, you are an amazing man. But you have to see what this does to me. I love you, no matter if we're married or not. I worry about you. You're going to be a father, I need to know you'll always put our son first."

The moment the words leave my mouth, I regret them. Everyone has a trigger, and I've learned over the last few weeks that questioning the type of parent he'll be is Henry's. His expression goes from one of anguish, to hurt, and finally anger. Grabbing his keys, he turns toward the back door and I shout his name as the screen door slams.

"Scarlett? Are you okay?" Taylor's voice pulls me from the memory, one that I will carry with me for the rest of my life. I know a drunk driver is responsible for the accident, but Henry was still angry and hurt. Because of me. He was on the interstate, making his way back into town. I told everyone he was going to get me ice cream and probably needed to clear his head first. The reality is, there was no reason for him to be outside of town. There was no reason for him to be on that stretch of road. If only I hadn't angered him, he wouldn't have left upset. He would still be alive.

"What? Oh, umm . . . it's all just a lot." Understatement of the year.

The sympathetic look Taylor gives me, makes me smile. He's such a good guy, and although he'll never know how much, Henry loved him. His behavior the last few years would lead some to question his love, but it's true. These men were brothers in the truest form, and as much as they loved one another, they were also each other's worst enemy at times.

"I should get out of here. Go home and start returning calls. I can't hide out here forever. Thanks again, Grant. I appreciate you letting me hold up here with my ice cream and never-ending sobfest," I say, walking to the coat rack by the door to grab my purse. When I slide it over my body, it skims over my baby bump as I pull it to the side. *Bump.* It's there but if I wear loose enough clothes nobody can really tell. I am waiting for the day I wake up and it's tripled in size. Now, my boobs are a different story. These things are a little out of control and the strap of my bag settles right in the cleavage only giving emphasis to their enormity.

I turn back to the guys, both standing with their arms crossed over their chests, looks of concern written all over their faces. I wonder if anyone in my life will look at me any other way. Doubtful. I can hear it all now. *"Poor Scarlett, raising that baby on her own. No man will ever want to take on such a burden."* The whispers and sympathetic head nods have already begun and are sure to only get worse as I approach my due date.

"Oh, stop. I'll be fine. I'm sad and hormonal. Pregnancy does funny things to your emotions. I need to get home, I'm sure there's a list of things for me to do. I think someone emailed me something. Maybe I imagined that. I feel like I've been dreaming so I could have easily made that up." By the time I stop rambling long enough to take a deep breath, Taylor is walking toward me, his hands lifting up and pulling me into him again. He runs his hand across my back; the motion is soothing.

"Scarlett, why don't you let us handle this stuff? Addy

will be here tomorrow, and you know her. She can't help but take over and control things. My sister is nothing if not organized and ready to dictate orders."

Laughing, the first real laugh in days, I step back from his embrace and smile. "Maybe I'll just go home and take a bath. I don't know if –"

"Why don't I come with you? You shouldn't be alone right now. I'll follow you to your house, and while you do whatever you need to do, I'll cook dinner and we can watch a movie. You still like those awful chick flicks? We could watch one of those."

"Are you sure? You've just arrived, and I'm sure you and Grant have—"

"Honey, we're all here for *you*. I'm sure. That okay, Cap?"

Taylor looks over his shoulder to Grant, who hasn't changed his stance. His arms are still crossed, and his expression is one of pity. Or most likely, sympathy.

"Yep, sounds like the best plan," he says with a nod, and finally releases his stance and places his hands in his pockets. "If you'd like I can pick up Twig and we can all sit around, share a pizza, or three, and watch a movie. Low on the cheese though."

"On the pizza or movie?" Taylor asks, and we all laugh.

"Both. Getting older sucks for dairy. You two go, get cleaned up. I'll grab the kid and we'll be by in about an hour with hot pizzas."

Skirting around Taylor, I walk up to Grant, pop up on my toes, and place a kiss on his cheek. "You're a good man, Grant Ellison. Thank you."

"No need to thank me. We're family. Family takes care of family. I'll see ya in sixty," Grant says as he pulls me into a quick one-armed hug.

Willing the tears to hold off until I can get in a nice warm bath, I walk past Taylor and out the front door. Hot on my heels, he stops at his bike and straps his duffle onto the back seat. I feel awful that he's only been here minutes and already moving on to somewhere else. I despise being anyone's charity case. It's embarrassing to ask so much of these men, but I have nobody else to lean on. My parents disowned me the minute I chose Henry over the future they planned. These military men are my family now, and I consider myself very lucky.

"Hey, Sugar?" I shout, catching Taylor's attention.

"Jesus, Scarlett. Not that name. I thought we had an understanding."

Shrugging, I smile and ask, "You remember the way, right?"

"I do. Drive safe."

Nodding, I click my fob to unlock my car and settle behind the wheel. I can do this. One step at a time.

Chapter 5

Scarlett

*H*ormones and death. Not the best of cocktails that's for sure. My emotions are all over the place, like their own little marathon. There have been moments over the last few days I've felt like I'm losing my mind. Thankfully Taylor and his sister, Addy, have been here to help me through it all. Addy was like an older sister to Henry and having her here the last few days has been a blessing. She's taken control of almost everything, just as Taylor predicted she would.

Over the years, Addy and I forged a friendship, and although we've both had a lot going on in our lives the last few years, we've kept up with each other via social media, checking in regularly. Her presence has been calming when I could easily fall apart.

I need to get dressed. It's a simple task, yet today it feels like the most complicated activity. I can't find the energy. Perhaps it's that I have to squeeze my pregnant body into a dress or, for the next few hours, I will need to find a way to smile and accept the condolences that are sure to be handed out like candy.

Candy. I need one of those hard ginger candies Addy gave me yesterday. They made a huge difference with the return of nausea. I blame the stress and crying, because well into my second trimester, a moment I greeted with the equivalent of a major parade, nausea has been a thing of the past. Unlike the first few months when I spent hours each day purging my system, these days, I'm more likely to devour an entire pizza or put hot sauce on almost every morsel of food on my plate than anything else.

Rising from the end of my bed, I walk to the dresser and see the dish of little pieces of greatness. Unwrapping one of the candies, I pop it in my mouth and turn to stare at the dress hanging on my closet door.

Mine. It's just mine now, not ours. I suppose it hasn't been ours for a while, but somehow, today it all feels final. Official and real.

A knock on the door pulls me from my thoughts. "Come in."

Addy pops her head in the room, a look of sympathy on her face as she takes in my lack of readiness. One look is all it takes for the tears to flow. Rushing to me, she pulls me into a hug, and I sob. I release the frustrations and fears I know today will bring. After a few minutes of emotional purging, I step back and offer her a small smile. The look I receive tells me I must look pathetic.

"Sorry. I know I'm running behind. I need about fifteen more minutes to get ready."

Sighing, she squeezes my hand and says, "There's no rush. We have time. Have you taken your blood pressure yet? I didn't like the earlier numbers."

Addy is a nurse, and when she arrived, Taylor told her

I had been complaining of a minor headache and not feeling well. I tried explaining to them I have cried a lot, and that was why I had a headache. The small human in my uterus was the culprit behind my constant nausea, and they should both calm down. Neither were accepting of my reasoning, and Addy immediately began hovering. She's had me checking my blood pressure every two to three hours and ordering me to rest and nap more than the average toddler would.

As overwhelming as hovering can be, I'm grateful someone is here to force me to take care of myself. It would be easy to ignore it all and just crawl in my bed and wait for this all to pass.

"I did. It was better than earlier. I logged it; the paper is on the nightstand." She walks to the side of the bed and picks up the paper, humming her approval of the numbers. My blood pressure was high early in my pregnancy, and I've had to take quite a bit of time off to rest. Light headedness, skyrocketed blood pressure, and a few dizzy spells last week has us all on edge. Everyone else more than me, but still, all of us are watching my numbers closely.

"Let's get you ready. The guys already left so it's just you and me. We'll take this as slow as you need."

I let Addy guide me to my bathroom and pull my hair into a low ponytail. Quickly, I wash my face and know there's no reason to bother with much makeup. A little powder, swipe of shadow across my lids, and lipstick will have to do. Returning to my bedroom, I step into the black maxi dress and shimmy it over my hips before pulling the tank-style straps over my shoulders. The jersey knit clings to my body, and my boobs look like one good sneeze may give a show to the entire town. Slipping on a short-sleeved cardigan, I deem the outfit complete.

As I take in my reflection in the mirror hanging on the back of my closet door, I hardly recognize the woman before me. Dark circles under my eyes show how little rest I've had regardless of the hours I've slept. My gaze lingers on my midsection and I'm reminded of the reason I need to take better care of myself. And that today will be harder than anyone can possibly understand.

"Do you want heels or flats? Maybe both just in case?" Addy asks, holding up a pair of wedges in her left hand and flats in the other.

"Flats. I will probably fall on my face in any sort of heel."

We both laugh at that, and it's a welcome sound. Nodding her agreement, she holds out the flats to me and I slip them on my feet before rising to brush non-existent wrinkles from my dress. With a deep breath, I catch her eye in the mirror and bite my lower lip as the tears start to appear again.

I don't want to do this. I can't sit through Henry's friends talking about how much he'll be missed. How sorry they are for my loss, for the loss to our unborn son. It's all too much, but it has to be done. It's my duty as his wife—widow. I'm a widow. A woman who a week ago was separated from her husband and the father of her unborn child. Now, I'm a woman facing life as a single mother and a widow.

"This sucks, Addy."

Squeezing my shoulder, she nods and guides me from the room. We go through the motions of closing up the house and gathering our belongings before heading to her car. The lights flash twice as the doors unlock. Slipping into the passenger seat, I settle back and pull on my sunglasses as she drives us to the funeral home.

"Henry Gilbert was my best friend. When we were snot-nosed kids eating dirt on the playground, we bonded over the important things in life: favorite cookies, coolest superhero, and why baths were stupid. We were five years old and that's how simple life was. How I wish we could go back to those days, when life was nothing but dirt and chasing the street lights so we didn't get in trouble. Our bond began in those years, and it was something that never broke. The day of Henry's eighteenth birthday we made a life-altering decision together. As brothers, we committed to serve our country and protect those we loved most."

Taylor's voice breaks a little and my heart aches for him. This isn't only my loss today, it's his. More than anyone else, he understands how I feel, the pain and the agony of never seeing Henry. Of never laughing with him or fighting with him until it hurts so bad you lose the fight. The overwhelming anger and pain from the loss of a man we both love runs deep in each of us. Somehow in our loss, the bond they shared is now part of who I am.

Most of the men and women here are from our town of Fayhill or military friends. Henry was often the life of the party, the guy everyone wanted around for good times. Funnily enough, I don't think he was the man they would call in the bad times. Empathy and patience weren't his strongest virtues, but he was loved nonetheless. Looking around this room, I'm humbled by the impact he has left on this world.

Taylor's sob pulls me from my thoughts, my eyes returning to the podium where he stands.

"The day Henry found out he was to be a father was one of the proudest days of his life. Building a life with Scarlett was his greatest accomplishment, but being a father was his greatest dream. I heard a change in him that day, the way he spoke of his wife and how much he loved her and they were building a family—"

I close my eyes and breathe deeply through my nose while tilting my head back. He has no idea how much I wish that were true. Grant squeezes my hand, giving me the strength to tune back into Taylor's eulogy.

"I will miss my brother, my best friend. But, most of all," he pauses, head tilted back, exhaling and sighing before looking toward the congregation, his gaze catching mine, "I will miss the ability to watch him become a father." Tears stream down my face in time with his own. "If we can take anything away from this loss, I hope it is that we should live life to its fullest. We all need to walk out of here and put our fears and self-inflicted obstacles aside. Live the life we want, the one we dream of, and make it our reality."

With not a dry eye in the house, Taylor steps from the podium. As he approaches our row, he pauses and looks at me. The loss in his eyes, the pain in his soul, mimics my own and I want nothing but to hold him and let him know I understand. I get it. Instead, I attempt a slight smile, and he does the same before proceeding down the aisle and out of the building. He doesn't sit with Addy or stand in the back of the room. He leaves. How I wish I could follow him.

Since there will be no burial, the funeral director thanks everyone for attending and informs them all are welcome at Grant's house for lunch and refreshments. Rising from our seats, Grant guides me from the pew and through a side door. This is the room set up for the family of the deceased, an opportunity to allow us a moment of peace from the other mourners.

"You okay, Red? Need anything? Bottle of water?"

Grant asks as I sit down on a large chair next to the window.

"That would be great. I just need a minute of quiet, if that's okay?"

"Of course," he says, handing me a bottle of water from the display on the side table. "I'll go let Addy know and be right back."

The silence of the room is welcome. There's no chatter, no one is sniffling, and I don't have to worry about how I look. Too sad. Not sad enough. Angry. Hurt. Lonely. Bitter. Alone. Closing my eyes, I lean my head back on the chair and rest my hand on my stomach and allow myself a few minutes of peace and quiet.

The sound of the door closing draws me from the slumber I almost fell into. Slowly I open my eyes and expect to see Grant's gray pants standing before me. Instead, I see Taylor Cain's sad eyes. Kneeling before me, he places his hand atop mine and smiles.

"You napping in here?"

A small chuckle escapes before I say, "If only. I'd love a nap right now." Instead, I sit up, his hand falling from mine. "Is it time to go?"

"It is. But, before we go I wanted to ask why the Gilberts are here."

"Henry's parents? They're his parents, Taylor. Why wouldn't they be here?"

A low rumble similar to a growl falls from his lips, and he stands, turning his back to me.

"I don't like it, Scarlett. Henry hasn't spoken to them since we left for basic. It was a part of his life he worked hard to separate from the one he built with you. I don't understand why they'd come. You don't see anyone else from that part of his life here. None of his friends or extended family. I'm surprised Lyle isn't here."

Standing, I step up next to Taylor, looking out the window. His gaze is fixated on Henry's parents. This is the first time I've met my in-laws and they seem nice enough. From this distance, I'd almost think it was Henry standing among the crowd if the man wasn't so thin. Mrs. Gilbert is petite with long hair teased high. As we look at them, his father laughs with one of the guys who works at a local ranch, and his mother reapplies her lipstick.

I place my hand on Taylor's shoulder, pulling his attention from what is happening outside. "I know they weren't the best of parents, but they seem to have gotten their act together. They deserve an opportunity to mourn the loss of their son."

Another growl is his only response before a nod and motion toward the door. I guess our conversation is over.

Chapter 6

Scarlett

A memorial service for your soon-to-be ex-husband and father to your unborn son is exhausting. Trying to maneuver the fine line of hostess and widow only adds to that feeling. It's been two days since Henry's memorial and I'm still tired. Addy dragged me to the doctor yesterday because I have had next to no appetite the last few days, relying on a single cheese stick and two apples for nutrition. She was worried about my stress level and wanted the doctor to tell me in no uncertain terms to get my shit together. Really, I think it was more about her witnessing the conversation for her own peace of mind.

It feels good to have someone like Addy on my side, making sure I'm taking better care of myself for the sake of my son. I was sad to see her leave this morning, but she has her own life to get back to in Lexington. A new town, a new love, and a new outlook on life, happiness looks good on my friend. Seeing her rebuild her life and find love again as a single mom gives me hope for the future.

I understand her concerns about my health and this

pregnancy. I'm scared. Scared that something will happen to the baby, that I'll lose him and truly be alone. Secretly, I'd hoped calling my parents to tell them I was pregnant would have reunited us as a family. I've waited years to be reunited with my parents and siblings, to be included in their lives again. Unfortunately, even the news that I was having my first child wasn't enough for them. To quote them: "We already have grandchildren." Maxwell and Eliza both blessed them with picture perfect grandchildren who look beautiful on their annual holiday card. The one I still receive even if Henry and I were never included.

Rubbing my hand in small circles across my abdomen, I take a deep breath and let my toes drag across the wooden porch as I swing in the last anniversary gift Henry gave me. A hand-crafted swing that I spend most evenings sitting on as I watch the sunset. Tonight, the sounds of Taylor in the kitchen fill the normally quiet backdrop of my sunset watch. He's been a rock since arriving in Fayhill just over a week ago.

Living in this town, building a life here, has created some of the best memories of my life. This home, while small, is full of both wonderful and devastating memories. The last few days with Taylor, the devastating memories have faded a little, letting new moments fill their space.

"Hey, Red. You hungry?" Taylor asks as the screen door slams, startling me. "Sorry, didn't mean to scare you."

"It's okay. Sit with me a bit first?"

I scoot over a little, leaving room for him to take the spot next to me. After I found out I was pregnant, my first thought was about all the evenings I'd sit on this swing, holding my child, rocking him or her to sleep. It's nice to start that tradition now.

"How are you holding up?" Taylor asks, his arm resting on the back of the swing. He tugs at my ponytail and I smack his leg. This is something he's naturally fallen into the role of: tormentor and friend. He's done a good job of pulling me out of my thoughts, making me laugh or swear at him, depending on the circumstance, all while making sure I'm not needing for anything.

"I'm okay. Trying to process everything. So many people loved Henry—"

"And you. They love you too. And this baby you're carrying. This town really rallied for you both. It makes me feel better about you being here, knowing so many people care about you."

Smiling, I twist in my seat trying to get comfortable. He's right. This town has been wonderful and kind to both of us but the way they've rallied and been there for me has been amazing. Vera from the diner in town made sure the gathering after the burial was organized, and I didn't have to worry about a thing. My new friend, Mercy, kept me company and ran interference if I needed a break from all the attention.

We sit and rock in silence for a few minutes before Taylor asks, "Did Henry's parents leave?"

"Yeah. I actually didn't see them again after I went to lie down during the party. Is it weird to call it that? I'm sure there's a different term but that seems more fitting for Henry."

We both laugh and continue to rock, neither of us speaking for a few minutes. Then I say, "It was the first time I met them. Did you know that?"

Shaking his head, a small frown appears on his face. "Pretty crummy time to meet the in-laws, huh?"

I let out an awkward chuckle as Taylor scrunches his

face. "Sorry. Yeah it was interesting to say the least. Henry refused to talk to me much about them but I know the basics. The drinking and drugs. How they treated him. They weren't what I expected. I think somehow, I had this vision of these horrible people, broken and loud. Demanding and argumentative."

Taylor's body goes rigid at the mention of the treatment of his best friend by the two people who were supposed to love and support him. I've always been curious about Henry's childhood, but when I'd push for information, we'd end up in a fight. Eventually I got tired of begging to be let into his past, so I let it go, focusing on the present and our own life. When I found out I was pregnant, Henry made promises to our child that worried me. Promises to never disrespect him, to always be proud of him, and to never embarrass him.

"Just be careful with them, okay? My last memory of them isn't too great. This version of them . . . it was strange. Like they got their act together after all these years. Yet, I did see his dad with a beer so clearly sobriety isn't a thing."

"I'll keep that in mind. I want to give them the benefit of the doubt. His mom asked me about the benefits. Wanting to make sure the baby and I would be taken care of. That was nice of her."

Grunting, Taylor stands from the swing, his back to me. Running his hands through his hair, he sighs, frustration evident, before turning. "Do not talk to them about the benefits or any payout."

"Taylor—"

"Promise me, Red. Don't do it. Any money you receive is none of their business."

I take in the sight of him before me. He's exhausted, sleeping on a pullout sofa bed does not allow for a decent night's sleep. As he raises his arms above his head, fingers interlocking around his neck, I wonder what it is about the Gilberts that bothers him so much. Sure, they weren't the best parents to Henry, and from what I've learned over the years, Taylor and Addy's home was an escape for my husband more than anything. A second family that was more like his primary family. But Taylor's obvious discomfort and worry gives me more pause than anything else.

"If it makes you feel better, fine," I concede. "Now, did you mention something about food? You know what sounds delicious? Some fried cheese sticks and chicken wings." I waggle my brows at him because, what man doesn't want to indulge in bar food?

Dropping his hands, he steps forward and extends a hand. "Addy would have my ass if I let you eat that. She said you need to limit your sodium intake and eat healthy. I was thinking I could grill some chicken, make us a salad."

Sighing, I take the offered hand and rise from the swing. Taking a step into his personal space, I poke my finger to his chest and smile at him. This man has sacrificed his own life to be here with me. To keep me grounded when I could so easily fall apart. His patience as I run from one emotion to another like the flip of a switch is something to be praised. Although, I think he's about over my need to slam doors. He stiffens as I poke him in the chest, a reaction that only fuels my sassiness.

"Sugar, I want some damn cheese sticks. I'll concede the wings, but I'm having cheese. I'm pregnant and have been dreaming of deep-fried cheese, don't let me down."

"Fine," he relents, "but we're posting a picture of the salad on social media so Addy knows I tried. By the way, using that nickname isn't earning you any buddy points, either."

Laughing, I walk through the front door and to the kitchen to retrieve my box of frozen cheese sticks before tapping the buttons to preheat the oven. As the numbers tick down, letting me know how many minutes until the oven reaches the right temperature, I begin pulling the little sticks from the box and line them up on a cookie sheet.

"You know, I've built a business on making these things. Why don't you let me do that while you pull out the stuff for a salad?"

"Sure, now that I've done the hard work." My eyes roll and lips scrunch as I abandon the snacks and walk to the fridge.

"Good to see you haven't lost your snark over the last week. I will admit, I was worried about you."

"Puh-lease. I'm sad, angry, and hurt, but we both know my snark and sass run deep, Taylor Cain. I will never lose that, you can guaran-damn-tee it."

His laughter fills the room, and I smile as I begin pulling the produce from the fridge for the most epic social media worthy salad.

"So, what you're saying is in all of these movies there must be either a single mom, a baking competition, or a stray dog?"

Taylor has been teasing me relentlessly over the last two hours about my choice of sappy romantic films. Sure, this is the fourth one he's suffered through in two days, but I also posed with a salad for social media, so I'll call us even.

"It's not a requirement but those three things are a common theme among these movies. Oh and there's often a CEO who has to visit a small town to either shut down a business or buy it. Something awful that may ruin the entire town."

"I still say we should have watched *Deep Water Horizon*. That movie is a classic."

"With all due respect to your classification of what is a *classic*," I begin with air quotes around the word *classic,* "I don't think that movie would keep my blood pressure down."

"Shit. I didn't think—" he says, running his hands through his hair. We've been sitting next one another on the couch, a bowl of popcorn nestled between us, as we watch movies. Right now, what I want to do is steal the bowl between us and smack him on the back of the head for teasing me about my choices of cinema. "I'm sorry, Scarlett. I didn't think of the premise. I'm such a dick. You're right. Sappy dog owner CEO stealing businesses is a better choice."

His tone is laced with regret and sadness. That's the one thing I'm truly getting sick of. The sadness. It's as if everyone I speak to is either looking at me with sadness in their eyes or their overall tone is dripping with it. The reality is, my life is sad. I'm the town's pregnant widow, left alone to fend for herself with no family to speak of. The only people around to support me are my husband's friends and the townspeople who have rallied to ensure I'm not alone. Geez, even thinking it myself, I kind of pity me.

"Do not apologize for treating me like a normal person, Tay. There's just so much . . ." I pause, choosing my words carefully, "all this pity and the never-ending apologies are killing me. I wish . . . I just wish . . . never mind."

"Don't do that. You need to talk through this. What are you talking about? So much what?"

"Nothing. How about we just finish this movie? I'm sure one day they'll release one that is the ultimate trifecta—CEO with a dog who enters a baking competition."

He doesn't say anything for a few seconds, long drawn out seconds, and when he turns toward the television, I release a long breath in relief. He's not going to push—never mind. Picking up the remote, he doesn't play the movie. Nope, he turns it off completely and shifts in his seat to face me.

"Talk, Red."

Groaning, I throw my head back on the couch and sigh. Dramatically. "Henry and I were separated. I planned to file for divorce after the baby is born."

Coughing or presumably choking on his popcorn, Taylor grumbles, "What the actual fuck?"

"It's not that big of a deal." I'm sure to him, and most people, it is a big deal, confusing and out of the blue. That just shows me how good we were at pretending. Burying our heads in the sand, ignoring the obvious. I've had months to come to terms with it all, and as I look at Taylor, I see it's news to him. "I mean, clearly it is, or was, a big deal to us. Neither of us came to this decision lightly. Truthfully, we've struggled for years, but this last year has been awful. I tried. Henry tried, even requesting a transfer to the Guard, taking himself out of active duty so he'd be home with me." I take a peek at Taylor. His mouth is agape, eyes wide, and brows quirked. Shocked.

"That's why we moved here. Why we changed our plans, to save our marriage."

"But I was here a year ago, when you moved in. I didn't

think anything was wrong."

Laughing, I sit up, or rather, try. I'm mimicking more of a turtle on his shell than anything, this couch is sucking me into it like a suction cup. Taylor reaches over and helps me to more of a sitting position. "We were both good at pretending. Not only with each other but those around us. Shortly after you left, we had a huge blowout. I was ready to leave then, but he made all the promises I needed to hear."

"Regardless of the effort, it just wasn't working. I guess . . ." Pausing, I contemplate my words, how best to explain this without sounding like a horrible person or making Henry sound like he gave up. "I thought moving here, to Fayhill where Grant and Connor were living, would help. There are quite a few soldiers who live in the area, and I hoped they'd help him."

I truly did believe that. Henry's life outside of our marriage had been all about his commitment to his country. I saw the changes in both Grant and Connor after they were discharged; the demons each fought were there, but a calm surrounded both of them. It was easy to see what a change in lifestyle had done for each of them. I wanted that for Henry, for us. I thought maybe it would save us. I was wrong.

"Then I found out I was pregnant. As much as I wanted it all to be okay, for this baby to be the answer to our problems," I say, willing the tears that have suddenly appeared to go away. "It was too late. I love Henry, Taylor. I swear I do, but I haven't been *in love* with him for a very long time. And this baby, our son, he deserved to have two happy parents who could raise him together without hating each other. That's what would have happened, we would have hated one another."

The tears aren't stopping, and the sobs come quickly. Removing the bowl of popcorn from its perch, Taylor sets it on the table in front of us and pulls me to his side. I settle in, allowing him to absorb all the pain and guilt I've held in all these days. The truth sucks, and I know how unlikeable it makes me, how people will judge us, but knowing someone else knows helps. It helps a lot.

I won't tell Taylor that one of the biggest kinks in our armor, in our marriage, was Henry's never-ending jealousy of his best friend. He hated how easily Taylor got along with everyone. How much he could make me laugh or diffuse a situation before it escalated. Their history and bond was never a question, but I'm not sure even those closest to him growing up saw how much animosity he held in his heart.

The one person whose arms I easily find comfort in now, is also the only person Henry equally loved and hated. Well, except maybe me. Sometimes I wonder if he'd already begun to hate me for the decision I made. There are times I hate me, so it only seems fitting he would too.

Chapter 7

Taylor

4 weeks later

I will never again take for granted waking up in my own bed each morning. It is fantastic. I'm a man of few words and don't often throw words like "fantastic" around but sleeping on that lumpy pullout at Scarlett's sucked. *Sucked.* That's a word I know well. A lot of things in life suck. Burying my best friend only weeks ago *fucking sucked.* Heavy emphasis on the suck part. Watching his wife, his pregnant wife, try to stay strong for everyone around her, to be the glue of our group, encouraging us to share stories and joke around like Henry would have liked, made my respect for her grow to an entirely new level.

Rising from my bed, I follow the beacon of freshly brewed coffee wafting through my small house. I've only been in this place a few years, but it works perfectly for me as a single man. I have no intention of sharing my space with anyone else except the occasional guys night with my teenage nephew.

I spend so little time here that this fixer upper I bought with the intention of updating quickly has become more of a work in progress. Actually, it's more like needs a lot of work with not much in progress. That's only partially true. I have managed to remodel the downstairs while also completely ignoring the work needed upstairs. Anyone who walks upstairs will enter a time warp to the mid-eighties. The bedrooms are a testament as to why rose-colored carpet and blue wallpaper should never make a comeback. I'm not sure who had the brilliant idea to layer wallpaper over existing wallpaper, but that person did not think about the future. Or how difficult glue is to remove from walls.

Originally, the house was boxy with nothing but half a dozen unnecessary walls. I can't remember how many times I ran into the random wall separating the living room from the kitchen after a long night at the bar. The weeks of demo were exhausting but rewarding. Seeing my concept come to life as I tore down wall after wall was gratifying. It was also fucking fantastic to take out my frustrations on those same walls. Now, instead of random walls separating the large space into smaller rooms, the open concept allows me to see the seventy-inch television from not only the couch but the kitchen, and if I angle it just right, the back deck.

In addition to the updated kitchen and main living space, the downstairs has a half bath and large bedroom with full bathroom. That's all I've needed to live comfortably. While I should probably consider starting on some construction upstairs, I haven't found a reason to justify the added work to my schedule.

Owning a bar was not something I thought I'd be doing in my thirties, but I won't lie that it's been one of the best decisions of my life. Although the hours suck, and I have next to no social life, I still love my job. I make sure to include myself into the schedule working at least four shifts behind the bar, two of which keep me there until closing. Plus I'm there six days a week handling the business side of things. Staying busy and not allowing a lot of down time helps me keep a handle on the havoc my time in the service put on my body and mind.

Pulling the carafe from the machine, I pour the rich brew into my favorite travel mug and seal the lid. My sister, Addy, teases me that I still use an old school coffee maker and not one of those pod things. She forgets what hours I keep, and not only do I rely on the ability to set the timer to auto brew, I'm a pot a day kind of guy. I'd be dropping a few hundred bucks in pods a month if I modernized my coffee habit. Taking a tentative sip of the coffee, I walk to the couch and throw myself down to flip on the television.

I relied heavily on my staff to keep the bar running smoothly while I was in Fayhill, but I'm on the schedule to close tonight. That's why I made sure to roll out of bed hours earlier than I normally would. I need to get in early, check the inventory, and pay a few bills before the happy hour crowd invades. Scrolling the guide on my television, I choose a second showing of this morning's sports show and settle in for a few hours of back and forth banter that will not only entertain me but also give me a headache.

Twenty minutes into a debate over some call in a college basketball game that I don't care about, my phone dings with a text message.

Scarlett: When you were staying here, did the wind whistle this loud?

Laughing at her random question, I immediately start tapping out a response to her message.

```
Me: Since I can't hear via text, I
don't know.

Scarlett: You shouldn't be sarcastic.
It's not attractive.

Me: Eh, I'll be fine. Yes, the wind
whistled a lot, and it was very an-
noying.

Scarlett: I hadn't noticed. It's very
quiet in this house now. I can hear
everything.
```

Instead of responding with another text like I'm a seventeen-year-old and my life's goal is using my gigantic fingers on a tiny keypad, I tap the phone icon next to her name and wait for her to answer.

"I don't know why you insist on actually using the phone for talking." Her response is dripping in sarcasm and I laugh. Pot meet kettle.

"Texting is to only be used in small doses. I could tell this conversation was going to be three messages too long. Now about this quiet house," I say, fading off to allow her to respond. The response is one of a sigh, then a slight groan, and finally a string of curse words.

"Are you okay? Do you feel lightheaded?"

"Yes, Doctor Cain, I'm fine. Geez relax. I freaking whacked my ankle on the table. Everything is just dandy. I'm lying on the couch with a bag of salt and vinegar— I mean, a platter of freshly cut veggies in my lap while watching season four, episode six of Housewives. It's called living my best life."

Smiling, I stand, coffee cup in one hand and my cell

in the other. Topping off my coffee, I listen to Scarlett recap whatever ridiculous shenanigans are happening on her show. I "oh" and "huh" a few times even though I have no idea what she's talking about.

When she finally comes up for air, I ask, "Do you want me to take more time off? I can come back for a few days, put the crib together or paint the nursery."

"What?" she asks, and I look at my phone to make sure I haven't lost my connection.

"Which part do I need to repeat?"

"All of it. My phone beeped with a call, and I looked at the screen. I didn't hear what you said. I assume you were offering to help me in some way, though."

Laughing, I take a sip of my coffee. "I sure was. You don't have to sound so annoyed by my offer." She grumbles something I can't quite decipher, but I do clearly hear the word *pathetic*. My mama didn't raise a fool, so I opt to ignore her comment and continue, "I'm happy to know there are others in your life who use the telephone for speaking and not texting."

Returning to the couch, I sit back down, my feet propped on the coffee table. A snort fills the line and I imagine Scarlett lying on her couch, rolling her eyes and likely flipping me the middle finger all with a huge smile on her face.

"Don't get too excited. It was an unknown number. I should get two or more calls before dinner."

"What do you mean? Are you getting a lot of calls?"

"Me and half the world's population. At least some of the spammers hang up before I can hit the ignore button."

Spammers aren't only about soliciting business anymore; now they steal your identity and even your voice.

My protective instincts take over and a million scenarios of people knowing Scarlett is alone and set to inherit a large sum of money from Henry's life insurance and military benefits.

"Red, what else is going on?"

An annoyed growl fills the line. "Nothing, *Dad*. Goodness, you're a pain in my ass. I'm fine. The baby is fine. I'm eating my veggies, mimicking a slug on the couch, and binging too much television. Stupid spammers are calling and hanging up. The wind whistled and knocked over my garbage can last night. Just your real-life shit."

"Scarlett—"

"Nope. I'm not arguing with you. I texted you because, well this wind is freaking me out. As much as I tease you about using the phone for talking, I kind of miss having someone to talk to. Grant is great, Connor tries, but you tolerate me more than anyone else. Quit being so overbearing, it's not attractive. I don't need a lecture, Taylor."

She pauses, a muffled sniffle in the distance. I can only assume she's pulled the phone from her mouth to ward off the tears. I won't lie and say I'm surprised. I've held her and had more tear-soaked shirts in the last few weeks than in my entire life. That's saying a lot because I work in a bar. Something happens about thirty minutes before last call with drunk twenty-somethings. I'm not sure what it is, but there are a lot of tears. A. Lot.

"I'm sorry. I don't mean to be overbearing or insinuate you aren't capable of caring for yourself. I just worry, okay?"

"Kay." More sniffles.

"Now, what I asked was if you want me to schedule myself off for a few days to come put the crib together.

Help you get ready."

"Oh"—another pause and a sniffle— "you don't need to do that, I mean, you've already done so much for me. You have your own life to live in Lexington. Besides, there's no time like the present to adjust to this new version of my normal."

The line is silent as I ponder what to say next, but she beats me to it.

"I've never had many friends. Military life is difficult to maintain many friendships, but it's never really effected me until now. I feel so alone."

"Scarlett, honey. You have a lot of friends. Family."

She doesn't respond immediately, but I hear her shifting and then the faucet running. "I know. It's just different. I have a lot to figure out. There's so much . . . I'm overwhelmed and just kind of sad." There's a pause, our breathing the only sound. Then she laughs. It isn't a humorous laugh, it's more a defeatist laugh, and then she says, "I need to find another hobby. The knitting club is great, but it's only once a week. Maybe painting? Sewing? I could make all the bedding for the baby."

The vision of an impatient Scarlett trying to master sewing makes me smile. Could she do it? Absolutely. Will it take her five times as long because she has the patience of a toddler with a four-word vocabulary? No doubt.

"The offer stands. I'll pencil myself out soon and come help you with the painting. But you know Cap and Connor will be there for you. Whatever you need."

"I know. I hate being so fucking needy, Taylor. It's pathetic. I'm sick and tired of myself. I'm really not a lot of fun. It's no wonder my husband didn't want to hang out with me."

Another sniffle fills the line, but this time it isn't muffled. I swear if Henry were still alive, I'd kill him for how he's broken this woman down. The young woman we met in a bar ten years ago isn't the same woman I spent the last few weeks consoling. Scarlett of a decade ago was snarky and self-assured. She gave him, and all of us, a run for our money. She was confident, driven, and one of the most beautiful women I'd ever seen.

She still is. I hate myself a little for thinking that about my friend's wife, but it's true. Her beauty shines in not only her appearance but her heart. The same heart that is broken. Not just because of the loss. After she confessed the status of their marriage, it was as if she couldn't stop herself. She revealed layer upon layer of the issues Henry was facing, that they both faced. I only slipped once, showing my frustration that I had no idea. Regardless of how strained our friendship was, both Henry and Scarlett knew they could come to me. Henry knew how fucked up I was when I was discharged. Medically or not, it was both a blessing and the worst thing that could happen to me. One day I was a soldier and then, in a blink of an eye, I was adjusting to not only civilian life but working to trudge through the chaos in my mind.

The bomb of their separation hit me harder than I would have expected. It also reminded of how detached from their life I've been these last few years. I wish I had known how bad things were; I could have helped in some way. As much as I wish I could have supported them, thinking of the demise of their relationship, the loss of love they had for one another, the same love I envied, tore me to pieces.

"You know he had his own demons. It was never about you. He loved you more than anything. I know he would have fixed things if he knew how. But, honey, you have to know his issues ran as deep as his veins."

Sighing, I wait for her to respond but hear a commotion in the background and then a song I know well. "Scarlett, are you watching *Curious George*?"

"No?" It's a question not an answer, and I can't stop the laugh that bellows from me. When I get my bearings, I take a long sip from my coffee. "Don't make fun of me, Taylor Cain. You were fine when I was recapping my other show. I like this movie. It's soothing. Plus it has the best music ever. Jack Johnson is dreamy."

"Oh, Red. You never cease to amaze me. Look, I've got to grab something to eat and hit the market before I head into the bar tonight. If you need anything, shoot me a text or call one of the guys. You know they'll be there in a heartbeat."

"Don't worry, Connor stopped by on his way to the job site today, and Grant has sent me a text every hour, checking in."

Smiling, I'm glad those two listened to me last week when I told them we needed to be on top of taking care of Scarlett. She'll never ask us for help until it's too late. We need to be there for her, to support her during this time.

"I bet Beth, I mean, Mercy, would be happy to hang out with you. Shit, that's still weird for me. What a small world."

I still can't get over the fact that in the largest state in the union, I ran into a former employee in the small town of Fayhill. At my best friend's funeral. Beth, now known by her first name, Mercy, had Scarlett pulled into a tight hug, whispering kind words in her ear when I walked up and did a double take. She didn't look as surprised to see me as I was her. Once I got my act together and stopped saying "This is a trip," she hugged me and introduced me to her boyfriend like it was just a regular day, and ending up in the same small town wasn't as weird as hell.

Knowing there was someone else I knew and trusted in town to care for Scarlett made leaving her easier.

"Some may call it kismet, Taylor."

"I don't know if it was anything like that, but it sure was a trip."

We both start laughing and finish our call before I head to the bathroom for a long shower. There's a breakfast burrito with my name on it just five minutes away. It's been too long since I've had my Rosa's fix, and I'm due.

Chapter 8

Scarlett

4 weeks later

I would never make it in prison. Life in a small concrete box with only a small window for sunlight. Let's be honest, my attitude and bitchiness these last few days would probably have me in solitary so there wouldn't even be sunlight. Nope, I'm not meant for solitude. I need people. Laughter, music, and conversation. Gosh, I miss conversation. As many problems as we had, Henry was my best friend and knew me better than anyone. I've managed to make a few friendships with the women in town, some in my knitting group, but it isn't the same.

The kind smiles and hand pats are almost more than I can take each day. Between my part-time job at the local dentist's office and the knitting group, I'm tapped out with sympathies. Everyone has the best of intentions, and I would never believe anyone in this town is judging me. Okay, not true, I don't believe anyone intends to judge me, it's just something that comes to people naturally.

Then, there are the expectations, perceived behaviors, and reactions a widow is supposed to portray. I don't think I have any of those. Instead, I scream and I yell. I talk to Henry and curse at him. Then I slip into a nice warm bath, and cry while I make promises to my son. I tell him stories of his father and his uncle Taylor.

Taylor. In the last few weeks, those talks in the bath have turned to me telling my boy how handsome his uncle is. How smart and kind and selfless he is. I regale him with stories told to me over the years by his father and those who know both men well. It's then that my tears return as I realize I'm happily telling my son about his pseudo uncle and not his father.

Hatred and self-loathing consumes me, then I tell myself to get my shit together and grow a fucking pair. And apologize to my son and remind him only adults swear and sorry in advance for his mommy's potty mouth when she's angry. Mostly, I remind myself of where I am in my life. That each new day isn't a promise, it's a reward.

Looking at my weekend bag, hands on my hips, and bottom lip tugged between my teeth, I contemplate my next move. A weekend in Austin doing some retail therapy, maybe a trip to a day spa, and some live music is option one. Mercy said she could sneak away, make it a girl's trip and introduce me to her old roommates. Option two is more of a risk. Drive to Lexington and surprise Taylor, visit with Addy, and not have to worry about being Henry's widow.

Decision made, I toss in a skirt, peasant top, and my favorite cowboy boots before placing my makeup and toiletry bags on top. Carrying my bag out of my bedroom, I check the back door to ensure it's bolted and flip on the light over the sink so the house isn't completely dark.

As I exit through the front door and take the first step, my neighbor, Mr. Stanton, is cutting across his lawn toward me, huge smile spread across his face. About seventy-five, Mr. Stanton has been one of the only people to offer his sympathies once and then move along with our lives. He still stops by once a week to bring me the extra coupons from his paper and waves each evening when he takes his daily walk. Maybe I should walk with him instead of sitting on my ass waiting for it to grow.

"Off somewhere, Scarlett?"

Taking the last step I reply, "Just a few days away. I need a little change of scenery."

"That's good. I look forward to my annual guys' trip. This year is Cabo."

Okay, I didn't see that coming. Who knew sweet Mr. Stanton went on guys trips to Mexico?

"Wow! Cabo, that's a true vacation. Sadly, I don't have such grand plans."

"Trips don't have to be grand to serve their purpose. Sometimes a new landscape is all we need to reset ourselves."

Truer words have never been spoken. I hope a few days outside of this house and its memories will reset not only my body but my mind.

"Did you have any more packages coming?" Mr. Stanton asks, pulling me from my thoughts.

"I'm sorry?"

"Deliveries. There was a young man at your door the other day, said he had a package for you that required your signature only. He stood there for quite a few minutes, knocking away on the door. Even caught him peeking in the window, probably hoping you were inside."

I don't recall having any deliveries due. Of course, I left the house with two different shoes on and forgot my purse at the grocery store the other day. Anything is possible with this pregnancy brain.

"No deliveries for me, but, if you see the courier again, would you mind asking him to call me to reschedule?"

"Of course. You drive safe and enjoy yourself. That little one will be here soon enough and your days will no longer be your own," he warns, gesturing toward my stomach.

Smiling, I nod and walk to my car, popping the trunk and placing my bag inside. Once I'm settled behind the wheel, I take a deep breath and pull out of my driveway. New landscape. New mindset.

The drive to Lexington is long. Much longer than I thought it would be. It may have something to do with my constant need to stop and stretch my body. And use the restroom. I cannot imagine making this drive on a motorcycle like Taylor did for Henry's funeral.

No wonder he was exhausted when he arrived. And ravenous. Snacking is usually my preferred way of eating. Grazing my way through the day with various chips, dips, crackers, and an assortment of cheeses is what Henry teased me about over the years. Now, I want nothing but to get out of this moving car, drink a large mocktail, and devour some red meat.

A new and strange craving of the last few days. I've wanted nothing but red meat in any fashion. Put it in a shell, on a French roll, or grill it up in steak form, I'm not choosy. Instead, I'm driving down this highway, my audiobook not helping my overactive hormones, and all alone. It's been miles since I've seen another car or truck. Deep in the back of my mind, I realize how irresponsible it was to hop in my car without telling anyone where I was going. A simple breakdown on this stretch of road and I'll be stranded. At least I had the forethought not to listen to one of my favorite true crime podcasts. With my luck, the most recent edition would be about a woman kidnapped on a road trip.

As my favorite narrator, Hawk Weaver, describes every inch of the heroine's body he plans to lick, I squirm in my seat. Hormones don't only make me cry at the drop of a hat and forget my groceries at the market, they also make me horny as hell. Another new development in the last few weeks of my pregnancy. I must have skipped over this part of my pregnancy books. Or chose to ignore it because it isn't like I have someone to help me through this hump.

"You're painstakingly wet, Love. Do you know what that does to me?" Hawk's voice is like the deepest darkest chocolate oozing down the side of a freshly baked cake, and I am here for it. I want to crawl in this book and let him do all of this to me. With his perfect British accent and deep gravelly voice essentially coating my body with each breath and syllable I feel like I'm living the life of the heroine.

Fine, I realize it isn't actually Hawk Weaver doing these things, and I also know my imagination is running amuck. I have no idea what he looks like in real life. He's an anomaly. Heck, for all I know he's a seventy-year-old man who wears dentures and lives with seven cats. But, for now, I choose to live in my own fantasy that this man exists and would only be happy to do sinful and amazing things to me.

The shrill of my phone interrupts the dirty talk filling my small car and startles me. Looking around, as if anyone is going to see me jumping in my seat, I tap the answer button.

"Hello?"

"Scarlett." Grant sighs.

"Hey, Grant."

"Don't hey me. Where the hell are you? I went by the house, and it's all locked up. That nosy neighbor was arguing with me about a package and a signature."

Laughing, I can't stop the snort that escapes. "Mr. Stanton is not nosy. I'm actually headed out of town for a few days. I forgot to call you this morning." Lies. I'm a liar. I did not forget.

"Oh. Where are you headed? I saw Mercy at the diner today, and she didn't say anything about you girls going on a trip."

"That's because I'm by myself." I mumble the end of my statement, hoping he can't hear me. I don't need a lecture but that doesn't mean I'm not going to get one.

"Red—"

"Nope, I'm not doing this with you, Grant. I'm going out of town for a few days and will be fine. Please don't push me on this."

A long silence with only his breathing filling the line has me wishing for more Hawk Weaver as my company. I tap the steering wheel a few times as I wait for my friend to gather his thoughts and, likely, attempt to muster a response that won't piss me off.

"Drive safely and let me know when you've arrived wherever it is you're going."

Smiling, I savor this small victory. Having three men looking out for me and my baby is great, but goodness, are they a little overbearing. And, not in the sexy book boyfriend way.

Chapter 9

Taylor

"Ashton Sullivan, I swear to all that is holy if you do not put that box down I am going to call Jameson."

Huffing and rolling her eyes, my senior bartender, friend, and royal pain in the ass employee sets the box on the bar and turns to face me. Hands on her hips, she looks absolutely ridiculous. Wearing a pair of maternity shorts and a flowy tank top, her dark hair is piled high on her head, while the expression on her face screams "Shut your mouth!" But it is the pair of slippers on her feet that make me laugh. Ashton has a few more weeks left in her pregnancy and refuses to stay home, regardless of how many times I remove her from the schedule.

"Taylor, do not tell me what to do. It is rude and makes me want to kick you in the nuts. Of course, after I birth these children, since they make it so I cannot wear regular shoes, nor can I lift my legs high enough to reach said nuts." Ashton scrunches her face and sighs as I approach her and guide her from behind the bar to one of the stools on the opposite side.

"I know taking it easy and staying home is killing you but, girl, you can't be behind the bar in slippers. We agreed when you got to this stage, I'd remove you from the schedule and you'd help me with the paperwork bullshit I hate. *From home.* Why can't you just hold up your end of the bargain?"

Filling a glass with water, I pop a straw in the glass and slide it across the bar to her as she sniffles. Dammit, not another crying pregnant woman. The difference between Scarlett and Ashton and their crying fits is that Ashton would rather have her fiancé comforting her than me. She's told me that on more than one occasion in the last few days. So, instead of pulling her into my arms like I would Scarlett, I hold a bar napkin out for her.

After blowing her nose, taking a drink of water, and sitting back in the chair and resting her hands on her stomach, she smiles at me. "Sorry. It happens when I least expect it. I know I shouldn't be behind the bar. I'm sorry."

"What did you do now, babe?"

A huge smile appears on her face as Ashton turns to face Jameson. He leans down and places a kiss on her forehead as he settles his hand atop hers. Watching my friends, together with their hands resting atop of where their two unborn children are pulls at me. These two are going to be amazing parents, and I have no doubt their children will be kind, smart, and so full of piss and vinegar we'll all be laughing as they toss back Ashton's very own snark and sass. Something tugs at me, not envy, but something that reminds me I'll probably never know that feeling. Parenthood isn't in the cards for me, and as much as I wish things were different, this is the life I've chosen.

"I didn't do anything, did I, Taylor? That was a blanket apology. I'm feeling apologetic."

"That's right, man. She's been weepy and apologetic all day."

Ashton and I exchange a knowing smile. If Jameson knew she had been behind the bar or trying to move boxes, he would flip his lid. He's worried she'll fall or hurt herself, or the babies, if she isn't careful. I can't say I disagree. But we are also talking about Ashton Sullivan here. She may be the most stubborn woman I know.

"You ready to head home? I want to get that second crib put together tonight," Jameson says, extending his hand to Ashton.

"I suppose. You'll be okay tonight, Taylor? We really need to get another bartender in here. Since I'm off the schedule, you're already shorthanded. It'll take at least two newbies to fill my spot while I'm on maternity leave."

Chuckling, I shake my head at Ashton. I hate to agree with her, but she's right. It'll take at least two mid-level bartenders to pick up the slack with her being out for a few months. If she even comes back. Something tells me once she holds her children in her arms, she'll call me and tell me to replace her permanently.

"We'll be fine. You guys have a good night."

Waving goodbye, they head toward the front doors of Country Road. Once the door closes behind them, I look around the expansive space, checking for any customers who may have entered while I was talking. Confirming there are only the few patrons already served, I quickly finish stocking the beers Ashton was carrying.

It's taken a lot of time, and I'm proud of what I've built and the staff that has stuck with me over the years. But Ashton is right. I need help. I guess it's time to put up a sign and get the word out that I'm looking for staff.

The happy hour crowd is settling their tabs, and I excuse myself from behind the bar for a quick break. It's the usual time Scarlett sits down for dinner, and I know from my time with her it's also the loneliest time of day. I understand completely, and that's why I work nights.

I open the door to my office, pull my cell from my pocket to call her, and see a text notification. Throwing myself into the chair behind my desk, I kick my feet up on the wood surface and tap the text icon. A text from Grant about an hour ago appears.

> Grant: Head's up, I think you have a visitor coming your way tonight.

A visitor? Maybe Connor is on his way to town. He mentioned wanting to see the bar, and it wouldn't surprise me if he showed up one day without much notice. Thankfully, my couch is comfortable.

> Me: Connor trying to sneak into town or something?

Tossing my phone on the desk, I thumb through the mail of the last few days when my phone signals a response.

> Grant: Red skipped town. When I spoke to her, it was very obvious she didn't want me asking many questions. I assume she's headed your way.

> Me: She didn't call me. I'll ask my sister and see if she's heard from her. Thanks for the heads-up.

```
Grant: Take care of her.

Me: Never a question. I'll let you
know when she gets here.
```

I scroll through my phone logs and don't see a missed call or any unread texts from Scarlett. It's hard for me to believe she'd just pick up and drive hours for an impromptu trip to Lexington. Before I can pull up Addy's contact information to see if she's heard from her, a knock at the door grabs my attention. "Yeah?" I shout.

The door slowly opens and one of the waitresses sticks her head in and says, "Sorry, boss. A few groups just walked in, I think Caleb could use some help."

Nodding, I rise from the chair and stretch my arms over my head, a long deep breath released, and shake off the exhaustion and worry that Scarlett is out alone, driving without anyone truly knowing where she's headed.

I lose myself in my job for the next hour. Pouring shot after shot while flirting with the female customers has lost the romance of my early years behind the bar. Yet here I am, going through the motions as usual. I've never been one to shy away from female attention, nor one to be lacking in it. Flirting has always come easy to me. A smirk accompanied by a wink and a lingering touch as I slide a shot across the bar has never steered me wrong. During my enlistment, I encountered a few women that were looking for more than I was willing to give. Addy has teased me for years that I've left broken hearts in my wake at every assignment. I don't know about hearts, but I do know there have been a few broken dishes when I've had to remind the women I'm not looking for forever.

The difference between now and those earlier days isn't just the years but what I want out of life. I accepted my life as a bachelor years ago. I never felt it was fair to bring a woman into my life when I wasn't sure when or where I'd be reassigned or if a deployment was imminent. Now my reasons for remaining single are deeper than any of that. It's less about geography and my obligations. Like many of my friends, what I've seen, how I've learned to process it all, it's not something I'd burden another person with. Sleepless nights, nightmares, and a broken body is my cross to bear.

It doesn't mean I wish things were different. Scarlett sent me a picture of her ultrasound from her recent appointment, and I sat for too long looking at the photo. The baby looks like an alien to me but he's also the greatest looking alien ever. She's going to make an amazing mother and that boy will want for nothing. He will know what it's like to have overbearing and protective uncles. His family by blood may not be around, but his family by choice will always care for him.

"Hey handsome," a petite blonde says from across the bar. Her too tight pink tank top is close to busting at the seams as she shimmies her body up onto the bar, tits practically spilling onto the bar top. I think her name is Lisa or Lila. Something with an "L." She's been coming on to me for weeks, promising she can rock my world.

"Hey doll, what can I getcha?"

"Well," she says with a purr as her fingers slowly tap their way across the bar top, "first, I'd like a slow screw against the wall, and then I'd like a beer."

It takes everything I have in me to not roll my eyes at her come-on. Poor thing thinks she's original. In all my years bartending, I've had a statement almost identical to that with that same shot as the punchline repeated to me at least three or four times a week. And, yet I've never actually made the shot for the person asking for it. Innuendos are cute when you're twenty-something. In my mid-thirties, they're embarrassing.

"Do you have a preference of vodka?" I ask as her eyes bat rapidly. She's likely trying to figure out why I'm asking about vodka. "For the shot, A Slow *Comfortable* Screw Against the Wall."

Defeat hits her when she realizes I'm actually going to make the shot for her and not give her an actual screw against the wall. "I've changed my mind. Just a beer is fine."

Smiling, I pull a chilled glass from the cooler and turn to the taps for a domestic light beer. I toss a cardboard coaster toward the young girl who is no longer displaying her tits like an appetizer on my bar and set the pint glass down. "Three bucks." Smiling, she sets three crumpled bills on the bar and spins on her heel, glass in hand. No tip. Got it.

The second wave of customers begins to slow, and I signal for Caleb to take a break. With a nod, he doesn't hesitate to slip from behind the bar and down the hall to the back door. I begin emptying the dishwasher and wiping down the counters when a throat clears from the other side of the bar. Lifting my eyes, I'm greeted with a beautiful vision of a messy bun, wide eyes, and a smirk I've missed.

"Can I help you, miss?" I ask, leaning forward, elbows resting on the bar top.

The smirk turns to a smile. With her head tilted, the wayward traveler says, "I heard this place has the best steak sandwich in Texas. What do you know about that?"

"I'd say whoever told you that is right."

"Thank goodness. I'm starving and need sustenance.

I'll have one of those and a large water, please."

"What're you doing here, Red?"

Puckering her lips and squinting her eyes, Scarlett looks around, seemingly taking in the activity around her. People are laughing and drinking, the noise level a decent hum, not too loud but loud enough to keep the customers here for a good time. Following her gaze, I see the flirty blonde from earlier looking my way as she winks. Scarlett mutters something under her breath and quickly turns back my direction.

"Can't a friend visit a friend?"

"Of course, but I'd like to know why I had to hear about you visiting from Cap. Who, by the way, you need to let know you've made it safely to your destination."

"I already did. And I'm sorry I didn't ask you first. I just needed a break, and maybe I wanted to see you and this place. It's fantastic, Taylor. I'm really proud of you."

When she looks at me like that with her kindness shining bright, it's hard to be upset with her. Instead, I walk from behind the bar and step up to her seat. Looking at me, she looks confused as I pull her into a hug.

Chapter 10
Scarlett

When I pulled into the parking lot of Country Road, I wasn't sure what to expect. From the outside, it looks like an old-school honky tonk from the 1980s. The parking lot is gravel and the vehicles range from large pickups with massive tires to small economical hatchbacks. I knew from the hour it was likely the after-work crowd and those who come here to kick off their weekends with a few drinks.

I contemplated calling Addy before going inside. The reality that Taylor would have likely spoken to Grant and known I was headed to places unknown did give me pause. Addy would be a great buffer for any lecture I would receive, and it's been weeks since I've seen her.

Instead of playing it safe, I decided to stand my ground and instead sent a quick text to Grant, letting him know I arrived safely. He admitted to ratting me out to Taylor and was grateful I did end up in Lexington and not somewhere else alone. By the time I opened the door to the bar, excitement and nerves filtered through my body. The thumping of the music from the speakers was oddly calming. So normal and expected from a bar, I welcomed the bass and made my way across the room.

Pausing a few steps from the bar, I stood to the side and watched my friend do what he does best. Charm the ladies with smiles and winks. His charisma like a cloud around him, the women are drawn to him like a moth to a flame and I can't say I blame them. Now, pulled to his chest, my cheek resting against his beating heart, I no longer hear the music that fills the room. It's only the thump of his heart in my ear and the whoosh of my own blood rushing through my veins that I feel and hear. My hands move in circles on his lower back and he shifts, clearing his throat before he steps back.

His hands move the tendrils that have fallen around my face away and for the briefest of moments, I forget who we are. I forget he's my husband's best friend and I'm a pregnant widow. For just another beat of my heart I see the man he is, the way his dark gray eyes widen. I want nothing more than to lift my hand to his cheek, feel the scruff on my palm. Instead, I do nothing and watch as his eyes flick from my own to my mouth and back again.

"You hungry?" he asks and just like that the moment is over.

Nodding, I smile and reply, "Yep. Starved."

"Steak sandwich it is."

I sip on my water with extra lemons and limes as Taylor moves about the bar serving customers. He's the perfect balance of professional bar owner and flirtatious bartender. The attention he gives to each patron is just enough that each feels like they are the only person he's taking care of. That's what he does. He takes care of each customer. Whether it's a handshake to a regular or a wink to a shy woman, I've yet to see anyone walk away from their encounter with him unhappy.

Leaning back in my chair, I rest my hands on my baby bump and yawn. It's been a long day and the adrenaline from driving here and seeing Taylor has easily evaporated. Exhaustion overwhelms me, and the realization I haven't made a reservation at a motel hits me hard. Like everything else these days, the realization strums up tears, and I have to suck in a deep breath to keep them from falling.

To my right, I see a tall and curvy brunette slide a piece of paper across the bar top toward Taylor. He smiles and accepts the paper. A slight tug in my belly cues up an emotion I haven't felt in a long time. I won't call it jealousy. Although, envy is an adjective I'm not afraid to admit.

Brazen and without a care, the young woman didn't even wait for a confirmation he'd call before turning on her heel and walking toward the door with her friends. Instead of pocketing the paper, he crumples it up and tosses it in the trash at the end of the bar. Relief. It's the next feeling I have and, instead of questioning why that's reasonable, I sit up and smile as he turns his attention to wiping down the counter.

"Hey barkeep," I shout, catching his attention. Smiling, he turns to me. "I realized in my haste to get out of town, I forgot to book a room somewhere. Is there a preferred motel here in Lexington?"

"Scarlett, you aren't staying at a motel. You'll stay at my place."

"No way," I screech. Coughing to cover up the squeal, I continue, "I mean, I don't want to be in the way. A motel is fine."

"Red, take this," he says, pulling a key from his keychain and holding it out for me to take. "I've already text you my address to enter into your GPS. Go to my place and get settled. I'll be home in about an hour, once things here settle down a bit."

Taking my phone from my purse, I look at the notifications and see the text he mentioned. Accepting the key, I glance back up at him, his expression leaves no room for argument and I nod in agreement.

"What about my sandwich?" I ask, my stomach echoing the query.

"I had it boxed up to go. I figured you were exhausted from the drive. Here you go." He lifts a white bag from the counter and sets it on the bar in front of me. I guess he's thought of everything. Sliding off the stool, I pull my purse across my body and pick up my dinner, tugging awkwardly on the straps of my purse before saying, "Thank you. I guess I'll see you?"

"I won't be long. Make yourself at home and I'll see you in a bit."

Before I can reply, another customer approaches the bar, taking his attention away from me. Giving myself a few beats to watch Taylor, I do as I'm told and leave for his house.

Taylor's home is a pleasant surprise. Sure, the expected monochromatic colored furniture, massive big screen television, and ramen noodles in the cupboards exist but so do splashes of color throughout the main living space, a large wooden art piece I assume was hand-crafted is hanging from the vaulted ceiling, and top-of-the-line appliances are nestled into their nooks in the expansive kitchen. An entire wall is nothing but what appears to be river rock, a fireplace in the middle of it with framed photos lining the wooden mantel. The picture of him and Henry as teenagers causes me to pause in my perusal. Picking up the frame, I run my finger along the faces of the two men who have given me more emotional support and care than anyone else in my entire life. My family included.

Setting the photo back in its spot, I continue looking around the main living space. It's warm and inviting, comfortable and homey. I long to nestle into the couch with a blanket, but what I need more is a shower. Leaving my suitcase at the foot of the stairs, I wander up to the second-floor landing, looking for the guest room. Opening the first and then second door, I only see rooms being used for storage. Rooms that haven't received attention or the makeover of the first floor. The third door is a bathroom that looks usable but without a shower curtain.

Meandering back down the stairs, I follow the long hallway to an open doorway. A spacious bedroom greets me. The room is easily the size of all my small bedrooms at home combined. I know this because the biggest bed I've ever seen sits in the middle of the room and does nothing to fill the space. A small door to the left, I assume the closet, is closed, but to the right I see an open doorway. Walking into the bedroom, the scent of lemon furniture polish mixed with a hint of sage and musk greets me. A pair of sweats is on the floor at the foot of the bed and I lean down to pick them up, placing them on the bed before walking toward the open door.

"Whoa," I whisper. Taking a step forward, I'm suddenly in a beautiful oasis. A room that would easily fit in any home makeover television show, this bathroom has everything you could dream of. Double sinks with separate mirrors to the left and a large multi-person shower to the right. Below a large window sits a clawfoot tub, and I can't help but clap my hands together in excitement at the long and glorious bath I'm about to take.

The room is white but not sterile. If I were to ever design the perfect bathroom, this would easily fit the bill. Next to the shower are open shelves lined with towels and a few decorative baskets. I loved the living room, but Taylor may find it difficult to get me out of this room.

Excitement I haven't felt in a long-time courses through my body and I practically skip to the tub, turn on the water, quickly grab a towel before adding a little body wash to the water to make some bubbles, and undress. Sliding my body into the suds, I settle in and let the tension I've been holding fade from my existence.

I doze, not really falling asleep but allowing myself to fully relax and live in this moment, for what feels like only seconds but is long enough for my skin to prune and the water to cool. As goosebumps sprinkle my skin, I rise up, and grab the towel I set on the side of the tub.

Patting my arms and body, I take in my reflection in the mirror. My skin is flushed from the bath and I notice the small changes pregnancy has done to my body. The light dusting of freckles I've had my entire life have darkened as have my areolas. My breasts, double the size they've always been, are heavy and full. I can't imagine what they'll be like over the next few months as my body prepares for birth.

Thankfully, Taylor invested in large bath sheets and I'm able to wrap it around my chest and tuck the end in. Stepping up to the mirror, I pull my hair from the bun on my head and run my fingers through the tresses, breaking up the small knots in the process. Turning on the faucet, I wet my hands and tap down some of the flyaways on my head before spinning on my heel.

Looking around the room, I realize I didn't bring my suitcase with me, so I have nothing to change into. Shit. I listen and don't hear anything in the house and assume I'm still here alone. Quickly, I pad my way out of the room and into the hallway.

Chapter 11

Taylor

Tossing my keys, phone and wallet on the counter, I open the refrigerator and grab a bottle of beer from the shelf. Twisting off the cap, I toss it in the trash and bring the bottle to my lips. It was a long fucking night but one that turned out to be pretty fantastic when Scarlett showed up. It was great to have her in my bar, simply people watching and sipping from her straw. I'll admit, I was thrown for a loop when she mentioned getting a motel room. The thought never occurred to me. As soon as I read Grant's text and saw she was headed this way, I assumed she'd stay here, and we'd resume the sleeping arrangements we had at her house. Me on the couch and her in the comfortable bed.

As I take in another draw from my beer, out of the corner of my eye I see her suitcase sitting at the foot of the stairs. Shit, I never told her to put her stuff in my room and use my bathroom. Groaning, I set the bottle on the counter and walk to her bag, pulling it behind me down the hall toward the bedroom. Just as I'm about to turn into the bedroom, Scarlett runs smack into me. Instinctively, my hand reaches out and I grab onto her, righting her so she doesn't fall.

With my hand wrapped around her waist, she gasps and her hands rest on my chest. Looking down, I'm hit straight in the gut with the vision before me. Her hair is a wild mane of red waves, skin flushed and wrapped in a towel. Startled, I can see her chest move as she breathes heavily. But, when she looks up through her wet lashes, bottom lip nestled between her teeth, I come unglued.

Lust and an unspeakable energy swirls around us like a tornado of emotions and attraction. My mouth is suddenly dry, the beer I just drank long forgotten. Without thinking, my grip on her hip tightens, pulling her a little closer to my body. The need to wrap her in my arms and taste that lip she's mutilating with her teeth is overwhelming. Instead, I release her and take a step back, the quick movement leaving her unsteady on her feet.

Clearing my throat I say, "Hey, I was just bringing your suitcase to you."

"Oh. Thanks. I guess I forgot to take it with me. That's been happening, I'm suddenly quite forgetful." She smiles sheepishly but I watch as her eyes dart to my lips. Heat fills my veins, and I know I need to get away from her before I do something completely stupid.

"Well, here you go. I'm just going to . . . yep, here you go."

Sliding her suitcase toward her, I turn and bolt down the hall to the kitchen and safety. A reprieve from the suddenly overwhelming attraction to my best friend's wife. Picking up my previously discarded bottle, I finish off the beer, toss the bottle in the recycling, and grab another bottle from the refrigerator.

I have to get my shit together. I cannot think of Scarlett that way. It's wrong on so many levels. Not only is she my best friend's wife, but she's carrying his child. And a fucking widow. Jesus, he's only been gone two months, and I'm already lusting over her. But goddamn, she looked like a fucking siren standing there in the dark. Knowing she was naked under that towel is doing nothing to dampen my desire.

"Gosh, what I wouldn't give for a glass of wine. That's wrong, isn't it?" Her voice pulls me from my own thoughts. Turning, I see her standing next to the counter. Dressed in a tight-fitting tank top that is clearly not maternity and a pair of loose-fitting sweats resting on her hips, she may look more sinful than she did in the towel. Fuck, I need to get it together.

"I don't think there's anything wrong with that. Indulging may be a different story."

Sighing, she pulls out one of the chairs at the counter and settles in. With her chin resting in her palm, she smiles. I watch her, waiting for her to say something about what just happened in the hallway. Instead, she smiles and says, "Thanks for letting me stay. That tub is amazing. I may never leave."

"You are welcome to it anytime. I'm not much of a bath guy. It was more for resale value."

"Well done. It's perfect."

I take another draw from my beer and wait. When she says nothing and only comments on the renovations I've made to the house, I breathe a sigh of relief at the realization she didn't experience the same thing I did in the hallway. That'll make it all a lot easier.

"I haven't done any work upstairs so while you're here, I'll take the couch. I'm just going to shower off the night.

Want to watch a movie when I'm done?"

Nodding, she smiles, and if I'm not mistaken, releases a long breath. Whether it's relief or disappointment, I'm uncertain. For her and me. Maybe my assessment of earlier was wrong, and she felt it too only she's much better at playing it off than I am.

"Got any popcorn in this bachelor pad?"

Laughing, I look to the takeout bag still sitting on the counter.

"For dessert. I'm going to need a snack."

Opening the pantry door and motion toward the stocked shelves. "Every snack imaginable. I have a teenage nephew who requires all of the processed food essentials whenever he stays over."

I step away from the door as she stands, and I awkwardly walk the long way around the kitchen island before retreating to my bedroom and what is going to be a very cold shower.

As the credits roll on the movie, Scarlett's soft snores fill the quiet. I sit and watch her doze. With her feet in my lap, she's curled on her side, head resting on the pillow I brought out for my makeshift bed. Shifting a little, her sweats have settled lower on her hips while her tank has risen slightly, exposing her baby bump. Her hair is once again piled on top of her head. While I miss seeing her wild mane spread across the pillow, with her hair off her face I'm able to see every freckle on her creamy skin.

I thought watching an action movie would lessen the

attraction I've felt for her all night. I was wrong. Nothing has diminished the ache I'm feeling. I hate myself for every second of it but can't deny it's there. Simmering below the surface of every word spoken and every movement, I itch to touch her. And now, I need to. I need to wake her and get her off this couch and into my bed for a good night's sleep. Tomorrow is a new day, and I will not envision her naked.

Slipping her feet from my lap, I rise from the couch and lightly brush my hand across her arm and up to her shoulder, trying not to startle her. Nothing. She doesn't even twitch. I try again with a little more effort. Still nothing except a loud snort of a snore causing me to chuckle. I could leave her here on the couch to sleep but I'd feel horrible knowing she's out here when I'm in the bed. Instead, I bend down and pull her hands so she's in a sitting position. Her eyes flutter open, a small smile appearing on her lips.

"Did I fall asleep?" she asks groggily.

"Sure did. Let's get you to bed, sweetheart."

Begrudgingly she stands and lets me guide her down the hall and into my bedroom. Pulling back the covers, I motion her to the bed and without another word, she slides under the covers and into the middle of the bed. When she turns to her side, facing me, eyes slightly open, she says, "You should sleep in here with me. It's big enough for at least five people."

There could not be a worse idea, so I say, "Sleep well, Red." As I exit the room, I hear her mumble a goodnight.

Once I return to the living room, I clean up our bowls of popcorn and drinks before making up a bed on the couch. Grabbing the remote control, I flip through my recorded shows for something to watch. It'll be hours before

I'm able to sleep, not only because my mind is still on the woman fast asleep in my bed, but because it's rare I manage more than a few hours of sleep a night.

Choosing the latest episode of my favorite courtroom drama, I settle in for a long night of television watching and mindless games on my phone.

Chapter 12

Scarlett

Rolling over, I burrow my face in the pillow. What the . . .

This does not smell like my lavender scented sheets. Slowly, I rise up on my elbows and peel my eyes open. And, they are not yellow. Shit. This isn't my bed. It's . . . Taylor's. How did I get here? I barely remember half the movie he put on last night, let alone how I ended up nestled into this amazing bed. Without a care, I sniff the sheets once more and smile. The scent is a cross between that sagey smell I encountered when I walked in the room and a fresh outdoor scent. Masculine. It smells masculine.

Flopping over onto my back, I look up at the ceiling and try to gather a smidgen of a memory of last night but fall short. What I do recall is the way his hands held me while I was wearing only a towel. The way his fingers gripped my waist and sent a jolt of awareness straight between my legs.

Listening to my audio book is off the table during this visit. There's no way I can listen to Hawk Weaver say all of those sinful things over and over and sit next to Taylor while we share a bowl of popcorn and watch action movies. Only action movies. Nothing romantic or with a hint of sexual tension between the characters. Nope, not for this girl. If anything remotely sexy appears on the screen, I'm likely to climb him like a tree and beg him to reenact my book.

I knew the moment I walked in the kitchen and he didn't say anything, the feeling I had in the hallway was completely one-sided. Taylor Cain is too much of a stand-up guy to ever be attracted to his best friend's wife. Besides, he's hot as hell and can have any woman he wants. That much was evident when I was sitting at the bar watching women slide him their numbers and put their cleavage on display. There's no way he's looking at my pregnant body and thinking of anything except of how I'm going to birth this child. Which is something I should start thinking about too.

Birthing classes, buying the necessities, and how I'm going to manage all of this on my own. At my last doctor's appointment, the nurse mentioned how she had her entire family in the room with her while she gave birth to her daughter only a few months ago. I held it together until I was in my car and then cried at the realization I have nobody to lean on during my birth. There will be no husband or mother holding my legs while I curse expletives like it's my job.

Kicking off the covers, I refuse to wallow in my reality just yet. I have four and a half months to get my affairs in order. Thankfully, the payments on the life insurance and other benefits have started rolling in, and I won't have to work until the baby is at least three months old. I made sure to set aside enough money to cover my basic bills to allow me time to recover and get into a routine with the baby until I figure out exactly what I'll be doing for work and daycare once the time comes.

Padding my way into the massive bathroom, I handle my early morning business before making my way out to the kitchen. The aroma of freshly brewed coffee and the sizzle of bacon greets me as I enter the main living space. Taylor is standing in the kitchen with his back to me. With his phone to his ear, he flips the bacon in the pan and grumbles a few one-word responses to whomever.

Once he tosses his phone on the counter, I clear my throat to announce my presence.

"Morning," I say with sleep still evident in my voice.

"Hiya. How'd you sleep?"

Looking at his phone and back at him I ask, "Everything okay?"

"Yep. It was my sister. She and Landon are out of town for the weekend while Mason stays with Landon's parents. I was thinking we could all cookout today, but since they're gone, you're stuck with only me."

"I think I can manage. I'm happy for Addy. From what she said, Landon is a great guy."

Opening the refrigerator, Taylor holds up a carton and I nod in confirmation. As he pours me a glass of juice he says, "Yeah, he is. We've been friends for a few years and while I never would have pegged those two for each other, it's a natural fit. After her dickhead ex-husband, it's great to see someone put her first for a change. And Mason. He's great for both of them."

"What about you? Do you think you'll ever get married?" I ask as I sip from my cup. The look on his face is a cross between horror and confusion. I can't help but laugh. "Calm down, I wasn't talking about today. I just mean in general, maybe in the future."

"I think that ship has sailed for me. Making room for another person isn't something I've managed, and I don't think I would even know where to start with that. Besides, I keep awful hours for anyone needing date nights."

Letting his response sit, I watch in silence as he goes about finishing a pan of bacon and whips up some scrambled eggs. Normally I'd ask if I can help, step in and make the eggs myself, but something tells me that offer would be shot down. Instead, I sit back in my chair, rest my hands on my belly, and watch. He's methodical in his process, watching the butter in the pan as he whisks the eggs. Once he pours the eggs in the pan he steps away and pops a few slices of bread in the toaster before sipping from his coffee cup.

I want to ask him if he does this routine often. Have a woman sitting in this seat as he makes her breakfast. I'd be surprised if the answer was anything except yes, but I honestly don't want to know. I like the idea that this moment is special, just something for us.

He must feel my gaze because he turns, and a slow smile appears on his face. That same emotion I felt in the hallway last night returns. My heart beats quickly and a heat rises across my skin like I'm standing outside on the hottest summer day. His gaze slowly takes inventory of me, settling on my chest before rising to my face. Opening his mouth to say something, he stops when the toast pops, and he looks at the pan.

"Shit!" he shouts before flipping the burner to off and lifting the pan from the flame. The faintest scent of burnt egg appearing.

I stifle a giggle at his frustration, and he shoots me a dirty look. His looks don't intimidate me, and I let the laughter bellow out of me. It isn't long before his own laughter fills the room. Once he's plated our breakfasts, he assumes the seat next to me, bumping my elbow with his. "How would you feel about a drive? Show you a little of Lexington."

"I think that sounds perfect. Will there be snacks?"

Seemingly amused by my question, he nods his head. "Yeah, Red. We'll get snacks."

Smiling, I lift my toast to my mouth and chew while never taking my eyes off him.

"Don't you have to work? I just dropped in unannounced. Surely you don't just happen to have time off to entertain me."

"I have it covered. What do you say, snacks and a drive?"

"Count me in. But first, I'm eating all of this then treating myself to another bath."

I dig into my breakfast and contemplate bringing up the idea of him marrying again but settle on saying, "It's a shame you won't cook for a wife like this. Your eggs are delicious."

Taylor keeps his eyes on me, no words spoken, just a stare. It isn't uncomfortable nor is it something I'll allow myself to wonder about. Instead, I smile and bring another mouthful of deliciousness to my lips.

When Taylor said we were going for a drive I thought he meant we'd meander around the town. Maybe he'd show me a few of the highlights, feed me, and then we'd be done. That is a big fat no. Yes, we drove through town, he showed me where I can get the "best damn breakfast burrito," what Country Road looks like in the daylight, and where Addy lives. When he started out of town, I teased him he was driving me somewhere remote to bury my body. I laughed. He didn't.

Instead, he told me to trust him, sit back, and enjoy the scenery. So I did. And I don't regret it. For the first time in months, I feel content. Relaxed and in the moment. I'm not worrying about how someone is looking at me, if they're judging my laughter or smile as too soon, there's no pity to be found and it turns out, Taylor and I have very similar music tastes.

Turning off the main highway, we hit a bumpy road, which is not great for my pregnancy bladder. I grip the handle of the door and rest my head back on the seat. Maybe if I pretend my bladder isn't in distress, I can will the need to relieve myself away. The moment the road smooths out and I'm no longer bouncing in my seat, I find a little reprieve, but the need still exists.

"Is there a restroom or a plethora of bushes where you're taking me?" I ask, dancing in my seat.

"Huh?"

Cocking my head, I point to my stomach and he cringes. "Oh shit. Sorry. I forgot. I mean, I didn't . . . my buddy has a cabin out here. I'll park there and you can use the bathroom."

"Are you sure? I'm not a delicate flower, ya know? I can make do like anyone else as long as you can find me a little privacy."

Ignoring me, he turns the truck down a small road and within minutes we're in front of a tiny A-frame cabin. A small shed that matches the color scheme of the cabin sits off to the side and other than a picnic table, there is nothing but land as far as the eye can see. Putting the truck in park, Taylor kills the engine and jumps out before running around to open my door. Once I'm unbuckled, I take his offered hand and step onto the gravel. Tugging me toward the front of the cabin, Taylor feels around on the frame before pulling down a key and opening the door.

Ushering me inside, he steps off to the side and I walk quickly inside the small place. I can see a door open to the left and assume it's the bathroom. Finally relieved, I take the small hand towel hanging on the wall and look at the small bathroom. It's little but decorated nicely with hints that a woman has added her personal touch to the space.

Opening the door, I step into the living room, and Taylor is nowhere to be found so I allow myself a minute to take in the space. The furniture is sparse but there's a couch, chair, and hutch against the wall. The kitchen is open with a few barstools at the counter.

"Jameson and Ashton are planning to add on to this space and make it more family friendly now that they're going to be parents."

Jumping, I turn to the voice behind me, hand on my chest.

"Jesus. You cannot sneak up on a pregnant woman. I almost pissed myself."

Laughing, he motions for me to follow him outside. I do as instructed, and when I step outside, I take in all that beautiful land before us.

"It's great, isn't it?"

"Yeah. Beautiful. Do you come out here often?" Rolling my eyes at the cliché of a pick-up line, I turn to him as he replies.

"Not as much as I should. Ashton has been my right hand at the bar, but now that she and Jameson are together and starting a family, she's not around and it's all falling to me." We walk over to the truck, and he pulls two bottles of water from the small cooler we packed. "Let's take a little stroll around the lake."

Walking side by side, I listen as he tells me about guy trips to this lake just a few years ago and how that has turned into couples and eventually will include children. We stop to skip rocks and just watch the beautiful scenery before us. I'm in awe of this place and how quiet and serene it is. I can imagine living somewhere like this, with the sounds of nature waking you each morning and singing you to sleep at night.

Stepping up onto a rock, I turn to ask Taylor if it's time for snacks when I begin to lose my balance. As I flail and begin to fall toward the ground, he swoops in and catches me. His arms cradling me to his chest, my hands landing on his shoulders.

My heart flutters.

My breath hitches.

My pulse races.

It's that same feeling as last night all over again.

Only, this time, Taylor doesn't let go of me as he rights us. Standing toe to toe, I lightly glide my hands across his shoulders and around to the nape of his neck. Glancing to his lips, I watch as his tongue slowly peeks out and glides across the bottom lip.

And then he steps back. Again.

Clearing his throat, he runs his hand through his hair and whispers, "Scarlett."

Confliction and frustration are evident in his movements. My heart drops at the realization he has no intention of pursuing whatever attraction this is between us. Disappointment replaces the lust I was feeling, but I won't let him see it. I'll plaster on a smile and pretend like nothing is wrong. That's the right thing to do.

"Snacks. I'm hungry. Let's go get some of those snacks," I say enthusiastically. Fake enthusiasm but still, it's there.

Stepping around Taylor, I begin walking toward the truck and my snacks because when in doubt—eat cheese and crackers.

Chapter 13

Taylor

All day she walked around in those goddamn shorts and that too tight tank top. Complaining about her "huge ass" did nothing but draw my eyes to her backside like a fucking neon sign. And then there was the thirty minutes or so of her stretching and lying in the sun. I'm not too proud to say I excused myself to the cabin for the restroom when in reality, I was reciting the alphabet backwards. In Spanish. All in an effort to diminish the growing hard-on in my shorts.

And I hate myself a little more for it. Scarlett is a beautiful woman, and I've never seen her as anything but a friend and savior to my oldest friend. Until this weekend. Now I see beyond her beauty and kind heart. I feel a primal need to touch and taste her.

It's wrong. I know it's wrong, disrespectful, and at the very least in bad taste. Regardless of how over she says their marriage was, I have a hard time wrapping my brain around the idea that she and Henry were planning a life apart while raising their son together. I'm not sure I'd be strong enough to do that, and I sit in even more awe of her.

As we drive back to town, the sounds of Eric Church fill the cab of my truck; the lyrics of the song playing aren't lost on me. Desperate. I feel desperate. Desperate for her touch and laugh. For more conversations about nothing and yet everything. Moments of quiet when neither of us feel it's necessary to fill the void. Comfortable. Content. In the moment. That's how I feel when I'm with her.

As we approach Lexington, I consider stopping by Country Road to check on things and grab takeout, but a quick glance to my right and I know I need to get her home and comfortable. She'd never say it, but I know a day exploring in the sun wore her out. It sure did me, and I'm not carrying another human in my body.

Just the thought of her nurturing and growing another person makes my heart beat faster. I'd never admit it to anyone, but I'm a little jealous of the moments she's having and pissed the fuck off at Henry for not being here to share them with her. Each time she rests her hand on her stomach, I wonder what she feels. Is it the baby moving? Is it a simple gesture she doesn't give much thought to? Earlier today, while she lounged on an Adirondack chair, her feet propped on my leg, and her hands loosely gliding across her stomach, I almost asked if I could touch her. If there was anything to feel. It seemed awkward and completely inappropriate, so I didn't. But the thought did cross my mind.

Turning into my driveway, I pull beside her car and put the truck in park. Stirring slightly, she shifts in the seat and slowly opens her eyes. With her head resting on the headrest, she turns to face me, a slow smile appearing on her beautiful sun-kissed face.

"Did I sleep the entire way home?"

"You did," I say, pushing the garage door opener. As the door slowly opens, I turn to her and ask, "Hungry? I was thinking maybe we could order a pizza."

"Sounds delicious," she says as I open the door and hop out of the cab.

Before I can make it around and open her door, she slides out of the seat and closes the door. By the time I round the corner, she's walking toward the open garage. Shaking my head, I motion for her to go ahead.

"Don't be grumpy. I am capable of opening my own doors."

"As much as that's true, I was raised to be a gentleman."

"Oh hush. That's saved for dates and women you're trying to impress," she scoffs, opening the door to the house.

Darkness fills the kitchen as we walk into the main room. Moonlight offers enough light to see where we're going but not much more. Although it's my house and I should know my way around here with my eyes closed, I still manage to run into one of the chairs at the counter, sending her into a fit of giggles. Groaning, I rub the spot on my knee that whacked the chair and walk over to the wall to flip on the lights.

As the room lights up, she says, "Do you mind if I shower really quick? That nap did nothing but make me more tired, and I think it would help."

"Mi casa es su casa. Have at it. I'll order the pizza. Any requests?"

"Anything except pineapple," she replies as she walks down the hallway. I allow myself only two quick seconds of looking at her ass before I move to the refrigerator, pull a beer out, and toss the cap on the counter. In only two drinks I finish the bottle and pull my phone from my pocket.

A quick call to the local pizzeria and a vegetarian and a meat lover are on the way, because you can really never have too much pizza. Plus, if I remember anything from my sister's pregnancy, she could change her mind three times in a five-minute period. I'm not taking any chances with Scarlett.

While I wait for my dinner companion to finish her shower and the pizza to arrive, I unload the breakfast dishes from the dishwasher and open another beer. I shoot a text off to Grant letting him know Scarlett is still here and seems to be doing well. Although we haven't really talked about it, I think not being surrounded by her day to day life is helping her process her new normal, whatever that is.

When the doorbell rings with the delivery, I start to shout for Scarlett to hurry but the soft hum of a blow dryer stops me. Placing the pizza boxes on the counter, I pull plates from the cupboards and ranch from the refrigerator. The soft patter of feet lets me know I'm not alone and I open the boxes as a low groan escapes her throat.

"You do love me. It smells amazing." Her dramatic inhale makes me laugh as she peers over the counter. "Two pizzas? I know the saying is 'eating for two' but I'm not actually going to eat enough for two."

Laughing, I lift the empty plate to her and motion for her to choose her slice. "There's nothing better than pizza for breakfast."

I watch as she concentrates on the two boxes in front of her. That lower lip is tugged between her teeth again, and it's only then that I take in her appearance.

"Red, are you wearing my T-shirt?"

A blush across her cheeks and a smirk are all I receive in response before she clears her throat and says shyly, "I didn't bring enough pajamas, and I'm a little sunburnt from today. This was loose and . . . I can change. I'm sorry. It was rude of me to assume."

"No!" I shout, startling myself. "Sorry. No, it's cool. I don't mind." I actually fucking like it a little too much.

Placing two slices of pizza on my plate, I open the refrigerator and grab a bottle of water for Scarlett, handing it to her as she smiles and makes her choice, pointing to the box with the veggie pizza. Following her to the living room, I sit in the spot next to her and pick up the remote control.

"Sorry, Red. It's my night for television. How do you feel about fish tanks?"

Rolling her eyes, she takes a bite of her pizza and says nothing in response. And once again, the comfortable silence and simplicity of being here with her joins us. There's a time I would have called this boring. Sitting with a woman, eating pizza, and watching mindless television instead of partying at a bar. And yet, this feels better than hitting on women and drinking my night away ever did.

After the first episode finishes, we both take our plates to the kitchen. Moving around each other in synchronized harmony, I place the pizza boxes in the fridge while she places the plates in the dishwasher. When I turn away from the fridge, she's in my space, bumping into me.

Reaching out to steady her, I say, "We have to stop meeting like this."

Once again, my hands are wrapped around her waist while hers rest on my biceps. This time, my hands have gathered the loose T-shirt, and her body is flush against mine. Looking up at me, her eyes go wide. Pupils dilated,

I know that look. I've seen it time and time again with women in my bed. Desire. Swirling around us, there's no denying the way her body melds to mine.

"Taylor." Her voice is a whisper, barely audible.

Lifting my hand to the side of her face, I brush her hair behind her ear, my fingers slowly descending to her neck and then shoulder. Lingering on her shoulder, I glance to her lips and watch as she licks them and ever so slowly rises on her toes, her lips closer and closer to mine. So close I can feel her breath. I can smell the spices from our pizza and can count the freckles on her nose. As her eyes close and the space between us diminishes, I slowly lower my mouth toward hers and then the realization of what is about to happen hits me like a ton of bricks and I release her, causing her to stumble.

A look of disappointment flashes across her face but she quickly schools it and stands up straight, shoulders back and a look of indifference on her face.

Hurt.

Something I've tried to keep her from feeling, but clearly it's something I've done. Needing to right the wrong, I lift my hand to reach for her but she steps back.

"I'm going to turn in early. Goodnight."

Pivoting, she hurries from the kitchen, leaving me alone and feeling like a total piece of shit for how I've made her feel.

Chapter 14

Scarlett

I've been hiding out in the master bedroom for three hours. Three long hours of passing multiple levels on my phone games, listening to Hawk Weaver read me a bedtime story, and tossing and turning because, while I've been in here for hours, I'm not tired. It's actually the opposite. I'm amped up and full of energy. Emotionally, it's a different story. I'm frustrated and embarrassed. Which also means I'm craving one of the ice cream bars I saw in the freezer earlier. I'm not above eating my feelings and emotions.

Sure, I could go out to the kitchen and get myself an ice cream bar, never speaking to Taylor. Avoiding all eye contact and opportunities to further embarrass myself. What was I thinking? Of course he doesn't want to kiss me. He is being kind and a good friend. There is absolutely zero reason he would be attracted to me. I swear my stomach grows an inch every hour and while Taylor Cain is one of the best men I know, he'd be crazy to look at me and see anything other than friendship.

Quietly, I crack open the bedroom door and peek out into the hallway. I can hear the low hum of the television from the other room, but the house is dark. Maybe that means he's fallen asleep. Taking my chances, I tiptoe down the hall. As I enter the main living space, the television giving just enough light that I don't kick a piece of furniture or trip, I slide into the kitchen and reach for the handle of the freezer.

That's not a stainless-steel handle.

It's a body.

Crap.

"Eep!" I shout and jump back, knocking into the counter. "Ouch."

"Shit. Are you okay?" Taylor asks, reaching out to touch me but he stops himself. Awkwardly, he pulls his hand back.

"I'm fine. I was just coming for some ice cream."

"Okay, well, uh . . . help yourself." Without another word, he turns and walks the opposite direction around the island. I watch as he resumes his spot on the couch, back pressed into the corner with his legs resting on the table in front of him.

Passing on the ice cream, I follow him into the living room and take the spot next to him. Sitting sideways, facing him, I watch as he takes a sip from his water and then places the glass on the table. I can't take my eyes off of him. While I was wallowing in the bedroom, he got half naked.

Sitting next to me in his shorts, sans shirt, with the glow of the television and moonlight lighting the room, I'm mesmerized and slightly taken aback. I've seen the ink on his arms but until this moment I realized I've never seen

Taylor without his shirt on.

There are moments you want to freeze in time. Your first kiss, your first love, the moment you hear your child's heartbeat for the first time—pivotal moments. And when your husband's best friend is half naked, sporting a tattoo that not only mesmerizes you but also sends a shiver of intrigue and awe up your spine. That's what I just experienced. If you were to ask me about my first kiss or my first love, I can't say if I'd remember the specifics. But Taylor Cain sitting shirtless in the moonlight is something I'll be able to recall for the rest of my life.

"Taylor, your chest." My voice is quiet, which seems fitting for the moment.

"It's armor. I know it's a little weird at first but there was a lot of scarring." Tilting my head, I squint my eyes as if that will help me understand what he means. "Honey, you more than anyone know the scars aren't always those that rest on the surface."

Tears well in my eyes. He's right, I know the scars he speaks of. They are the same ones Henry bore and the ones I feel making their mark on my heart. Scars run deep in each of us. Maybe that's why we connect so seamlessly. His scars. My scars. Everything we've been burdened with, it all sits between us. A mountain of issues and a plethora of chaos, but I want nothing more than to touch him. To run my fingers across the intricate design that covers his chest. The artist who did this work is a genius.

Without allowing myself a second to pull back, I extend my arm, my fingers only a fraction of an inch from his chest with my gaze fixed on the three-dimensional ink. Before my fingers make contact, I look up and catch his eye. For once, I see a look that matches mine.

Lust.

Desire.

Taking that as an invitation, I allow the contact of my skin upon his. The warmth of his chest warms my fingertips and I cease breathing. My heart beats rapidly. It's barely a moment but one I want to remember.

Feeling embolden, I rise to my knees, my hand gliding across his skin. His breath catches, but he doesn't stop my perusal of his body. I know there may never be a moment like this again. Without a second thought, I pull my left leg out from under me and slide it across his lap.

Settling atop him, my hands rest on his shoulders, his lightly sitting on my hips. Moving my body, I continue my hands-on motion across his upper body, but it's no longer about his tattoo, about the scars, or anything other than this moment with him. Needing him to move his hands, to touch me, I twist my hips, a gentle push into his lap and he groans, his head leaning back. With his eyes closed I take the opportunity and rest my lips on his chin and then the corner of his lips.

It's a test. An out for him should he choose. The hesitation on his part is nothing compared to the desire I feel. It empowers me, allows me the power to take what I've wanted, what I've dreamt of. My fingers thread through his hair as I continue to kiss him, my tongue sliding across the seam of his lips as my body touches his. It feels like an eternity but can't be more than a heartbeat before his grip on my hips tightens and he relents, opening his mouth.

Swirling tongues, each touch pulling me further into an abyss of emotion and desire, I make a mental note of every moment. Flooding my mind and body, every touch of his tongue draws me deeper into the darkness of passion. My nipples are hard and sensitive, the friction of the shirt touching them, hindering on the border of pain and passion. When his hands slide beneath the T-shirt, his shirt, and find the naked skin of my backside, I push my pelvis into him again, the friction everything I need.

Slowly, I pull back and look him in the eye, my fingers still gripping his hair. Contemplation and an entire conversation takes place between us without a single word spoken. Rising from the couch, he takes my hands in his, lifting them to his lips. Shivers run up my spine at the contact. Somehow it feels more intimate than the teenage makeout session we were just having. The look in his eyes, enthralling and lustful, takes my breath away.

Taking a step out of his personal space, I turn and link our fingers. Pausing briefly, I give him an out. A chance to stop this before I take another step. When he doesn't say anything, I link our fingers and walk toward the bedroom. This is a risk; everything will change, but I don't have it in me to care. I'm selfish and needy. Wantful. It's more than desire; it's need. Looking over my shoulder, I catch his gaze and slow my steps, mesmerized by the look in his eyes as I wait for him to stop me. I'm giving him another out. Instead, he tugs me to him, our lips meeting again. These kisses are more intense, emotional and sensual; the desire to move my body is overwhelming.

With one hand wrapped around my waist and the other threaded in my hair, he walks me backward. His lips never leave mine, and I love every second of our contact. When we reach the bedroom, he lays me on the bed, the covers pulled back from my hours spent in here earlier. The coolness of the sheets sends a chill up my bare legs, and my nipples harden more, begging for attention. Sensing my needs, Taylor kneels between my legs and tugs the shirt up and over my head. I want to cover myself, embarrassed by the size of my breasts, but the look in his eyes stops me. Leaning down, he tugs the erect peak into his mouth, his tongue swirling around it, and a flood of wetness covers my panties. Lifting my hips, I wrap my legs around his waist.. pulling his body to me. It's then the reality of our situation hits me. Or, rather, hits him.

My baby bump makes this position awkward, and I half expect him to lift up and apologize. To stop the amazing things he's doing to my body because of regret and humility. But he doesn't. Instead, he flips us so I'm on top of him, my legs straddling him. When I lean down to kiss him, I'm stopped mid-motion by his hands gripping each breast, and he begins feasting like a man starved.

The sensation and pleasure is too much, and I feel my orgasm building. When his erection hits my core in the right spot, a whimper escapes and I roll my hips, grinding against him. His breathing labors, mine mimicking the sound, and as the wave of my climax rushes through my body, I let out a mewl that would give a cat in heat a run for her money.

Every fiber of my body lights up like a Fourth of July firework. It's been months since I've been touched, but it's been even longer since I've come with such vigor. Resting my face into the crook of Taylor's neck, inhaling his scent and realizing I've never felt more at home than I do in his arms. His hands slide up and down my back, soothing my thumping heart.

A soft kiss to the side of my head pulls me from my thoughts. Sliding up onto my elbows, I look at the man before me. His usually gray eyes are bright and clear blue, but his expression is hard to read. Shifting my hips, I smirk as he groans and throws his head back. Moving my head slightly, my lips graze his chest and I poke my tongue out to taste the saltiness of his skin. The tattoo no longer holds an ominous presence around us and is, instead, begging for my touch.

My hands skirt down his sides and just as they reach his waistband, I feel his hand on my wrist. Pausing, I look into his eyes and stormy gray has returned, replacing the clear blue.

"Scarlett." His voice is gravelly and the tone remorseful and sad. "We can't."

Sitting up quickly, he takes in a breath at my fast movement, but I don't care if he's uncomfortable. Shame falls over me like a veil. Crossing my arms across my chest, I sniffle back a tear of embarrassment.

"No, don't do that. You're beautiful, and this isn't because I don't want you," he says with his hand reaching up to grip my cheek.

All of it is too much. His touches, my heart—the beating and breaking—shatters the dam of tears, and they freely fall. Without words, I lift myself off him, but he doesn't let me go far. Instead, he sits up with the discarded T-shirt in his hand. Slowly he pulls it over my head as I sniffle and let him.

"Red, look at me." I do as instructed and he smiles. "We need to talk about this but not right now. If you don't mind, I'd like to hold you tonight."

Nodding, I lie on my side, my back to his front as he spoons behind me, pulling the covers over us. His arm curls around my side, resting just above where my son sleeps, and I don't bother stopping the flood of tears as they drip onto the pillow.

Chapter 15

Taylor

It isn't the bright light of the morning sun that wakes me. It's the silence. No longer the comfortable silence of the last day with Scarlett here, I'm greeted with the dead silence of an empty house. Rolling onto my back, I stretch my arm out to her side of the bed and only find coldness.

Her side of the bed.

How easy it is to think of her here in my bed. Giving her a piece of it like she gave me a piece of her last night. It took every ounce of self-restraint to not devour her. To not claim her as mine and make love to her. Thinking of her now, on top of me, kissing me, running her hands across my chest as she grinded her hips makes me hard. But then the same thought crosses my mind.

Henry.

I wouldn't have ever thought of Scarlett like this when he was alive so why now? His death doesn't give me permission to lust for his wife. It absolutely does not give me permission to have the feelings I do for her. The overwhelming need I have to protect her, care for her, and make her laugh. Every time she laughs I feel like I've scaled the tallest mountain.

It's too soon. She's too fragile. Regardless of the status of their relationship, they were having a child together. They loved one another, and I have no right to insert myself into that part of her life.

Frustrated, I climb from the bed and handle my business before walking out to the kitchen. As I pass through the living room, I eye the couch where she first touched me. Or rather, where I let her. Ignoring the jolt of desire the memory stirs, I start a pot of coffee and look around for signs of her. Her purse isn't sitting on the counter where she left it, and her shoes aren't resting by the door. My assumptions are confirmed when I see a note on the counter.

Pouring myself a cup of coffee, I pick up the piece of paper as the doorbell rings. Hope fills me and I set the paper back down and make my way to the front door. Pulling the door open, hope dissipates when my sister's smiling face greets me.

"Jeez, grumpy much?" Addy asks as she pushes her way through the door, knocking me off balance. Following her and the scent of something sweet from the box in her hands, I pause when I see she has the note in her hand. Turning to face me, I see the look of confusion on her face and know I have a lot of explaining to do.

Extending my hand, I take the paper and read the short note that hurts me more than I would have expected.

Taylor,

Thank you for letting me stay for the weekend. I needed the break from my reality but it's back to life for me. And for you too.

No hard feelings, I get it.

Scarlett

That's just it. She doesn't get it. Hell, I don't get it. Looking up from the note, I see my sister standing with her back against the kitchen counter, a bear claw lifted to her mouth, and a quirked brow and invitation for me to spill.

"Is it too much to ask you to mind your own business?" I ask. A snort is my answer. Before I spill the beans on everything from Scarlett's admission on the state of her marriage to a PG version of what happened last night, I pull out the counter stool and take my own pastry from the box.

Thirty minutes, a lot of requests from me to my sister to stop gasping and grunting at every other word I speak, my story ends with Addy laughing. Not just a little sarcastic giggle or a "you're an idiot" snort. No, this is a full-out belly laugh that does nothing but annoy me.

"I fail to see what is funny, Addison." Full name and a straight face doesn't stop her. In fact, it only encourages her more. Taking the opportunity to ignore her, I refill my coffee cup and take a sip while she rights herself.

Dabbing her eyes with a dishtowel, she takes a few deep breaths before saying, "Oh brother dearest, you are so clueless."

"About what exactly?"

"You offended that poor girl. All she wanted was a little affection and instead you shot her down."

"I didn't—"

"Didn't what? Shoot her down? Of course you did. Gosh, Tay sometimes you're truly clueless. Look, if there's anything you hold in spades it's integrity and the need to do right by others while protecting those you love. Always putting yourself last. It's why you gave up that scholarship to enlist. Your commitment not only to your country but to your friendship with Henry. It's who you are, and it's why we all love you."

She takes in a deep breath and slowly releases it, her eyes sympathetic and her lips forming a tight smile. Her tone is sincere and genuine, but her words make me feel reprimanded. "Baby brother, this time, you've screwed up. Scarlett has been through the ringer, and while some may say it's too soon for her to feel something for another man, none of us know what she's going through. The pregnancy hormones alone are enough to make each day, heck, each hour, an emotional roller coaster. Add to that her loss and loneliness, she just wanted to feel loved, special."

Gathering her thoughts before she speaks again, she looks to the left. Like somewhere outside of this room the words will appear. "Maybe it's more than that, I don't know. What I do know is she was asking for something, and you flat out denied her. She's probably humiliated."

Stepping toward me, my big sister places her hand on my arm and pulls my attention from my cup. "Scarlett is a good person with a huge heart. All she ever wanted was a family to love and to be loved unconditionally. She had that taken from her, but with you, maybe she saw an opportunity to have it again, if only for a short time."

Staring at my sister, sincerity the only emotion on her face, I contemplate what she's said. Instead of sitting here in silence with my sister while she shakes her head in disbelief, I grab my phone from the counter and pull up Scarlett's contact information. Addy mumbles her approval as I listen to the line ring, and then her voicemail picks up.

"Hey, Red. It's me. I just wanted . . . well, I wasn't expecting you to be gone. I wanted . . . Call me back, okay?"

I sound like a bumbling idiot. Like a teenager calling his crush. I guess in a lot of ways I am. Minus the teen part. That ship sailed long ago. Regardless of how much time has passed, the feeling is the same. Confliction, worry, and fear. Each emotion brewing under the surface as I play out the last few months in my mind. The way she clung to me the day I arrived in Fayhill to the simplicity of our banter as we shared a pizza, each moment special even when they seemed mundane. I feel more myself with Scarlett than I have with any other woman, possibly ever.

Addy stays for another hour, telling me about the trip to a bed and breakfast she and Landon stayed at this weekend. They cut the trip short so she could spend time with Scarlett, and although she didn't get the one-on-one time with her, I feel like she enjoys teasing me just as much. By the time I kick her out of the house, half the morning has passed, and I only have a few hours before I need to be at the bar.

I call Scarlett one more time, but when her voice mail answers, I don't leave a message. Instead, I shoot off a quick text to call me when she can. Since I don't know when she snuck out of here, I have no way of knowing when she'll stop and be able to call me. Hell, I don't even know if she will call me. If what Addy said is true, and she is embarrassed, I may not hear from her.

Taking a preemptive measure, I make one more call before facing my day. On the second ring his greeting is short but typical. "Sugar."

"Cap."

"Touché. What's up? Everything okay with Scarlett?"

Pausing, I choose my words wisely. No way I can respond with, "Oh well, after I sucked on her tits and made her come, she snuck out of my house like a thief in the night." Instead I say, "She's headed back to Fayhill. I just wanted to give you a heads-up."

"Thanks for the warning. It's been strange without her here for a few days. How's she doing?"

"Good. I think the change of scenery helped. We went out to a buddy's property and relaxed yesterday. Crashed early."

For the next few minutes we catch up, and I manage to answer his questions about Scarlett without confessing my sins like we're at church. It's what he says before he hangs up that sends me for a loop and has me frozen in place.

"Henry would want her to be happy, regardless of what that looks like to outsiders. The last few years were hard on them. I thought this baby would be a blessing, but I don't think it changed much. I'm glad she is turning to you. I hate to see her punishing herself for something out of her control."

"I care about her. Both of them. It's my job to take care of Henry's family." It's the first time I've spoken those words out loud. I've thought them for weeks and vowed to myself I would make sure they are always taken care of but saying them to Grant gives them a different meaning.

Chapter 16

Scarlett

"*Hey, Red. It's me. I just wanted . . . well, I wasn't ex-pecting you to be gone. I wanted . . . call me back, okay?*"

The message never changes regardless of how many times I play it back. The first time I listened to it, I was at a rest stop stretching my legs. I could've answered his call but didn't. I could have answered Addy's text message, but I didn't do that either. I'm sure they both assumed I was driving and technically I was on the road home just not at that exact moment. It sucks that I missed seeing Addy, but I couldn't stay.

After one of the most epic orgasms of my life, I fell into a deep sleep. Dreams that were more haunting than happy pulled me from that slumber, but it was the full bladder and layers of regret that didn't allow me to fall back asleep. Reminders of the line we crossed were emphasized by the appearance of Henry in my dreams. The dreams themselves weren't anything special, just mundane every-day moments, but anytime the man who was Henry would begin to speak, saying something sweet or loving, I would look back at him confused. Then his face and body would morph into Taylor. Yet, when his body and face changed, his voice remained the same and the kindness was replaced with hurt, anger, and disappointment.

It doesn't take an internet search for me to know what the dreams mean. I regret what happened. Except I don't regret what I did or who it was with, I simply regret the moment he looked at me and turned me down. The moment I laid my heart out in the palm of my hand for him to take and he refused. As much as I've denied them, my feelings for Taylor have grown by leaps and bounds over the last few weeks. When he stood on the podium at the funeral giving his eulogy, I was moved by his love for Henry and their history together.

As we spent more time together and he allowed me to be lost in my emotions, I appreciated him more. It was the night he held me without judgment as I told him about the end of our marriage that things shifted for me. Going to see him this weekend was a gamble. I didn't plan on jumping him, and while it may not have been my finest moment, it was great just the same. Nothing may come of it, and I may have damaged our friendship, but to touch him, to feel his skin on mine, it was more than I imagined.

Sitting here on my couch, my phone in my lap, I contemplate calling him back. What will I say? "Sorry for throwing myself at you?" I'm not. "Sorry, my attempts at seduction fell short and you weren't into it?" That sounds pathetic.

Instead, I opt for a quick text message.

Me: Got your message. I'm home safe and sound. Thanks again for the reprieve from my life.

And now a quick text to Grant because, honestly, I'm surprised he wasn't here waiting for me when I got home.

`Me: I'm back. Exhausted and turning in early. I'm making fajitas this week, I'll let you know what day.`

Once the response from Grant comes through with a dozen thumbs up emojis, I toss my phone on the table and head for the shower. Stopping before I make it out of the living room, I realize I didn't check my mail from the last two days. Sliding on a pair of flip flops, I head out to the curb. As I thumb through the mail, I see Mr. Stanton walking across his lawn toward me.

"Hi, Mr. Stanton."

"Hello, dear. Did you get your package?"

Looking at him confused he smiles and then points to my front porch. A square box sits off to the side of my front door. I hadn't even noticed it when I walked out.

"Oh, I'm glad the delivery guy made it back. I came in through the back door today, so I didn't even see it. Thank you."

Patting me on the shoulder he smiles and returns to his house. Stepping up to the porch, I bend to pick up the box. Lighter than it appears in size, I carry the package inside and set it down on the table along with the mail. The return address doesn't have a name, only a post office box that I don't recognize. Tugging at the tape, I pull the strip across the package and pull the box.

Nestled in a layer of tissue paper is something I know well. Emotions bubble up inside of me as I lift the envelope sitting inside. Sliding my finger under the seal I pull the card out and I recognize my sister's scrawl.

Scarlett,

I thought you may want this. Mom has a box of your things in the attic as well. Congratulations on motherhood. Again, we are very sorry for your loss.

Regards,

Eliza

Regards. Not love or even sincerely. Nope, *regards*. How formal and practical. As I pull the tiny hand-knit blanket from the box, a wave of nostalgia hits me. I don't have memories of my life with this blanket, but I've seen photos of me holding it like a protective shield. It's gender neutral, colors of gray and yellow, because my parents didn't know if I was a boy or girl. Apparently, I wanted to keep them on their toes, questioning everything, even in the womb.

Ignoring the fountain of tears, I pull the blanket to my nose, inhaling and hoping for some sense of home to hit me. Instead, the musty odor makes me sneeze. This blanket was important to me when I was little. By all accounts, it was my comfort. The one item I relied on for peace. My parents didn't save and preserve it. They probably packed it in a cardboard box not unlike the one my sister shipped it in and placed it in the attic with all the other discarded items of our childhood.

Cast away like I was, it's simply a possession they no longer deemed necessary. Anger is something I held on to for a long time when I thought they were only disappointed in me. Now, standing in my kitchen holding this blanket I know it isn't about me, it's about them. I will never make my son feel this way. He will never know what it's like to not be enough. To always be second best and never fulfill the expectation of his parents.

I place the blanket back in the box and go back to the front door, locking it before heading down the hall to my bathroom for a quick shower and a little time with some mindless television. Kicking off my shoes, I begin stripping out of my clothes when the closet door catches my eye. The door is closed. I rarely close the closet doors. This is a topic Henry and I argued about often. My inability to close the closet door and his refusal to rinse the sink after shaving.

Slowly, I place my hand on the door knob to the closet and take a deep breath. Apprehension keeping me from opening it. Why am I frightened? It's not as if someone is hiding in here, that's ridiculous. I must have subconsciously closed the door before I left. *You're welcome, Henry. See I do listen.*

Opening the door, I peek inside, and nothing seems to be out of place. Turning to walk away, leaving the closet open like I prefer it, I finish undressing, tossing my clothes into the laundry basket before stepping into the bathroom. Turning the knobs, I set the temperature to very warm and step under the spray of the shower. I let the water pound on my shoulders, washing away the emotions of the last few days. Once I've stepped out of the shower and toweled off, I wipe the steam from the mirror and stare at myself in the mirror.

My face is fuller and my freckles a shade darker than usual. It's the light in my eyes that catches my attention. For the first time in months, I see hope and determination staring back at me. Buried with my past are the pain and frustrations I've carried all these weeks.

I know there is nobody else in this world who will

make sure we're cared for, who will be responsible for our happiness and future. That is my responsibility and as much as the thought exhausts me, I make a vow to myself and my son to give it my all. A night of television and a good night's sleep in my own bed are the first steps to a new beginning. Starting tomorrow, I have a life to get in order and a baby to prepare for.

Chapter 17

Taylor

Six weeks later

The soft lull of music from the bar and tapping of the keys on my computer are the only sounds I hear. It's how things have been at night for the last six weeks. Long gone are the dinnertime phone calls with Scarlett, and in their place is new employee paperwork.

I've managed to hire two new part-time bartenders and establish a new routine around here. Without Ashton on the schedule to pick up the slack, I've been handling more of the business side of things and only covering the bar on busy nights or if someone calls out. Thankfully, the calling out has been less and less, and we've fallen into a new normal around here. I could use one more full-time employee to allow myself some days off, but I can't entertain that idea until I'm confident my current staff is up to par. Besides, they covered me more than was reasonable in the weeks following Henry's death. Allowing me time to be there for Scarlett.

Now, she's barely a blip in my daily life. The weekend

she spent here was a turning point in our friendship. She's pretending it never happened while strategically placing walls around us, keeping me at arm's length. She's refused my offer to come to Fayhill and help her with things around the house or to come here and spend a weekend with Addy.

I'm ready to pack up a bag and show up at her house unannounced to force her to talk to me. I want to ask for her forgiveness for how I reacted to our night together. I want to hold her in my arms again and listen to her tell me the back stories to all of her ridiculous television shows. I want to see her laugh, to make her laugh, and I want to ask her how we move forward. What we do.

She isn't far from her delivery date and I feel so detached from her life. A crater sits in my heart where she is supposed to be. Where her laughter and smile fill the space. I don't allow myself time to question what that means, although my sister has plenty of ideas. Each I've shot down.

Last weekend she spent two days with Scarlett in Fayhill watching movies and having what she called "girl time" but I know was actually more about her checking on her well-being. As much as she tried to reassure me, and Grant has insisted, I need to see her for myself. To know she's okay.

A soft knock on the door pulls me from my running thoughts of Scarlett and the paperwork scattered atop my desk. "Yeah?" I shout. The door opens and my sister pops her head inside.

"Is it safe to come in? No hussies throwing themselves at you?"

Rolling my eyes I sit back in my chair, arms crossed over my chest. "One time, Addy. One misunderstanding and you'll never let me live it down."

"Nope. And it may have been a misunderstanding to

you, but that poor girl was devastated when she thought I was your girlfriend and she had to put her boobs away."

Laughing, I motion my sister inside the room, and she takes the seat across from me. A few weeks ago when Addy came by to drop off my nephew Mason's fishing gear, she happened to catch a customer in my office, trying to proposition me. I was in the middle of turning her down when my sister appeared, and the young woman assumed she was my girlfriend. I didn't correct her, grateful to have an out that didn't include me telling her I simply wasn't interested.

"What brings you by?"

"The gang is all here. It's Ashton's first night out since the babies were born. I doubt she'll make it an hour, but we forced her to put on pants and leave the house."

"Ash doesn't wear pants," I remind her.

"Semantics. Anyway, I wanted to stop in and see how you're doing. Have you talked to Scarlett?"

Shaking my head, I grab the mouse and begin clicking aimlessly at the screen in front of me. Addy is going to suggest I get in touch with my feelings and why not speaking to Scarlett is driving me nuts. Why I ask daily how she's doing, if anyone has seen or spoken to her.

"It's killing me to see you like this. Your fucking pride is really annoying, you know that? You need to grow up and go see her. Tell her how you feel. If you love her like I think you do, there's no better time than the present to make the grand gesture."

"Love? Who said anything about love? I mean, sure I love her, she's Henry's wife. I just worry about her. It's my duty to take care of her, and she won't let me."

Rising from her chair, Addy scoffs and turns to grab

the door. I guess this conversation is over. Before opening the door, she turns to face me. "Taylor, you are a good man and deserve happiness. I wish you'd love yourself half as much as the rest of us and do something for yourself. Choose love without regret."

Not allowing me a chance to respond, she walks out and closes the door behind her. I sit for a few minutes, allowing her words to float around the room. Love without regret. I'm stubborn, this much is true, but it isn't fair for me to even contemplate feelings outside of friendship for Scarlett. No matter how much I care or how much I miss her, it's wrong and inappropriate. Pushing the door closed on my feelings, I get back to work, but my phone buzzes on the desk next to me.

Looking down, I see Scarlett's name and don't hesitate to answer.

"Red, I was just—" Her sobs fill the line and my heart drops. These aren't the same cries of sadness I've heard from her. "What's wrong? Scarlett?"

"I went through Henry's things. I . . . boxed up his clothes. I'm sorry, I shouldn't have called."

Taking a deep breath, overwhelming relief fills me as I sit down in my desk chair. The sound of her sobs sent my heart racing, fear consuming me. I'm grateful she isn't hurt or scared.

"You shouldn't have done that alone."

"I didn't. Mercy was here. I just . . . I can't bring Logan home from the hospital with Henry's ghost at every turn. I want his presence here for our son, but I can't continue to slide his shirts over to hang my own anymore."

She's nesting. I remember my sister commenting on it the other day, saying the time would come when she started purging everything. Ashton tried pulling that shit in the bar in her last month here and it took me three shifts to find the cutting boards from where she'd put them for "convenience."

"Logan? Did you decide on a name?" I ask, hoping the topic of her son will help settle her anxiety.

"I'm testing it out. What do you think? I was also considering going a little old-school. Maybe Oliver or Matthew."

"I think your son is going to do amazing things, and his name won't matter. Well, unless his name is Banana or Shallot."

My teasing causes her to laugh, and it's a welcome change to how our conversation started. When she gains her composure, she says, "Thank you for making me laugh. That's why I called. You never judge me. Well, you may if I name my son after produce. Plus, you give me permission to purge my emotions without judgment. Then you make me smile. I'm lucky to have you, Taylor Cain."

"Ah, Red. You're going to make me cry." I fake sniffle and she laughs again. It's beautiful music to my ears when there is such a dark cloud hanging over the conversation. Choosing a baby's name should be done with both parents involved. I unscrew the cap of the water bottle on my desk, lifting it to my lips as she speaks.

"What are you up to mister big-time bar owner? Flirting with all the ladies? Handing out screaming orgasms?"

Choking on my water, I cough and wipe the dribbled water from my chin. Her giggles fill the line, and I shake my head. A light tap on the door doesn't allow me to make a sarcastic and possibly inappropriate response. "Yeah?" I shout.

The door opens and my bartender for the night, Caleb, opens the door. "Yo boss, it's getting pretty nuts out here, and we need another bottle of Jack."

"I'll be right there," I tell him and wait for him to close the door. "Scarlett, I've missed you. I'm sor—"

"Tay, I can't. I'm emotional and hormonal, and it's no telling what will come out of my mouth. I wasn't sure you'd answer. I have so many regrets."

Regrets. Love without regret. "Scar—" She continues talking, never hearing my attempt to speak.

"—and he's moving like crazy. The other day I could see a foot. It was surreal. It's all so real, and I'm overwhelmed. Most of all, I needed to hear your voice, to know I could call without judgment."

"Never judgment, Red. I promise. Look, I've gotta run. You going to be okay?"

"Yeah, I will. Thanks for listening. For everything."

The line goes dead before I can respond; before I can promise her we'll be okay.

Chapter 18

Scarlett

*C*alling Taylor yesterday was a mistake. I've been doing well these last few weeks, able to compartmentalize my feelings and the changes I'm making. Okay, so really I've done a phenomenal job of pretending nothing happened between us and keeping him at arm's length.

Until I was sitting on the bedroom floor, listening to a sappy love song that Henry used to play for me when life was good. When we were happy, and I believed in forever kind of love. I was holding his favorite sweatshirt to my face, inhaling the scent of him and lost it. I sobbed to the point I couldn't catch my breath. I felt so alone. Broken and lost. The baby kicked, and I needed someone. I needed to be pulled into a warm embrace and comforted.

Without someone here to comfort me, I picked up my phone and called the one person I knew would be there for me. Regardless of what happened that night in his bed, Taylor Cain is the only person I wanted to talk to.

Flooded with emotions I'm not ready to face, I ended the call abruptly, abandoned my purging, and crawled under my covers for a long cry. Today I'm paying the price. A sob-fest hangover is not my best look. As I get ready for a doctor's appointment, I almost don't recognize the woman staring at me in the mirror. Her eyes are puffy and vacant, her hair a tangled mess. I'm exhausted after a restless night of sleep. Dreams I've become used to, but last night's were different, more intense and focused on Taylor. That's what I get for calling him. I should've called Mercy like I told him I had.

I lied.

It seemed easier at the time but now it's just another thing I regret. I thought I could handle sorting Henry's things; it would be easier to do alone. I underestimated my ability to break down.

Splashing cold water on my face, I go through the motions of putting on makeup and hiding the dark circles under my eyes. Running my fingers through my hair, I spray a little product and braid the sides before piling it high on my head.

Exchanging my loose-fitting sweats and tank with a maxi dress, I slide my feet into a pair of sandals and head for the door. Today I get to see my son on the ultrasound and that means it's going to be a great day. As I'm walking out the door to my car, my cell phone rings. Glancing at the screen I see it's a blocked number and let it go to voicemail. Another voicemail that will be white noise. No words spoken. No noise. And just like every day for the last few months, another voicemail I'll delete without a second thought.

Sitting in the obstetrician's office, I try to ignore the couples sitting around the room. Women are in various stages of their pregnancies with their significant others sitting with them, hands resting on arms, legs, and bellies. Partners. There are few women alone like me but none with the obvious final trimester stomach like me. Instead of wallowing in the thoughts of fear and loneliness that have hit me like a ton of bricks over the last few days, I focus on the excitement of hearing my son's heartbeat and seeing his precious face on the screen.

The realization that it won't be long until I'm holding him in my arms fills my heart with both excitement and fear. Becoming a parent is scary business but something I plan to excel at. The man of the hour is currently doing some sort of calisthenics in my stomach, the flutters making me squirm in my seat.

I read a lot of books on pregnancy and the various stages of movement but nothing prepares you for the real thing. It's weird as hell. And awesome. But, mostly weird. Last night I saw a handprint from the inside out and turned the lights off to avoid seeing it again. I don't need that visual in my head before I fall asleep.

In many ways it felt like this part of my pregnancy would never arrive while in others, it flew by so quickly. I suppose that's part of life. When you dreamed and wished for something and receive it, time speeds by, and you feel like you've almost missed it all. That's where I am. Looking in the mirror this morning, it was difficult to remember a time I didn't have these boobs and this massive belly.

"Scarlett."

The sound of my name from the far side of the room grabs my attention. Rising from the chair, I walk toward the smiling nurse holding a small tablet. I know the routine well: weight then blood pressure before I change into my little *gown*, a term they should really retire since there's nothing about the scrap of fabric they give you that remotely resembles a gown.

Once I confirmed I gained a few pounds since my last visit and my blood pressure is only slightly elevated, but nothing compared to what it was a few months ago, I slip out of my dress and replace it with the *gown* before sitting on the paper sheet atop the table. As I wait for the doctor to enter, I play a little on my phone and scroll through my social media. Photos of my friends fill my feed along with some random advertisements for yarn. I'm not sure I'll ever officially make a blanket or garment my son will be able to wear, but the need to click on the ads and choose some new material is almost desperate.

Two rapid knocks on the door are my warning before Dr. Green enters the room. His demeanor is fatherly and always tugs a little at my heart. His kind eyes take me in and that's when I see it, the sympathy. I was here two weeks ago when he determined it would be best for me to slow down, spend more time sofa surfing, and living a life of boredom.

"Scarlett, how are you, dear?"

Plastering on a smile, I reply, "I'm good. Thank you. Ready to meet this little guy." My hands rub large circles on my stomach, and I'm rewarded with a sharp jab to my side. "Oomph. I think he's destined to be a soccer player or martial arts master. He's quite the kicker."

Dr. Green laughs as he taps on his small tablet. Fingers scrolling, the room becomes quiet before he takes a seat on the rolling stool in front of me. Looking at me, he says, "How is everything really, Scarlett? This is such a stressful and difficult time for you."

"It has been quite a few months. I'm finding each day a little different than the last. Some better than others."

"I understand. Your blood pressure seems to be better. Are you still taking it three times a day?"

"I am. As you predicted, it tends to spike in the afternoons. I've grown accustomed to naps during Dr. Phil," I say sheepishly. Dr. Green laughs, so I continue, "I am bored, though. Do you have a prescription for that?"

Dr. Green walks to the sink and washes his hands all while telling me to enjoy the time I have. The peace and quiet before my son arrives. I suppose he's right, as much as I hate it. He pushes a button on the wall and within minutes, the nurse appears in the room and we begin the examination.

"You're measuring right on time. Is he moving a lot?" Nodding, I watch as Dr. Green touches his hands across my abdomen and is greeted with a hearty kick, causing us all to laugh. "Well, looks like someone has thoughts on my touching him. Do we have a name for this little guy?"

"Not quite yet. I want to meet him first. Is that strange?" I ask, suddenly unsure if that's not the norm with new moms.

"Nothing strange at all. I've had parents wait until five minutes before discharge to name their child. It's a huge responsibility. Well, Master Gilbert, I wouldn't be surprised if we met sooner rather than later."

Gasping, I try to sit up but fail. Or flail is more like it. "What?"

Motioning for the nurse to dim the lights, he turns on the ultrasound machine and points at the screen. "Your little man is in position and it's just a waiting game. While more time is never a bad thing, we are absolutely in the safe zone for delivery."

Instead of responding to this news, I look to my left and watch as my baby fills the screen. I love seeing him and knowing he's safe and secure in my womb. His little hands are out in front of him like he's praying, and I don't bother to stop the sudden influx of tears.

The nurse hands me a tissue, and I return the gesture with a smile of thanks. Once the doctor has printed a few pictures from the ultrasound, he offers a hand to help me sit up on the table. Sniffling, I dab my eyes with the tissue. He pats my knee while the nurse grips me around the shoulder.

"Scarlett, I know this is a difficult time for you. It's important to have a support system, do you have that?"

Nodding I say, "I do. Henry and I have a lot of friends. I'm grateful for the concern, but these tears are more about seeing my baby and knowing he's going to be in my arms soon than anything else."

"I'm glad to hear it. Please continue to limit your activity and rest as much as possible. Once this one is born, you'll be glad you did. Give us a call if you begin to feel unwell or if there is a lack of movement. We're here for you, Scarlett." I nod because if I speak, the tears will start again. The nurse hugs me once more before they both exit the room. Looking down at the photo in my hand, I smile.

"We're going to be okay, buddy. I feel it. I'm sorry you won't know your daddy, but he loved you very much." I'm rewarded with another kick and a sudden hankering for some pie from The Mess Hall.

A slice of pie and a cup of decaf coffee later, I'm sitting in the small diner in town. My friend Mercy is bustling around serving the handful of customers while I sip on my second cup of coffee and scroll through my phone: checking emails, claiming my lives in every game in my arsenal, and reviewing all of my social media accounts.

I stop my scroll on a picture in my feed of Addy and Taylor. Standing in Country Road, she's hugging him while he looks moderately annoyed. The standard for those two. The caption reads "Little Bro love." I pause on the photo longer than is probably reasonable for a friend. Taylor's handsome face, so full of life, stares back at me and a twinge of envy prickles as my neck. I miss him. I miss his hugs and his comfort.

Shaking off the thoughts, I snap a picture of the ultrasound photo and attach it to a text message for Addy. I make sure to let her know the doctor is happy with my progress and while I still need to take it easy, everything seems to be going well.

My next message is to my son's honorary uncles, Grant, Connor, and Taylor. The responses are quick with confirmation my baby is going to be a star athlete and is already handsome like his uncles.

I hover over my sister's name next. I don't bother reaching out to my parents or my brother, each making their opinions and thoughts of my life choices clear. My sister, though, sent the gift and since then we've spoken a few times. Our communication is sparse, but I think her maternal instincts make it possible for her to show me a small sliver of family connection. I'm not sure if it's the loneliness or the emotions from today's appointment, but I have a strong need to feel connected to my family, so I suck it up and hit her contact information.

Halfway through the second ring, voice mail picks up. I've been sent to voicemail. Ignored. This shouldn't surprise me, but it hurts, nonetheless.

With a shaky hand, I set my phone down and take a sip from the water glass sitting untouched on the table.

"Hey, you okay?" Mercy asks as she slides into the seat across from me.

"Yeah. Just tired, I think. I should go home and rest. Doctor's orders and all that."

"Okay, pie's on me. Still want to hang out later this week? Maybe Saturday evening?"

"Yes, please! I love Grant and Connor, but I need some girl talk."

She winks, and I grab my phone and purse before scooting out of the booth. We hug, and I walk out of the diner, waving my goodbyes to the other customers. By the time I settle behind the wheel of my car, my adrenaline from the day begins to plummet, and I know a nap is in my immediate future.

Pulling up in front of my house, I pull my mail from the box before parking in the driveway. Mr. Stanton waves from where he's kneeling before his flower beds. Smiling, I take my mail and drag myself into the house.

As I sort through the mail, I pull a square envelope from the pile. I've been receiving random gifts from other friends we've made through the years, and this is likely another gift card. I should add finishing thank you cards to my to do list.

Looking at the envelope, it isn't the writing that catches my attention, it's the sender's name. "Gilbert" is scrawled across the upper left of the envelope and my heart skips. I haven't heard from Henry's parents since the funeral.

Sliding my finger under the seal I tug the card from the envelope. As I open it, a newspaper clipping falls to the floor and lands next to my foot. Bending down, I retrieve the paper and note the photo. Smiling, I look back at a young Henry. This young man in the photo is the one I met in a dive bar a dozen years ago. His baby face and huge smile were what drew me to him. His arm is slung over Taylor's shoulder, and they look happy as clams.

Glancing down at the text under the photo I read: "Hometown boys making us proud." It must be a clipping from their local paper. Proudly, I take the picture and place it on my refrigerator. Turning my attention back to the card, I look for a note from the Gilberts but instead, it's blank. Not even a standard greeting from the card's creator. Just blank.

It was nice of them to send the clipping. I don't have many keepsakes from Henry's years before me, and this will be something our son will love to have. Setting the card on the pile of mail, I make my way to the living room and my favorite napping corner of the couch.

Chapter 19

Taylor

Saturday nights at Country Road used to be my favorite shift of the week. It's just a bunch of people out for a good time. The early part of the evening is primarily couples while the singles venture out later in the night. Regulars and new-to-town folks on nights like this are what keep my doors open and why I love owning this place. Watching strangers meet for the first time and knowing there's a chance I'll see them back week after week, sometimes together, is one of the best parts of the job.

Invitations to engagement parties, weddings, and baby showers come my way monthly. I won't say meeting your future partner in a bar is easy, but there's something about this place, the way friendships and love stories find their beginnings here. It's special.

Handing a group of guys their change, I catch Jameson and Ashton approaching the bar. "What are you guys doing here? Shouldn't you be changing diapers or something?"

"Dude, she has been bugging me for some of your nachos smothered in extra cheese—"

"And jalapenos. Oh and bacon. Maybe some tomatoes. Gosh, I'm hungry."

Shaking my head, I turn for the taps and pour Jameson's preferred IPA. When I slide the glass his way, I ask Ashton, "And for you, mama? Leaded or unleaded?"

"Leaded. Margarita on the rocks, please. Only one tonight."

"She's so excited for a margarita; it's all she's talked about since her parents showed up to babysit." Laughing, I listen to my friends tease each other before setting her cocktail on a napkin. "Anything else, your highness?"

"Yes, can you maybe add some extra chicken to those nachos? I'd love you forever."

"Sure thing," I say with a snicker as I punch in their order for the kitchen. I go about my business for the next few minutes, unloading and reloading the dishwasher while pouring a few more drinks. I hear my name called and turn to Caleb. He's standing with Ashton's nachos in one hand and the bar's phone in the other.

"Thanks," I reply, reaching for the platter when he thrusts the phone in my direction.

"It's for you. I couldn't hear well but someone is crying and asked for you. A woman. What'd you do, man? Break a heart?"

Confused, I take the phone and tell him to take the nachos to Ashton. Lifting the phone to my ear, I click the button on the cordless phone and walk toward my office.

"Hello?" I shout into the phone.

Sniffles fill the line. Commotion in the background sends my pulse racing. I'm not on my cell so I don't know who's calling, but it's a woman. Fuck. My sister? Did something happen to my nephew? Then I hear it. The wail I heard many nights as I held Scarlett in my arms while she cried.

"Red? What's wrong? Are you okay?" My instinct is to grab my keys and head for the door. Only, I don't know what's wrong or where I'd go.

"Taylor, I'm sc . . . sc . . . scared."

Blood pulses in my ears and my breathing increases. "What's happened? Honey, tell me what's wrong."

"Someone was in my house. It's safe here. Why would they do that? Who was it? Taylor, I can't . . . Oh God—"

Motherfucker.

"Scarlett, where are you? Are you alone?" I'm reaching for my keys when Grant's voice booms in my ear.

"Sugar. I'm here with her. She's okay. Honey, stay here with Mercy, okay? I'm going to talk to Taylor."

Tossing my keys back on my desk, I run my free hand through my hair in frustration. Inhaling through my nose, I pace the office, waiting for an explanation.

"What the fuck is going on, Cap?" Visions of Scarlett scared and crying flash before my eyes and rage sends my blood boiling. The need to get to her is overwhelming. To protect her and the baby.

"Relax. It's okay. She's okay."

His calmness does nothing to ease my need to get to her. If anything, it infuriates me. How can he be so fucking calm? She's losing it, I can hear her crying in the background.

"Tell me what the fuck happened, Grant," I growl.

"It doesn't look like anything was stolen. She's safe.

I'm taking her home with me tonight."

"That doesn't tell me what happened, Grant."

Coughing, he lets out a chuckle, which only adds fuel to my existing fire. "Wow. You've used my name twice in one call. I've been trying to get you to use my name for years." An actual growl is my response. Why is he taking this so lightly?

"Fine. She came home from dinner and says she knew instantly something was wrong. The porch light was off, which isn't normal for her. Then when she got to the front door, she noticed the curtains in the window were shifted. But when she went to put her key in the door, it opened right away. Thankfully, Mercy was with her and waiting in the car. Scarlett rushed from the house and locked herself in the car. They called the cops and then me."

"I will close down the bar and be there in a few hours. Fuck, why is Fayhill so fucking far away?"

"Jesus, you're a fucking mess. Calm down. You won't do anyone any good if you're swearing up a storm and trying to go Rambo on everyone. I'm going to . . . shit. Hold on."

Leaning my head back, I listen to the dead air, my heart racing as a thousand scenarios of what is transpiring run through my mind. Grant's voice becomes clearer, panic lacing every word. Fuck.

"What's happening?" I shout, jumping from my seat.

"Honey, breathe. It's okay. Taylor, I've got to go. I think we need to get Red to the hospital. She doesn't look good."

The last words I hear him say before the line goes dead is "It's too soon . . ." The baby. Shit.

Rushing from the office, I make my way back to the

bar and sigh in relief when I see Ashton still perched on her stool. She catches my eye and her wide smile falls as I approach her.

"What's wrong?" she asks, panic lacing her question.

"I have to leave. I have to get to the hospital. I have to—"

"Taylor, breathe. What's wrong?" She's standing before me in seconds, her hands on my arms. She's a tiny little sprout, barely reaching my chest but her presence is big and welcome.

With two deep breaths, I exhale and croak, "The baby. I have to go. Scarlett needs me. I can't leave the bar. Fuck, I need more bartenders. Shit." Looking around, I see how busy the bar is and know I can't just walk out.

"I don't know that you should drive like this. You're shaking."

"Ash, I have to go. I'm going to close. Everyone will have to fucking suck it up."

"No way. You'll have a riot on your hands." Turning to Jameson she says, "Babe, sorry but how do you feel about a working date night?" I open my mouth to stop her, tell her it's not her job, but before I can, Jameson hops up and does an awkward fist pump.

"I have always wanted to pour a beer behind this bar. Dreams do come true. We've got this man," Jameson says as he motions me out of the way.

I turn my attention back to Ashton as she places her hand on my cheek, "You go calm the fuck down, and when you think it's safe to drive, go. It'll be fine, and we'll cover as long as you need us." She pushes me out of the way, points at Jameson, and then leans over, taking a large bite of food before dumping her fresh cocktail for a glass of water.

Taking Ashton's advice, I didn't immediately leave for Fayhill. Instead, I called my sister on the drive to my house. She was as freaked out by what happened as I was but went quickly into nurse mode while I packed a bag.

By the time I threw a bunch of random stuff in a bag and was standing in my driveway trying to decide between climbing on my bike and breaking every speed limit law between here and Fayhill, or being sensible and driving my truck, my phone rang with an update from Addy.

Scarlett's in labor, but it's early and slow going. It isn't that I'm questioning her doctor's opinion but from everything I've read, she isn't due for another four weeks. That's a month away and yet he doesn't seem too concerned about her well-being. Something Addy found funny and worth mocking me about. Regardless, I flew out of Lexington like a bat out of hell. I may have chosen to leave my bike behind, but I'm still pushing the limits with what is a reasonable speed.

I shaved off about an hour of what my drive would normally take and make it to the hospital around the time I'd be climbing into bed after closing the bar. Parking my truck in a spot just outside the entrance to the hospital, I read Grant's last text message with Scarlett's room number.

Approaching the nurse's station, I take a deep breath and plaster on a huge smile. Getting in afterhours may require charm I'm used to playing behind the bar. The older woman sitting behind the computer glances at me and then turns to look at the large clock on the wall. Her brows furrow, and I know she's going to tell me it's too late, or I suppose, too early for visiting hours.

"Good morning, ma'am," I say in greeting. Okay, so maybe I'm laying it on a little thick. I'm fucking amped and tired at the same time.

"Sir."

"Would you mind directing me to room three twenty-six? Scarlett Gilbert."

"Sir, visiting hours are long over. I'm sorry, you'll have to come back after eight a.m."

I'm about to plead my case when Grant turns the corner. He looks exhausted and worse for wear. A look of relief crosses his face as he approaches me, hand extended. "Karen, this is Taylor. I'll take him back."

"Oh, I didn't realize. Go on ahead, Grant. Do y'all need anything?"

Shaking his head, he leads me down a hall. We stop in front of a door marked 326. Turning to me he says, "She's okay. Sleeping right now. I waited for you to get here because I knew you'd want to see her for yourself."

"What did the doctor say? And, why did Nurse Ratchet bat her lashes at you like that?"

Rolling his eyes he scoffs. "Karen is a friend. I spend some time here volunteering, and I told her earlier you would be here late. As for Red, the doc said the stress of the last few months and then tonight's scare likely triggered the labor. Before you freak out, she's completely in the "safe zone" of delivery time. Now we just wait for the little guy to make his appearance."

All the tension I've been carrying since I heard Scarlett's wails on the phone earlier drops from my body and exhaustion overwhelms me. She's going to be okay.

"Grant, I don't think I've ever been so scared as I was listening to her on the phone. Then you shouted about the baby and every bad scenario played out in my mind. I'm relieved it's a better outcome than my imagination was coming up with."

"Me too, man."

We both know I won't be leaving anytime soon so Grant agrees to go home. I promise to call him if anything changes. As I watch him retreat down the hall toward the elevators, I turn back to Scarlett's door.

With a deep breath, I open the door and peer inside. Lying on the bed, her red hair a tangled mess on the pillow and a peaceful look on her face, is Scarlett. Her hands rest protectively on her stomach. Tears form in my eyes, but I suck them back. If something happened to her, to them, I'm not sure what I'd do.

Quietly, I move to the chair next to the bed. As I slide it closer to the bed side, her hand slips from her abdomen and lands on the bed. Slowly, I sit down and take her hand in mine. Placing a chaste kiss to her fingers, I lean forward, elbows on the bed and watch her sleep. Relief and protectiveness overwhelm me as I lay my head down on the bed next to her and let the sounds of the machines surround me.

Chapter 20

Taylor

Finger-light touches on my head stir me from a deep sleep. Blinking, I let my eyes adjust to the bright room. Beeps and hums of machines and a giggle greet me as I sit up quickly, blood rushing to my head. Scarlett's beautiful face greets me, a huge smile on her face. Looking down, I note I'm still sitting in the awful chair beside her bed. I must have fallen asleep as I lay here last night holding her hand.

"Morning." Her voice is a little raspy in the pre-dawn hours. I look over to a nurse who is smirking while she taps away on a small tablet.

"Hey. How are you feeling?"

Shrugging, she looks at the nurse instead of responding. Turning her attention to us, the young woman in scrubs says, "Your wife and baby boy are just fine. Contractions seem to be pretty steady, are you doing okay?" Scarlett smiles and nods to the nurse. "We'd like to get her up and walking, see if we can move this along a little."

I open my mouth to correct her mistake when Scarlett interrupts me to say, "Thank you. Is it okay if he walks with me?" She confirms my role as walking partner is fine, and once she's gone, I turn my attention to Scarlett, brow quirked.

"I don't want to explain it all over and over. While you were sleeping, I heard the nurses talking. It's almost shift change. We can explain it to whoever will be with me all day and into delivery because, I'm having this baby today. These contractions suck."

Ignoring her attempt at humor I say, "You scared me, Red."

She pushes up on her hands and adjusts her body, settling her hands on her stomach, fingers laced. "I was pretty scared myself. I'm sorry you came all this way. I hate being a bur—"

"You are never a burden. I'm sorry it took me so long." It's a simple statement, but I mean more than just my drive from Lexington. "So, sounds like we need to get in a little cardio."

Rolling her eyes, she snorts. My smile is instant at her reaction, which earns me a look that is meant to be menacing but is more cute than anything. "There will be a steady shuffle in the hallway and that's about it. I'm getting ready to birth a baby, Sugar, not prepare for the CrossFit Open."

She pushes the blankets from her legs and slides to the side of the bed, her feet dangling off the side. I stand and grab her elbow, helping her settle on her feet. With a hand on her back she sucks in a deep breath and slowly releases it. Lifting her eyes, she looks up at me sweetly and I pull her to me. Wrapping her hands around my waist with her head resting on my chest, she begins to cry softly.

We stand wrapped in each other for only a few minutes

before she squirms out of my hold. "I'm going to thank you in a few minutes for that hug and everything else, but I have to pee so bad. If I don't move it, we're going to be calling maintenance for a spill on aisle pregnant lady."

Laughing, I step aside and let her shuffle to the bathroom in the far corner of the room, her IV pole by her side. Before she steps through the door I say, "I'm going call Grant while you're in there. Give him a quick update."

She smiles and enters the bathroom, closing the door behind her. Pulling my phone from my pocket, I press Grant's contact information and halfway through the second ring, his voice fills the line.

"How's our girl?" No pleasantries. We're both in work mode, soldier mode. To others, it may sound clipped and even rude but for us it's about the facts. There's no time or room for emotion.

"She's in the restroom. We're going to take a walk to see about moving labor along. I only have a minute so tell me what you know."

"From what I can gather from the sheriff, it was a crash and grab. The house was ransacked and shit everywhere. Nothing big was taken so we assume it was kids and they needed to get in and out quickly."

"Damage?" I ask as I walk to the window and peer out the curtains. The sun is rising in the horizon. Colors of blue, pink, and purple paint the sky, promises of a new day. A day that will welcome a new life. Perfection.

"Nothing major. Broken glass from a picture frame looks to be the extent of it. Mostly just a huge mess that needs to be cleaned. Once the sheriff gives the go ahead, Connor and I will start cleaning but be ready to head to the hospital when it's time."

We talk for a few more minutes before the bathroom door opens and I turn to see Scarlett. With a clipped "Gotta go," I end the call and slide my phone back in my pocket.

Looking at her standing before me, dressed in a plain hospital gown and fuzzy yellow socks on her feet, I'm not sure there has ever been a woman more beautiful. Exhaustion lays on her like a blanket, but beneath the fear and stress of the last twelve hours is a strong and determined woman. With a hand on her stomach, she pauses, holding my gaze. A slow smile spreads across her face and I know things are different. The way she left my house all those weeks ago changed something in me. In us.

She's always been my best friend's wife, my friend, but the moment we kissed everything changed. Being here with her, experiencing these moments as she prepares to welcome her son, means something to me. She means something to me. I know there is nothing I won't do for her. I will care for her, protect her, and most of all promise her. Promise her safety and love, in whatever form she'll take it.

We walk for what feels like hours but is only about thirty minutes. During our walk, or shuffle as Scarlett referred to it, we mostly make small talk, ignoring not only the reason for triggering her labor but also about how we left things when she was in Lexington. We laugh, and by the time I guide her back to her room and help her settle in the bed, she's exhausted. Apparently, while I slept, she was awake and now that there's "movement" in her labor she's exhausted.

As she settles into the bed and the nurses scramble around her checking machines and the IV, I settle into the couch under the window. Flipping through my phone, I check emails and the local news. By the time the nurses filter out of the room, I'm yawning to the point my eyes are watering and know I need at least a few more hours of sleep. Turning to my side, I hear giggles from the bed just a few feet away.

"Something funny, sweetheart?"

"You didn't hear a word they said, did you?"

"Enlighten me," I retort while trying to figure out how I'm going to get comfortable when this couch is half my size.

"That turns into a makeshift bed. Just pull the cushions. I think—" She doesn't finish her sentence before letting out a long drawn out yawn. "Going to try and sleep."

Rising from my seat, I turn and look at the couch and see the small handle-looking strap for pulling the cushions into a bed. That's going to be much more comfortable than that stupid chair I was in the last few hours. Spinning, I take a step to the bed and Scarlett, her eyes closed and a small pucker on her pink lips.

Slowly, I lift my hand and push the hair from her face before leaning down and placing a kiss on her forehead. As I pull back, a tiny hand grips my wrist and draws my attention. Looking down, I see a pair of beautiful brown eyes, clear and bright, staring back at me.

"Thank you for being here. It means the world to me. I'm sorry I left like I did."

"I'll always be here for you. I promise."

Smiling, her eyes flutter closed, and I say, "Sleep well, beautiful. We have a baby coming."

Chapter 21

Scarlett

L abor is not beautiful nor is it amazing. At least not for me. It's painful, and I don't want to do it anymore. I've screamed, cried, and begged for someone to make the agony stop. Not one person in this room has complied with my demands. The nurses are very sweet and gentle, and I want to punch them in the face. Turns out, birthing a small human makes me violent and very angry.

And emotional.

The tears are uncontrollable, and if I'm not careful, I'll drown my little boy with them as soon as he makes his presence known. Which, according to Dr. Green, will be in two more pushes. Two more pushes. I feel like I've been at this for an entire day, and I suppose in many ways I have. It's hard to believe what a roller coaster the last twenty-four hours have been. And through most of it, Taylor has been with me.

I still can't believe he dropped everything to be here. I never voiced it, but I had no plan for this moment. I knew Grant and Connor would be here in some form. Likely waiting in the hall because nobody wants to be around a wailing woman pushing a human from her body. It wasn't until I woke from my nap and saw Taylor next to my bed that I realized how alone I've felt all these months.

Life is strange; sometimes, even surrounded by friends and those who care about you most, loneliness can consume you. I've experienced it firsthand and that loneliness is stifling. But actually being alone, with nobody in your daily life, in your corner supporting you, that's something I'd never experienced.

About a month ago, I pulled up the medical center's website to enroll in birthing classes. It was then that the realization I had nobody to list as my partner hit me like a lightning bolt. There is no baby's father or significant other to wrap their arms around me and help me practice breathing exercises. No partner to rub my back when the worst of the contractions hit during labor.

But now, as I glare at the previously kind and supportive Dr. Green, a man who is now a smiling masochist, I feel Taylor's large hand on my lower back. His touch is comforting and is helping keep me grounded so I don't lose my shit completely. Leaning down, his breath is warm on my ear as he whispers, "You've got this, Red. Just a few more pushes and he'll be here. You'll hold your son."

Bearing down, I say a prayer and a few curse words before the overwhelming pressure dissipates, and cries of a baby fill the room. Sobs rack my body, my chest heaving as I lay my head back on the pillow. Looking up, I catch Taylor looking at me, his hand pushing the stray hairs from my sweaty face and nothing short of adoration in his tear-filled eyes.

Quickly, he leans down and presses his lips to mine. It's a short kiss, nothing passionate or romantic but in this moment, it is everything and more. It's the promise of what's to come and helps fill my heart to the brim. Hope overflowing along with the love I know dwells deep in my soul.

Before I can say anything about the kiss, a wailing naked baby is nestled on my chest. Love. Undeniable and all-encompassing love is on my skin, his pink face scrunched up in anger and, most likely, fear.

"Hi sweet boy, I'm your mama," I whisper as I place a kiss to his head. I only have his body on mine for a few seconds before the nurse swoops him away with promises to return him soon.

Taylor clears his throat, pulling my attention back to him. "I'm going to go out and update everyone."

Confused I ask, "Everyone?"

"Cap and Twig have been here since late afternoon. Mercy and Vera showed up a few hours ago with enough food to feed half the floor." My eyes light up, and he chuckles. "Yes, they set aside food for you. Anyway, there are a few other folks out there I don't know but you had quite the crowd last I saw."

"If you'd like to step out and update the family, Scarlett and . . . the littlest Gilbert, will be all ready for visitors in about thirty minutes," Dr. Green tells Taylor. As he shuffles out of the room, Nellie, my new evening nurse taps me on the shoulder, drawing my attention from Taylor's retreating back.

"That one's a keeper. I'd kill for a man to look at me like he looks at you. But this guy here, I think his look is a little bit more special," she says as she places a blanket-wrapped little man in my arms, a knitted cap on his head. He's like a little chubby human burrito, and I know there will never be another love like I feel right now.

"Girl, that's one fine male you have there." Vera's over-the-top statements shouldn't surprise me. Yet, here I sit. Mercy smacks her in the arm, eyes wide as she hushes her. "What? He may only be a couple hours old, but he's a handsome little devil." Vera pops a french fry in her mouth and smiles while chewing.

We all break out in laughter, Mercy's snort startling the baby a little as he sleeps in my arms. I'm grateful to have changed out of that dreadful hospital gown and into my own clothes. I'd kill for a shower but the little bird bath I gave myself at the sink will have to do for tonight. The adrenaline I had earlier is quickly fading, and it's entirely possible I'd fall asleep standing beneath the hot stream of water. My nurse, Nellie, stood watch while I brushed my teeth three times and relented when I begged her to help me braid my hair before allowing anyone in to see me. One may call that a little high maintenance, but I call it being a good friend. Nobody needed to see the hot mess I was after labor. I saw it first-hand. Not pretty.

"Oh," Vera says as she elbows Mercy in the side, "you thought I meant the hottie with the stormy eyes and lustful gazes at our Scarlett. He's not hard on the eyes either. But this little man . . ." she continues as she stands and extends her hands, a silent request to hold the baby. "He's the real deal. You've done good, honey. This guy is a handsome little fella."

"I can't argue with that. Thank you both for being here. I didn't realize how difficult this would all be." The tears start again and before I know it, Mercy is holding me tightly as I sob, and Vera is whispering to the baby. I wish I knew what she was saying, but knowing her, it could be anything from a promise to show him all the wonders of sparkly vampires or how she's going to teach him how to bake the best pies in the state. The thought of both makes me laugh.

We sit and talk, cooing over the baby for another thirty minutes before the ladies excuse themselves to go home. Opening the only diner in town at dawn means they're already looking at a long day tomorrow. Like the passing of the guard, Grant and Connor step into the room. Without trying to be obvious, I peer around them looking for Taylor. I haven't seen him since he excused himself to tell the waiting room of the baby's birth. Maybe I imagined the feelings I saw when he looked at me. Or, maybe I was projecting how I feel on him.

"Hey, mama bear. Let me see that little soldier." Rolling my eyes, I place the baby in Grant's arms. I need to decide on a name, calling my son "the baby" is already getting old.

Connor places a beautiful assortment of flowers on the counter and steps up to place a kiss on my cheek. "Congratulations, Red."

"Those are beautiful, Con. Thank you both for coming."

"You know there's nowhere else we'd be today. Now, for the important question—does this guy have a name yet?"

Sighing, I rest my head back on the pillow and let out a long breath. "Nope. I've said them all over and over and nothing feels right. Oliver, Logan, and Matthew. Great names, but sadly, I don't think any of them are his."

Connor and Grant spend the next ten minutes throwing out every baby name under the sun, each getting more ridiculous as they go. I attempt to intervene when they move on from names to call signs. A quiet knock at the door stops us all.

"Hey, Sugar," Grant says as he smiles, his eyes darting between the two of us.

"You okay for another visitor?" Taylor asks. I notice he's changed clothes and his hair is a little damp on the ends. My heart flutters knowing he didn't leave. He stayed. And apparently took a shower. Lucky bastard.

"I think we're going to take off. Hey little man, you be kind to your mama." Grant places a quick kiss to the top of the baby's head and hands him back to me. I hate that Grant is alone in this world. He's such a good man and would be an incredible father. I've always seen him as a later-in-life dad, stepping into a family that needs him and his big, kind heart.

"Then there were two," Taylor says as he approaches the side of the bed.

The baby begins to stir, and I reply, "Technically, three. You showered."

"I did. It had been a while, and I was starting to feel like the nurses could smell me coming down the hall."

The silence between us is slightly awkward so I take a risk. Because if there's a chance to lay it all out, it's when I can blame my irrational decisions on hormones.

"Want to sit with us?"

His hesitation is only a few beats before he slowly scoots onto the bed next to me. It's a tight fit but we make it work. Nestling into his side, my head resting in the crook of his arm, I feel every fiber of anxiety and stress leave my body. His beating heart a sweet lullaby. We lie like this, the baby nestled in my arms when he speaks.

"So, going with Logan?"

"Nope. It doesn't seem right."

Shifting, I move the baby so he's in front of me, his little bundled feet resting on my abdomen. With his head in my hands, I look down at him and ask, "What is your name, sweet boy?"

"Honey, you don't have to decide tonight."

"Nicholas Henry Gilbert."

"Nicholas?"

"It just popped in my head," I say, looking at Taylor, his brow quirked and a smirk on his face.

Humming, Taylor rubs his hand across his smooth chin, my eyes tracing each move. "I like it."

"Yeah? I'm trying to do right by him. Unlike my parents. They weren't very original with my name, now were they? Can't do that to my son."

"I always assumed you were named after a certain fictional character. A smart mouthed independent lady with a southern drawl." I scoff at his description of my actual birth namesake. My parents had no way of knowing the teasing I would endure when they named me Scarlett along with my fiery red hair. "It's a strong name and if this grip is any indication, he's a strong boy. Like his mama."

Leaning my head back onto his shoulder, I look at my son. There are so many possibilities for him. His life is only beginning, yet I think of all things I want to teach him, the lessons he'll learn.

"You did great today. I was so in awe of it all. Thank you for letting me share it with you."

Lulling my head to the side, I look up at Taylor, his face only inches from own. Slowly, he leans down, and my heart skips a beat. His breath is minty, and I suck in the coolness of it, preparing for his lips. I feel the thump of his heartbeat as my eyes slowly close. But a certain little person will have none of that and begins to stir in my hands, a whimper and a slow cry replaces the buzzing of sexual tension in the room. Laughing, I pull away and open my mouth to speak.

"Nuh uh. Take care of him, we have plenty of time to talk. I'll clean up these bags of food and give you some privacy."

Gently, he rises from the bed and begins gathering the trash. When he's gone, I adjust the baby to the crook of my arm and open my nursing pajamas. With a hope and a prayer, I guide Nicholas's mouth to my breast, hoping this latching will take the first time. I'm not that lucky and it takes a few tries but eventually he's suckling, and I relax.

"I'm sorry your daddy wasn't here for this day, baby boy. I have so much to tell you about him. He'd be so excited to hold you and love on you. Never doubt that. Never doubt how much you are loved by all of us."

Chapter 22

Taylor

Zipping the small suitcase, I look to where Scarlett is humming a song to Nicholas as she snaps his little pajamas. His little body wiggles, and I pause to watch them. Being here these past few days has been amazing. I almost blew it by kissing her just hours after she gave birth. What kind of asshole kisses a woman in a very important moment of her new parenthood? Apparently, me.

I avoided snuggling up to her in her bed and kept a safe distance by sitting on the couch, changing the baby's diaper while she was showering, and absolutely not imagining her naked while she was doing so. Of course, I did tell Nicholas how amazing and strong his mother is, and I made sure to tell him about his father. Gripping my finger, he was the perfect audience as I told him story after story of Henry's and my childhood shenanigans. Stories flowed from me, some I'd forgotten, with ease and it felt like, in those moments, Henry was here with us.

Scarlett gently settles Nicholas into his little carrier

and clips the buckles as I approach the bed. Smiling up at me she says, "I think we're all set. Tay, do you think he forgives me for the . . ." She holds her hand up, making a scissors motion with her fingers.

I grip her fingers in my hand and shake my head. "Do not make that gesture when referencing a man's genitals, even if said man is only two days old. But yes, honey, I think he forgives you."

Sighing, her shoulders relax, and I laugh at her reaction to which she responds to with a smack across the chest. "Do not make fun of me, Taylor. That was traumatic."

"You think that was traumatic? Maybe we should ask Nick what he thinks. What do you say buddy? Going to have nightmares?"

"Don't listen to Uncle Taylor. He's not a nice guy."

I gasp in mock horror at her statement, and she relents and says, "Fine. He's actually a very nice guy. And handsome." The last part is a mumble, not meant for my ears but I hear it nonetheless.

"Hey, Gilberts. Oh and Taylor. Are y'all ready to get out of here?" Nellie asks as she pushes an empty wheelchair into the room. Nellie has been Scarlett's nurse most of her stay, and when I returned from her house this morning with her car, they were enjoying a cup of tea together while Scarlett told her all about Henry. There wasn't a dry eye in the house, but this time while she cried, I didn't see the same Scarlett as the times before. Those tears were of memories and loss, but she wasn't broken like she was following the accident.

"Hey Nell, do you think we could have a quick minute? I wanted to talk to Taylor about something. I need like five minutes."

"Sure thing. I'll be back."

After Nellie has left the room, I turn my attention to Scarlett. Her fingers twist the hem of her loose-fitting shirt, nerves evident. Reaching out to grab her wrist, she stops mid twist and I take her hand in mine, my thumb rubbing across her knuckles.

"What's wrong?"

"I don't think I can go back there." She alternates on her feet, unable to sit still. I hate seeing her like this, distressed and worried. "The house, it's . . . I can't do it, Taylor."

Sighing, I release her hand and pull her to me, keeping my opposite hand resting on the baby carrier on the bed. Her chuckles into my chest cause me to step away.

"I think you can hug me with both arms, he isn't going anywhere."

"Are you saying my one arm hug isn't sufficient?" I tease and she wipes her tears from her cheeks. Taking her chin between my thumb and forefinger, I capture her eye. "For the record, I didn't expect you would want to go back to the house that's why we're going to Grant's to discuss things. Does that work for you?"

Nodding, she releases a breath, and I know I just gave her a small gift. A chorus of voices outside of her room draws my attention. I recognize Dr. Green in the crowd and want to grab him before he moves along.

"I'm going to grab Nellie so we can get out of here." I rush from the room and find Dr. Green halfway down the hall. I nod to Nellie as I pass the desk and whisper shout the doctor's name. He turns from the group and excuses himself as I approach.

"Mr. Cain. How are Scarlett and Nicholas doing?"

"They're great. We're heading out now. I just wanted to know if it's safe for Scarlett and the baby to travel?"

"I don't think—"

"Sir, it's only to Lexington. While we had a positive result here, she was brought in because of the extreme stress she's been under. Not only Henry's death but also the break in at her home. Until the sheriff can confirm it's safe for her to be in that house, I can't in good conscious-ness let her stay there. My sister is a nurse in Lexington, and I can guarantee she will be checking on both Scarlett and Nicholas. We're close to a hospital if necessary."

"I was going to say I don't think that will be a prob-lem," he says with a smile. "Nicholas will need to be seen by his pediatrician in the next few days, but I won't need to see Scarlett for six weeks, barring any problems." Relief washes over me. I can take her to Lexington. Get her out of this town and away from the home she so clearly does not want to go back to.

Thanking the doctor, I promise to have Scarlett discuss the trip with her pediatrician before we leave town. Step-ping into Scarlett's room, she's settled into the wheelchair with the baby carrier sitting on her lap. Peeking into the carrier, I see Nicholas fast asleep and walk beside her as Nellie guides us out of the room and toward the elevators.

Scarlett and Nicholas are fast asleep in Grant's bedroom as we sit on his porch and share a few beers with Connor, who is telling us a story about some online dating fiasco. It's been a long time since I just sat and relaxed with friends. The last few months have been busy and chaotic for us all.

Death has a ripple effect on the people who mourn the loss of a loved one. Each of us have seen death and its destruction in our lives, but this one has been a little harder for each of us.

"Don't scoff at my dating woes old man," Connor teases Grant. "One day you'll finally put yourself out there, your days of living your life like a monk behind you, and it'll all make sense. Dating is a fucking bitch, but sometimes the reward is sweet."

"Or lands you a restraining order," I counter, and we all raise our bottles in agreement.

"So we've dodged the conversation long enough. While Red and the baby sleep, we should probably figure out a plan. I'm happy to have them here as long as needed. Or, I can stay at her place with them until she feels safe."

"Cap, I think she knows that but honestly, I'm not sure we'll ever get her back in that house. I didn't tell her, but she talked in her sleep last night. It's more than fear from the break-in. I think it's Henry and everything they went through in that house."

Both Grant and Connor mumble their understanding before taking a long draw from their bottles. Connor finishes his beer and sets the empty bottle on the small table with our collection of previously discarded brown bottles before uncapping another.

"Besides, I don't care what the sheriff says, this break-in isn't sitting well with me. I think we should install some cameras and see if they come back." I look from Connor to Grant, waiting for either to disagree with me. I've thought about this for two days, and aside from staying here myself, this is the best plan to see if the bastards come back.

"Agreed. The whole vibe is off. I'll pick up something tomorrow and put them up. She can stay here, and I'll move in there until she knows what she wants."

"I was thinking of taking them to Lexington," I say to Grant, his expression unreadable. Unlike Connor, who is smiling like the cat who ate the canary. Shaking my head at his obvious approval, I turn my attention back to Grant, waiting for a response. I respect Grant Ellison as both my former captain and as a friend, but I don't need his approval for this plan. I'd like it, but I don't need it.

"You ready to take all this on?" he asks, turning his gaze toward the house. "It's a lot when it's not your family."

"That's where you're wrong. They are my family, Cap. It's my dut—"

"This is more than some obligation you think you have to Henry. I know you don't need it, but you have my blessing. I care for that girl like a sister, hell, I'm almost old enough to be her father, and I want nothing but for her to keep smiling like she did today. Keep her safe and make her smile. We'll work with the sheriff and figure out what's happening here."

Shooting a look to Connor, he nods his agreement. I rise up from my seat and extend my hand to Grant. He stands and takes my hand, shaking twice before pulling me into a hug. "I think he'd be a dick about it, but eventually even Henry would admit this is what's best for them. For all of you."

Chapter 23

Scarlett

Something I've learned as a new mother is there is no one solid answer to a single baby question. I've talked with friends, spent time online searching, and all I've learned is for every question, there are ten answers. I suppose, at the end of the day, I need to accept that each new mother and baby have their own story.

Our story is a little messy, very tearful, and nothing short of exhausting. And I love every minute of it. The weeks since his birth have been a whirlwind to say the least. Taylor has been a godsend, and I'm not sure I'll ever be able to repay him for the sacrifices he's made for us. Beyond completely changing his schedule to be home at night, he's also spent most nights on the couch while I've claimed his bed.

Sure, he's insisted that with his difficulty sleeping, it only makes sense for him to spend his time on the couch. But I know he's full of it. There is nobody in the world who thinks a couch trumps a bed. Especially this bed. It's cushy without being soft and the sheets are like soft little puffs of comfort. Memories of the time in this bed during my last stay hover above me like a cloud of confusion and bliss. I'm choosing to ignore the confusing aspects and focus my attention on my son.

Nicholas is fast asleep in his bassinet to the side of the bed while I lie here, staring up at the ceiling. I counted sheep. I thought of waves crashing and soft lullabies. Nothing worked. Instead of sleeping while he sleeps, I think of the things I could be doing around the house to repay Taylor for his hospitality. The realization that I can't hide out here forever and need a plan filters its way into my mind like the bright sunlight through the curtains.

Sleep alludes me but a shower beckons me. Slipping off the bed, I peer at my sleeping boy, his little body wrapped tight like a human burrito, as he sleeps peacefully. A twinge of jealousy pings into my soul. I didn't know it was humanly possible to be this tired and still function. Or semi-function.

I don't think my mind is wired to sleep during the day, regardless of how desperate I am for it. Hopefully, that will change soon, but until then, a warm shower will have to do. Quietly, I tiptoe out of the room into the master bathroom and turn the faucet to hot, letting the room fill with steam. Taking one of the shower bombs from the gift basket Addy brought over yesterday, I toss it into the corner of the shower and let the aroma of lavender fill the space.

Massaging the shampoo into my hair, I enjoy the sensation of my nails scraping my scalp. Gosh, I could go for a massage right now. The tension of the last few weeks compounded by the knowledge that my life is in a major upheaval and out of my control has my body consumed with knots.

I'm not sure if it's the warm water, the lavender filling

the room, or my acceptance of exhaustion, but I know I'll be able to sleep for at least a while, so I quickly rinse my hair and turn off the water before exiting the shower and toweling off. Wrapping my robe around my body, I begin combing my hair. Listening for the baby, I don't hear anything, so I turn on the blow dryer on low and begin drying my hair.

One of Addy's words of new-mom wisdom is to expose Nicholas to as many daily sounds as possible. She says if he hears the blow dryer, vacuum, and other random sounds around the house he'll always be able to fall asleep in an active house. Since she's one of the only moms I know, I take that advice to heart and give it a go. The upside to her being right is I will be able to handle household chores while he sleeps. Downside is I can't hear him with the blow dryer on, so I won't know if he's crying. That realization doesn't sit well with me, and I declare my hair dry enough and turn off the dryer. Peering into the bedroom, the sight before me steals my breath.

Standing in the room, holding my son to his chest is Taylor Cain in all his shirtless glory. The contrast of Nicholas's white blanket and Taylor's tan and beautifully inked skin, is shocking but something I can't take my eyes off. Rocking back and forth, he's patting the baby's back, whispering in his ear. The slight smile tells me whatever he's saying is probably not meant for this mama's ears, so I allow them a few minutes of one on one time. This opportunity also grants me more time to ogle, or appreciate, the man before me.

It's been nearly six months since Henry's passing and while I hate that he's not here for these moments and isn't the one comforting our son, I'm grateful for the man who is. Each night, when Nicholas wakes me for his middle of the night feeding, I've been telling him about his father. Quiet stories of the man I loved for so many years fill our nights and most of them end with me crying myself to sleep.

Regardless of where we were in our relationship, he should be here, sharing these moments with me. Changing diapers, wiping spit-up, and reassuring me my body will return to some sort of normalcy is something I know he would have loved. Overwhelmed by the thoughts of Henry, I retreat back into the bathroom and turn on the faucet, splashing cold water on my face.

After composing myself, I step into the bedroom and spy Taylor with his back to me, swaying back and forth attempting to sing to the baby.

"Are you singing Celine Dion to my son?" I ask in mock horror. Spinning on his heel, Taylor smiles sheepishly.

"It's the only thing I could think of on the fly. Don't mock my music choices, I think he likes it." I step up to him, looking at Nicholas's sleeping face and smile. Lifting my hand to his back, I rub a little circle before pulling my hand back and stuffing it into the pocket of my robe.

"Did he wake up? I didn't hear him."

"Yeah, he was fussing a little when I opened the door. Obviously I couldn't help him with what he really wanted so I tried the next best thing. Turns out your son is a fan of nineties ballads."

Laughing, I contemplate taking Nicholas from him or changing into some clean clothes. The idea of clothes reminds me that Taylor is standing before me half naked. "Uh, something happen to your shirt?"

"I didn't think it was good for Nick to inhale all the booze and grease that is probably all over my shirt, so I tossed it in the laundry there before I picked him up."

Something about that simple gesture, knowing he immediately thought of the baby before anything else hits me in the gut. Refusing to cry at such a simple, yet sweet, gesture, I clear my throat and say, "I'm going to get dressed then I'll take him."

Before he can respond, I grab a pair of leggings, a tank top, and clean pair of panties from one of my two drawers in his dresser and scurry to the bathroom to change. Distance from this moment is necessary if I want to keep from throwing myself at him. There is nothing sexier than a half-naked man holding a baby, especially when that man is Taylor Cain.

Once I've pulled my clothes on and tied my hair high on my head, I return to where Taylor is holding Nicholas and motion with wiggling fingers for him to give me my fussy little man. As I settle on the bed with Nicholas and unwrap him from his blankets, Taylor disappears from the room without a word. Assuming he'll return, I grab the discarded blanket and cover the baby as he begins nursing.

Proving me right, Taylor appears just a few minutes later with a bottle of water and, sadly, a fresh T-shirt. Uncapping the water, he sets the bottle on the side table and peers down at the lump under the blanket.

Looking up at him, I smile. "Pretty strange, huh?"

"He's amazing, Red. Truly. You made a human. It's fucking amazing. Shit, sorry. I should scale back on the cussing."

Barking out a laugh, I cover my mouth as the baby unlatches and whimpers at my outburst. "I think he's a little young to pick up on your potty mouth. Thanks for your help. I hate that we're taking over your house and free time."

Motioning for the bed next to my feet Taylor sits and rests his hand on my ankle. "You aren't taking over anything. I want you guys here. I'm just sorry it's under these circumstances."

"You've given up so much for us. Changing your work schedule from nights to days—"

"Scarlett," he warns, and I bite my lip to keep from continuing on. When I agreed to come here while we wait for the sheriff to finish his investigation and for me to decide if I can move back into the house, I expected to just take over the upstairs of Taylor's house and give him his space. But he insisted on changing everything to ensure he's home with us. Beyond the sacrifice of his bedroom, he also hasn't worked a closing shift in the weeks we've been here.

"Fine. What—" I begin when my phone starts buzzing on the dresser. Taylor stands and grabs it. I can tell by the look on his face it isn't a call from Grant or anyone else in Fayhill.

"Who is it?" I ask as I switch Nicholas to my other breast.

"Unknown. Is this still going on?" he asks incredulously.

Squirming under his glare, I ignore the question and peek under the blanket, pretending to check on Nicholas. After a few beats, he clears his throat. Lifting my eyes, I see an expression that hasn't greeted me in over six months. It's a look I recognize from Henry. Frustration, stress, and a sprinkling of anger.

"Scarlett."

"It's an unknown number, Taylor. I hit ignore and go about my day. No biggie. Hell, Jamaica called me the other day too. It's solicitors or political bullshit. I ignore it, the call goes to voicemail, and they don't leave one."

"How often?"

Shrugging, I adjust my tank top and pull Nicholas up to my shoulder to burp.

"Red," he implores, his expression changing to one of concern, and I fold like a house of cards.

"A few times a day. It's a lot less than it was a few months ago. Maybe they realize I'm not buying what they're selling."

Growling, he laces his fingers behind his head and exhales loudly as he lifts his chin, gazing at the ceiling. He stands like that while I pat the baby's back a few times. Shifting my position, I shimmy to the edge of the bed, a motion that catches his attention because he moves quickly to my side, reaching to help me up. Laying Nicholas in his bassinet, I turn to face the brooding man before me.

"Look, I appreciate you going all alpha here. It's ridiculous and unnecessary but appreciated, nonetheless. Phone calls happen, Taylor, they don't have to mean anything. Right now, I'm more concerned about how fucking tired I am. I'm going to curl up and take a nap. By the looks of that luggage you're sporting under your eyes, I think you could use one too. Why don't you kick off those shoes, take that pillow and join me for an epic nap? Or at the least, a few minutes with your eyes closed until this little dictator declares naptime over."

"Red . . ."

"Nap, Taylor. I need one," I say with finality and pull back the covers, slide into the bed, snuggle into my side, pointing to the pillow on the far side of the large bed. Grunting his opposition, he does as instructed and walks to the other side of the bed and kicks off his shoes before gripping the collar of his shirt and pulling it off in one swoop.

My eyes go wide at the view, and he must take the look as one of horror or confusion because he says, "If I'm going to nap, I'm going to do it right and be comfortable. Fair warning, I'm fucking exhausted and snoring is likely."

"Noted," I say through a yawn and close my eyes, welcoming the sleep to smother my exhaustion.

Chapter 24

Taylor

Pulling an old concert T-shirt over my head, I don't even bother stifling my loud and lengthy yawn. I've purposely eased myself out of these closing shifts since Scarlett and Nicholas came to stay with me five weeks ago. I wanted to be here for her, to help her adjust to motherhood but also to remind her they are safe in Lexington with me.

The first three weeks were hard on me. Change is not something I dabble in. Structure and routine are my comfort zone and my preference. Owning my own business allows me the ability to maintain that level of structure in my life, and I've built a schedule for myself that works with my need for not only routine but my bouts of insomnia. With Scarlett and a newborn in the house, I've had to quickly adapt to the unknown and learn to be fast on my feet. Unfortunately, this means I've hardly slept and, most days, I'm dead on my feet. But I wouldn't have it any other way.

They're here and they're safe. That's what matters.

Although I'm able to protect them from tangible and visible threats, it's the unknown that leaves me feeling uneasy. I know she isn't telling me, but Scarlett is still getting calls at all hours of the day. She finally listened to me and blocked most of the numbers, but she insists it's simply easier to ignore the call and move along than continue to block every number. We've agreed to disagree. Honestly, we're both too exhausted to do much more than that.

While I've established a zombie-like existence, Scarlett and Nicholas have developed their own routine during the day while I'm at work. Each morning as I stand before the coffee pot, grumbling and willing the brewing to happen at warp speed, she's already fixed herself breakfast, strapped Nicholas into the sling across her chest, and taken an early morning walk. I can only assume after I leave for the bar, they spend the day napping and doing yoga. At least the streaming history tells me there's yoga being played, whether it's being done, I'm not sure.

A few nights a week she's cooked or waited for me to get home to grill. It's all very comfortable and domestic. It's not something I ever thought I'd personally experience, yet here I am. Although, I do remind myself it's temporary and the reason I haven't purchased new beds for the upstairs bedrooms. That and I really like the idea of sharing my bed with her.

Saying that, even to myself, feels wrong, but it's the truth. After the nap we shared in my bed after the first few weeks they were here, I never slept on the couch again. But that is also why I'm so tired each day. When Nicholas wakes during the night, we both get up. Scarlett insists I should sleep; it's her job to care for him alone, but it has yet to happen. I'd never tell her, but those late-night feedings are my favorite. After picking up the baby from the bassinet, she always climbs back in the bed with him to nurse. The room is dark, and I can't see anything, but the intimacy of the act has stirred something in me. Something paternal and something toward Scarlett I can't quite name.

I'm bummed I won't be home tonight for that moment. One of my new bartenders called out due to a family emergency, and it's my turn to cover his shift. So, I'm strapping on my dormant Friday night bartender hat and heading to the bar for a closing shift. On about five hours of broken sleep. It's going to be a long night.

Walking out of the bedroom toward the kitchen, I pause when I see Scarlett at the stove, her back to me, a wooden spoon in her hand stirring whatever cooks in the pot. Her hips sway side to side, legs dipping as she slowly adds her shoulders to the mix. Fuck me running. Pregnancy has done her body good. Or maybe it's the yoga. It doesn't matter because she has curves for days, her ass perfect and full in tight fitting pants. She's wearing one of those tight-fitting maternity tanks that makes her tits look like the most edible fucking things ever.

"Oh shit!" she shouts, reaching for her phone and turning the music down, while dripping sauce on the floor. "Double shit."

Laughing, I walk over to the counter and pick up a discarded dish towel and begin wiping up the drippings from the floor and anywhere else they may be. When I rise, she's standing before me with her hand on her face, her very flushed face.

"I didn't hear you walk in."

Shrugging, I take the spoon from her hand and dip it in the pot before lifting it to my lips. "Mmm. That's good. Save me a bowl, will ya?"

Her eyes are focused on my lips, and I can't help but smirk. Playing with her a little, I slip my tongue between my lips and lick up any sauce that may have dripped on my lips. "Red?"

"Yeah, huh?" she stammers, eyes jumping up to catch my own.

"A bowl? Save me one?"

"Oh, sure. Of course. It's going to be weird without you here tonight." Taking the spoon back, she turns to the sink and rinses it off before returning her attention back to the pot.

"Addy's coming by, right?"

Nodding, she doesn't say anything. I reach my hand out and place it on her shoulder, drawing her attention away from the food. Sighing, she shifts on her feet before meeting my gaze.

"What's wrong, honey?"

"I'm getting too comfortable here. I should figure out what I'm going to do about my house and everything. Obviously there's no danger at my place. Nothing has shown up on the cameras Grant and Connor installed, and when I called the sheriff earlier today, he told me there didn't seem to be anything more he could do, and he was closing the case."

"First, you don't have to make any decisions right now. You've just had a baby and have a lot of adjustments happening. No reason to add to those." I won't tell her the idea of them leaving and returning to Fayhill not only makes me uneasy because we don't know that it's safe but also because I like having them here.

Scoffing, she steps over to the cupboard and begins pulling bowls and plates from the shelves, placing them on the counter. I like this. Her here in my kitchen, moving around seamlessly like she belongs here. Just as it feels having her in my bed, these moments of what most people consider everyday life leave me believing there could be something more for me than I prepared myself for.

"Look, you've been here a few weeks and barely ventured farther than a walk down the road. What do you say about us doing something tomorrow night? Just us. I'm sure Addy will watch Nick for a few hours. You and I can go out to dinner, let someone else do the dishes for a change. What do you say?" She opens her mouth to argue but I stop her.

"Nope. It's just a few hours. He takes an evening nap and will be good for a solid three hours before he needs to be fed. Besides, you started pumping and there should be enough in case we are late getting back. Come on, say yes, Scarlett."

"Yes, Scarlett."

"Smartass."

"Better than being a dumbass, Sugar."

She winks as she turns on her heel and goes about setting the table. Grabbing my keys from the counter, I toss them in the air and catch them before saying, "Speaking of asses. Yours looked pretty good dancing in my kitchen, Red."

I leave her standing in the dining room, a bowl in her hands and an open mouth on her face. She loves getting in the last word just as much as I love leaving her speechless. Laughing, I open the door to the garage and let it close quietly behind me as I walk out to my truck for a long night serving drunks.

As the final credit card is run and the last cab pulls up in front of the building, I let out a long sigh of relief. Although I'm dead on my feet, I also feel slightly energized from the night. That may also be a result of the three energy drinks I've had since I left my house earlier, but regardless, I'm exhausted and wired at the same time.

Caleb nudges me out of the way as he loads the dishwasher with glasses. "Why don't you close everything out, and I'll handle this."

"You sure? I don't want to be a slacker," I say.

"Dude, you look dead on your feet. Go to your office and handle the math shit, I'll make sure everything's done out here."

I don't argue with him. I quickly close out the register and pull the till from the drawer before doing the same with the second unit at the far end of the bar and retreating to my office. I just finish the final report when there's a knock at the door. Caleb sticks his head in the door and says, "We're all done out here, boss. I sent everyone home. You need a ride?"

"Nah, I'll be okay. Thanks though, I'll walk out with you." Logging off the computer, I walk toward the door. Thank God I have tomorrow off, I don't think I could do this two nights in a row. Pausing at my office door, I set the alarm and flip the light off before following Caleb down the short hall and out the back door. Locking the door, I turn to him and extend my hand.

"Thanks for keeping shit running around here in my absence. I appreciate it. You've been a life saver these last months. We should talk about you taking on more duties full-time."

Groaning, he pulls his hand back and runs it through his short hair before dropping a bomb. "I wanted to wait until things were back to normal, but I think it's best I let the cat out of the bag. I'm getting married."

Confused, I shake my head in disbelief. "What?"

"Yeah, my girl and I got engaged a few months back and decided on a destination wedding."

"Well, congrats man. I honestly didn't realize you had a serious girlfriend. I feel like a dick."

"Nah, she lives out of state. My hometown as a matter of fact. That's kind of the second part of my news. I'll be moving back to Colorado. She's starting medical school and my dad wants me to come back and work the family business with him."

The realization of how little I know about my employees hits me like a ton of bricks. I knew Caleb just finished his last year of college, but I didn't know he was dating someone. Hell, I didn't know he's from Colorado. Normally I consider myself an in-touch boss, but these last few months I've been so consumed by my own shit, well Henry's shit, I don't know what is happening around me.

"I hate to see you go. How long until you leave?"

"Two months. I feel bad with all you have going on and Ashton not back but—"

"Don't worry. I'm happy for you. Let me know if there's anything I can do."

Shaking my hand, he says goodbye and climbs into his car, leaving me standing next to my truck. Looks like it's back to the drawing board and looking for another bartender. Thoughts of how I can adjust the schedule and maybe convince Ashton to come back and help me with the managing side of the business for a while distract me as I drive across town toward my house.

As the garage door rises, I yawn again. I hate to say

it, but maybe I'm old. In my mind I shouldn't be tired. I should be preparing to eat something, play a few rounds of Call of Duty, and drink a few beers before I head to bed. Instead, I'm thinking a beer sounds like a bad idea, but a hot shower and my bed is perhaps the greatest idea I've ever had.

Quietly, I enter the house through the kitchen, a single light over the stove illuminating the room. An aroma of spices lingers through the space from Scarlett's dinner, but I'm too tired to indulge in a bowl. Dropping my keys, phone, and wallet on the counter, I kick off my shoes and walk toward the bedroom. Slowly, I open the door and enter the room. Scarlett is fast asleep in the bed. Lying on her back with an arm flung over her head, I pause and let the moonlight peeking through the curtains cast a light upon her. Slipping off my jeans, I toss them in the hamper followed by my shirt before walking into the bathroom.

Once I've taken a quick shower and brushed my teeth, I slip on a pair of my athletic shorts I keep hanging on the back of the door. Normally, I'd sleep in my boxers but when Scarlett and I started sharing a bed, I chose to sleep in either shorts or pants. As I flip the switch, I hear Nicholas stirring in his bed and quickly move through the door to check him. Eyes wide, he's moving around but not making much noise. Glancing toward Scarlett, I see that she's stirring but not waking up. If he's stayed on his schedule, this isn't his feeding time. He's likely just woken himself up and needs to be comforted.

Picking him up, I hold him to my chest, rocking back and forth. My hand feels massive on his small body but the moment I wrap him in my hands, he settles. Soft coos and a long exhale with an audible sigh tell me he's relaxed and falling back asleep. We walk the room a few times, careful not to wake his sleeping mom.

As I bend to lay Nicholas down in the bassinet, I look over to the bed and catch Scarlett looking at me. Her head is resting in her hand, a coy smile on her face, and my mouth goes dry.

Chapter 25

Scarlett

I wish I had a camera for the moment I just woke to. Seeing Taylor comforting my son, holding him to his chest, without a second thought; it's stirring something deep inside me I've tried to ignore. Over the last few months, I found myself falling. Falling deeper into some unknown emotion I didn't know was possible.

Guilt was my first response to the flood of feelings. How could I feel something so profound for a man while I carried another man's child? Then he was there with me for the birth, and I couldn't deny it. When he kissed me off pure instinct only moments after Nicholas was born, I knew I loved him. I knew this was my new normal. Fighting the feelings for a man who is supposed to be forbidden.

Anger soon followed the acknowledgment of my growing love for Taylor. I was angry I'm not supposed to love freely. Not supposed to love *him*. Like an angel and devil perched on my shoulder, words I know my mother would say whisper in my conscience, *"What would people think if you moved on so soon after Henry's death? And with his best friend. Scandalous and unbecoming, Scarlett.* "

The realization that no matter how many years separate me from my family, the fact that their opinions of me are still directly related to how I feel about myself only piss me off more. Until last night I thought the feelings were one-sided. Sure, we had that random kissing session a few months ago, but that was just a blip in our friendship. A moment we haven't spoken of since. Too embarrassed to bring it up, I've locked it away and focused on the now and where we are in our current situation.

Then, after he blatantly flirted with me in the kitchen last night, I felt a shift in the atmosphere. Something was different. He was different. Playful and sexy. The fine lines around his eyes appearing for the first time in weeks, a sure sign he was happy sent flutters to my stomach. I vowed in that moment I wasn't going to allow other people's judgments or perceptions to stop me from pursuing something that may make us both very happy.

I expected Addy to be shocked and horrified when I confessed my feelings to her, but she surprised me. Instead of gasping in offense that I could so easily care for another man so soon after Henry's death, she smiled, pulled me into a hug and thanked me for trusting her and being honest. *Honest.* That one word opened the floodgates and I confessed the last year and a half of my life to her. We cried, we laughed, and she told me I was only days from being six weeks post delivery, and unless I was hiding some horrible discomfort, I had the green light for some, *"Activity with my brother I don't want to talk about because he's my brother, but you know what I mean,"* before she proceeded to do a bad rendition of seventies porn music.

My plan is to approach the subject tomorrow night, or tonight I suppose, on our pseudo date. He may not call it a date, but I consider it one and I figured it's the perfect opportunity to tap deep into my past and pull out all the flirting stops. Then, I wake up to him shirtless and holding my son, comforting him back to sleep. Waiting until tomorrow night seems like the worst idea.

I turn to the other side and watch as he rounds the bed and slowly crawls on top of the freshly washed sheets, pulling the covers up to his waist. I don't speak, only watch him as he settles in, one arm thrown over his head while the other rests on his abdomen. His rock hard abs with the lightest dusting of hair at the waistband of his shorts move with each breath he takes. Looking to his face, I see he's closed his eyes.

Tugging my bottom lip between my teeth, I shift a little so I'm closer to him, the warmth of his skin radiating and sending a chill up my spine. He opens his eyes and turns his head to look at me. My eyes roam over his face, attempting to decipher what he's feeling. If the lights were on, I could use his eyes like one does a mood ring. Deep gray for anger and pain, light heather for humor and light-heartedness, and stormy gray with bright blue chips for passion and lust.

Saying a little prayer, I'm hoping for the blue chips as I tentatively reach my hand out to rest atop his. My fingers brush his forearm, and I feel his skin prickle with goosebumps. Shivers of my own skirt across my body, compounded by the heat I feel inside.

"Thank you for that," I whisper.

He doesn't say anything and instead turns to his side facing me, my hand falling to the bed between us. With his head resting on his arm, the other resting next to mine, he simply stares at me. Is he letting me take the lead here? Well, two can play that game. Instead of saying anything, I look back at him, a smirk on my lips.

It isn't quite a staring contest, but after a few beats I can't stand it anymore.

"Do you remember the first time we met?" I ask.

"Hmm . . . I think it was a few weeks after you and Henry started dating. I met up with you guys at a bar for a game."

Smiling, I move my hand a little, our pinkies touching. "Nope."

"Maybe a get-together at someone's house then? A party?"

A giggle escapes, but I quickly suck it back, not wanting to wake Nicholas. "Wrong again," I whisper while moving a little closer so I can keep my voice low. At least that's what I tell myself as I rest my hand just under his arm, still on the bed but closer to his stomach.

"We met the same night I met Henry."

Brows furrowed, he doesn't say anything, so I continue, "Earlier in the night, my friends saw you. They were cooing at how hot and sexy you were, and how they wished they had the lady balls to go up to you and your group of friends. I drew the short straw."

"And met Wolf," he offers, and I shake my head.

"I kind of followed you to the bathroom and pretended to be reading something on the wall."

"Did I speak to you?"

Nodding in affirmation, I inhale slowly and lift my hand to his side. I feel the moment he sucks in a breath and lets my hand sit on his waist.

"I kind of fake stumbled, and you helped me, asked if I was okay. I thought . . . I thought for a minute there was something when we looked at each other. I was a silly girl who read too many romance novels and believed in an instant connection with another person. Then you smiled, and I became a sudden mute. Words weren't something I had access to, so I scurried away."

Pausing, I wait a beat for him to interject. When he doesn't, I continue, "By the time I returned to the table with my friends, they were in hysterics because I came back without even knowing your name. So much for having lady balls."

"Red, I don't remember that, but we did have a connection. Sure, I didn't know it then, but we hit it off when you started hanging around us. We've always been friends."

It's now or never I suppose. Shifting my body closer, I move so we're only inches from each other. I can feel his breath on my lips and memories of the last time we were this close in this bed flood my mind.

"What if I don't want to be friends anymore?" I ask.

Instead of waiting for him to respond, I lean forward, my lips landing on his. When he doesn't move his lips or even his hands, my heart sinks. Pulling back, I open my mouth to apologize when he grips the back of my neck and says, "Fuck it," and pulls me to him.

In one swoop, my body is flush with his, my leg flung across his body, his kiss consuming me. Soft kisses are short-lived when he licks the seam of my lips, and I open for him. Groaning, his hands tangle in my hair, mine following suit, tugging at the fine hairs at the base of his neck. We kiss, our tongues dancing as our bodies begin to move.

Without breaking the kiss, I push my leg farther over his body, which moves him to his back. Lying atop him, I pour myself into the kiss; I express every feeling and emotion I've ignored for months. I give him me. Just me. Not his best friend's wife. Not his friend. Not the woman he's trying to save. Me. All of me.

His hands run up my sides to my breasts. When his thumbs find my sensitive nipples, I whimper, which causes him to pull back abruptly. Catching his wide eyes, I smile and place a peck to the corner of his lips and then the spot next to his ear. "They're a little sensitive," I whisper in his ear before I tug his earlobe between my teeth.

"Red, we can—"

"No. Don't say we can't. I need this. I need *you*. Please, for one night can we just be us? Can we stop pretending and *just fucking be*?" Desperation accentuates each word, but I am desperate. I need to get out of my head, and I need to know I'm not crazy. That there is something between us well beyond friendship.

"I don't want you to have regrets. You know I never want you to feel like I'm taking advantage of you."

That makes me laugh. I've been giving out signals, or what I thought were signals, this entire conversation, and he thinks he's taking advantage of me? God bless this man.

"Do you want me?" I ask but stop him before he can speak. "It's a yes or no question. A nod or a shake of the head response will do."

With a quirked brow, I wait for him to respond. Slowly a smile appears on his face and his head moves up and down. Leaning my head down, I capture his mouth with mine and sigh into the kiss. Just as quickly as I kiss him, he flips us so he's lying on top of me. The pressure and warmth of his body blankets me and I relax into the bed. Legs wrapped around his waist, I run my hands up his back, the muscles flexing with each pass.

His lips move from my mouth to my neck and the moment his tongue peeks out to lick the sensitive spot below my ear, I let out a moan.

"Shh, baby. You don't want to wake the little man."

Heeding his warning, I draw my lip between my teeth. All this stifling is bound to give me a fat lip by the time morning comes. Lifting my hips to find friction, he groans and instead of offering the same advice, I tug his hair.

His lips move from my neck to the top of my tank, his hand cupping my breast. Gently, his thumb circles just below the nipple and then he lifts his head up to look at me. The expression makes me nervous. Apprehension.

"Is it too soon? Maybe we shouldn't . . ." Taylor looks off in the distance, and I take his face in my hands, returning his eyes to mine.

"Hey," I begin, "it's safe. I promise. Well, except I'm not on birth control, but I saw some condoms when I was cleaning so I think we're okay. I want this, I promise."

"This changes everything."

"Do you want me?" I ask.

"More than anything."

"Then have me."

No other words are spoken as he kisses me. This time, his lips are strong and consuming. His hands are everywhere and not enough places. Lifting my tank over my head, he tosses it aside and ever so gently slides his tongue across my nipple, the sensation sending a pool of desire between my legs. I could come from this feeling alone. He moves his attention from breast to breast and I throw my head back, ecstasy overwhelming me. It's like an out of body experience, this man nestled between my legs and his glorious mouth sending me to new heights. When I can't take it anymore, I begin tugging at my sleep shorts, trying to pull them off.

Understanding my need, Taylor lifts up, and in one swoop pulls them off along with my panties and throws them in the direction of my tank top. The realization that he's seeing me naked. My post baby body has more marks and loose skin than it did months ago, sending my hands instantly to cover as much as I can.

Not having it, he tugs my hands from where they've fallen and slowly slides them up above my head, his fingers interlinking with mine. Leaning down, he kisses me. It's sexy as hell and slow enough to drive me crazy. Unhurried, he drags it out until my body relaxes and then he says, "You are beautiful and amazing. Never hide yourself. Every part of you is perfect."

I don't bother stopping the tear that falls to the pillow. I don't know if it's possible but, in this moment, with those simple words, he holds all the power with my heart. Whether he heals me or destroys me, I am his.

Nodding in understanding, he quickly stands and discards his shorts before pulling open the nightstand. I watch as he sheaths himself and give myself time to peruse the vision before me. Tall, chiseled, and perfect, his body is a work of art. The actual artwork on his chest almost shines in the moonlight, and I itch to touch it. As he slides back on top of me, my hands slide across his chest and I lift my head and place my lips over his heart. Repeating the movement on the opposite side, I look at him and it's then, in the darkness of the room, that I see the blue chips in his gray eyes.

Slowly he slides into me and I throw my head back. As a moan begins to make its way out of my mouth, I tug a pillow from the side of the bed and cover my face, letting the sounds fall freely from my lips. Laughing, he pulls it from my face and kisses me. "I'd rather swallow your moans than have you suffocate yourself. But don't worry, you feel so fucking good I'm about to embarrass myself."

He moves his hips, rotating them a little as I lift my own to join the rhythm. The feeling of him inside me is more than I can take. My orgasm builds quickly, my breath hitching as I fight it off to no avail. A whimper escapes as he buries his face in my neck and follows me over the edge.

Our breaths are quick and in tandem as he lifts his head and kisses me slowly before looking me in the eyes. "Are you okay?"

"I've never been better."

Chapter 26

Taylor

Being here, nestled between her legs with her naked body spread out beneath me, I've found the heaven everyone talks about. Her heart shares the same beat as my own, and I can't stop myself from kissing her. I've done everything in my power to not follow through on my desires. On the attraction I have for her. The overwhelming need to touch her, to kiss her, to beg her to be mine. I lie here, wondering why I was so determined to avoid this. Why did I think neither of us deserved this moment?

Scarlett shifts her legs, and I realize I'm hardly holding any of my body weight off her body. "Shit, I'm sorry. Stay here, I'll be right back," I promise before dropping a quick peck to her lips and moving to the bathroom. I discard the condom and wash my hands before grabbing a towel and returning to the bed. Scarlett is standing over Nicholas's bassinet, and I pause. She's slipped her tank top back on, but she's bottomless as she lifts her eyes to mine. With a smile, she walks toward me.

"I was just checking on him. He's still out like a light."

"I grabbed you this . . . in case . . . I mean, I didn't know if . . ." I reply awkwardly, holding the towel out before me. Jesus, I'm like a fucking teenager who just dry-humped the popular girl on the couch in my parent's basement. Muttering and talking about a fucking towel.

"Thanks. I'm going to clean up. I'll be right back."

Slipping past me, her hand grazes my stomach and my dick jumps at the contact. It's only then I recall I'm standing bare-ass naked. I step aside and let her pass before I walk to the side of the bed and slip on my shorts again. Before sliding back into bed, I flatten the sheets and rearrange the pillows. I'm pulling the covers to my waist when she climbs onto the bed.

With about a foot of space between us, she lies on her back, sheet pulled to her chest, hands folding properly on her stomach. Slowly, I slide my hand across her chin, cupping her cheek, drawing her attention to me.

"You okay?" She nods. "You also planning to sleep way over there?"

"I wasn't—"

"Come here," I say, nudging her my direction. She turns, her back to my front, and I wrap my arm around her waist. Kissing the back of her head, I whisper in her ear, "Sleep, baby. That little guy will be up in less than two hours."

Sighing, she relaxes into my hold, and its only seconds before her breaths even out and she's asleep. I don't have the same luck. My body is exhausted, but my mind is in overdrive. I won't even talk about my heart or conscience. Both are bursting, and it's a conflict I'm not sure how to quiet.

Like most nights when I can't calm my mind, my sleep

comes in spurts. Each of those fragments of sleep are interrupted by a nightmare. Usually, my nightmares are flashes of memories. Moments in the desert with rapid gunfire or explosions. Screams and crying. Tonight, it's different. Instead of the fear and anxiety those dreams usually bring, I'm filled with guilt. Nothing but guilt. Henry came to me, his anger and hurt laid out before me like a mat. I assume the mat is a metaphor for his heart. I've stood on it, stomped it, and left it alone as I walk away.

Jarring awake, I feel the warmth of Scarlett's body still pressed against mine. Her hands are still linked with my own, and I try to calm my racing heart. My mind is in a desperate battle with my feelings for her, and I'm not sure what to do. I feel so strongly for her, wanting to protect her, to care for her, to make her laugh, and listen to her talk about nothing and everything. I want to be for her what she's been for me. My salvation.

Then I remember. I remember who she is. Who *we* are. How can I fall for my best friend's wife? How can I look at his son, hold him to my chest and love him like he's my own? I shouldn't. Yet, I can't seem to stop myself.

Making love to Scarlett was absolutely one of the most intense moments of my life. Each caress of her skin, the way her body molded to mine. It was more than I've had with another woman. Scarlett stirs a little and I tighten my hold on her. She softly hums before relaxing again. Placing a kiss to her shoulder, I think of the words I spoke at Henry's funeral, *". . . live the life we want, the one we dream of, and make it our reality."*

Maybe it's time I take my own advice for a change.

The smell of freshly brewed coffee wakes me. Or rather, the sunlight filling the room wakes me, but it's the coffee that has me standing from the bed before slipping a T-shirt over my head and heading to the kitchen. As I enter the living room, I hear the music of the baby's mobile on his bouncy seat and Scarlett's voice. She's talking to someone, so I glance around looking for a friendly face. When I don't see anyone, I clear my throat and she turns her head, cell phone pressed to her ear. Smiling wide, she turns back around and opens a cupboard, pulling a coffee mug down to fill it. Walking up to her, I place my hands on her hips and bend to place a soft kiss to her shoulder. She giggles and then slides out of my grasp.

"Sorry, *Grant*, what were you saying?" Her gaze shoots to mine, eyes wide in warning, as she hands me my cup of coffee. Taking a sip from the cup I notice her eyes follow the cup as I pull it back from my lips, a blush creeping across her chest. Me drinking coffee makes her blush, duly noted. "Yep, he just walked in. Let me hand you off. I'll talk to you soon. Tell Connor he better be watering my lawn, or I'll make him clip it like Mr. Stanton—on his hands and knees."

Setting my cup down, I take the phone from her extended hand and hold it against my shoulder. Without a warning, I grab her by the waist and tug her to me, her body flush with mine. Capturing her lips, I savor the taste of coffee and maple syrup on her tongue and moan. Fuck, I'm hard for her already, and it's been less than a minute of seeing her. Pushing off my chest, she points her finger at me before waggling it like I'm naughty and walking toward her son.

Lifting the phone to my ear I say, "Mornin', Cap."

"Morning, *Sugar*. You slept late."

"Yeah well, I haven't been doing many closing shifts so last night kicked my ass. I was fucking exhausted. How's it going?"

"Not too bad. I hadn't talked to Scarlett for a few days; thought I'd call and check on her. She sounds good. A lot better than last week. I guess she's getting into a routine."

"Something like that," I agree, never taking my eyes off the woman in question. She's bustling around the house humming to herself. It isn't until she pulls on the baby sling that I realize she's heading out for a walk.

"Hey, Cap. Let me call you back from my phone. Scarlett and the baby are heading out on their walk, and she needs to have her phone with her." I tap the end call after he agrees and walk toward her.

"Mornin'."

"Hey," she says shyly. Which is funny since she wasn't shy last night.

"Here ya go."

Taking the phone from me, she slips it in her pocket and says, "I'm only walking down the street, it'll be fine."

"Never leave home without a way to call someone if you need it. It isn't safe, honey."

Sighing, she shrugs but doesn't argue. She knows there's no point in arguing with me when I'm right. We haven't talked about the break-in, and while she hasn't said anything, I know she's still getting those calls and hang ups, because a few days ago when she silenced the call during dinner, I grabbed it from her and checked the history. She attempted to scold me for violating her privacy, but the moment I scrolled the call history and looked up at her, she stopped and shrugged. Twenty-seven calls from the same number and another dozen from various others.

Solicitors my ass.

"I was thinking of having Addy come over around six, will that work? Let you feed Nicholas before we head to dinner."

"Oh, you still want to go to dinner?" she asks.

"Of course. Why wouldn't I?"

"I wasn't sure if—"

Slipping the sling over her head, I toss it on the couch before wrapping my arms around her waist and bending my knees, so we're eye-level. I search her eyes, looking for a glimpse of what she's thinking. Her brown eyes are wide, and if I'm reading them correctly, full of worry.

Sliding a hand up her back, I wrap it around her neck and pull her closer, kissing her slowly. After a few swipes of my tongue, she melts into me and opens her mouth. It's not a long kiss but enough that she knows I'm serious.

"I want to go out for a nice dinner with you. I want to laugh and talk and be together. If you want that, of course." Her eyes glisten with unshed tears as she nods slowly. "Good. Now, go on your walk, and I'm going to call Grant back. I'll run by the bar and check on a few things and get in a workout before we get ready."

"Okay. We won't be gone long." I pick up my coffee and take a sip while watching her as she settles the baby into the sling and pulls her hair from where it's tangled in the strap. It's these little moments, the ones that are so domestic, that give me pause. It's nothing I ever expected to have in my life, but damn if it doesn't all feel right.

Tapping on Grant's name, I wait two rings before he answers. "I thought you forgot about me, I was about to bake a cake."

"Fuck off. I had to get some damn coffee."

"Is that what we're calling it?"

"I don't know what you're talking about. So, anything new with the cameras?"

Sighing, I hear rustling in the background and assume he's settling in on the couch. If he's getting comfortable, this can't be good. He clears his throat and stuns me. "I told you it's been days without any action. I stopped by there this morning and checked the one we moved to that new spot in the backyard. The memory card is full."

That has my attention. The trail cameras he and Connor put up work on motion sensors and will only take pictures if there's movement. The one facing the front of the house has been a dud, only offering a few shots of what may be a person lurking around the house. And cats. A lot of neighborhood cats.

"Did you check it yet? Able to identify anyone?"

"Not yet. I will make it a priority this afternoon. I'm already late for an appointment but will get on it first thing when I get home."

"Let me know as soon as you do. Those fucking calls keep happening. I've respected her wishes and tried not to make a big deal about them, but that's about to change. My gut says this is all connected, and something is off. Someone is fucking with her."

Grant's quiet as a door closes in the background and I hear his fob unlocking his truck. The engine roars to life and the distinctive sound of the Bluetooth connecting confirms it'll be hours before I know if we finally have a lead on the break-in.

"I don't like saying this, but I have to agree. I didn't want to say anything before because you're a bit of a hothead when it comes to Scarlett, but I think someone's been at the house. Some of the flowers were stepped on and Connor thinks there was a footprint in the back where he let the water run too long and it made a muddy mess."

"Get me those pictures, Grant. I want to get this fucker and give her some peace of mind."

Chapter 27

Scarlett

Our morning walks are always my favorite part of the day. Taylor doesn't live in a traditional neighborhood, and there are stretches of road between each home. He's close enough to have neighbors but far enough we can barely see the other house and surely can't hear anyone sneeze or swear at the contestants on a game show. Just thinking of Mr. Stanton makes me smile. Actually, thinking of Fayhill in general makes me smile. My house, not so much.

I'd rather do just about anything than go back there. It isn't only the break-in that has me reconsidering where I call home. When Henry passed, I planned on staying there in our home, the one we planned to raise our family in. But, little by little, as time went on, it felt less and less like a permanent part of my future. Not even a part of my present most days.

The fact of the matter is, I am a lost ship at sea. I have no home base and no single location I can call home. Until I came to Lexington. I haven't ventured much into the town. Just a grocery run here and there, mostly staying close to home. *Home.* That's what I feel when I wake in Taylor's house. The warmth and comfort I feel here makes it hard to imagine ever leaving.

As I reach the half-mile mark on my walk, I turn and smile at Helen and Fran, who are venturing out on their own morning trek. I met them on one of my first days out for a walk. Of course, those first days I was barely making it to the next property before turning around and heading home for a nap. But, I'm adding on a little more each day and, like clockwork, encounter them on the other side of the street at the same point each day. There's comfort in this simple routine, and I welcome it. Normalcy. When I met Helen and Fran, they didn't know who I was. They didn't see me as the poor widow or the single mom. They simply saw me as a woman out for a walk with a baby strapped to her chest. I didn't know how much I needed that until I encountered it.

Waving, I continue on the rest of my walk and ponder exactly what happens between Taylor and me now. Last night was incredible, but I'm not naïve enough to believe it means anything more than what it was: two people finding comfort in one another. The attraction between us has been building for months, and I had a lot of regrets after the first night we were together that I didn't pursue something then. I wanted to. I almost did. And then I chickened out.

Last night I took a chance, and it paid off in spades. When Nicholas stirred in his bed this morning, I startled, and although it sounds horrible, I didn't move immediately. I stayed nestled in Taylor's arms and relished the feeling for a few beats before untangling myself to tend to my son. We snuck out of the room, leaving Taylor sleeping and headed to the kitchen.

My nerves were like a live wire as I waited for him to

wake up. Would we pretend nothing happened? Would he say he had regrets? When he walked in the kitchen, my heart beat rapidly, flutters of nerves and excitement running through me, and then I saw the look in his eyes. Happiness. Contentment. The same emotions I felt reflected in his gaze and I was relieved. And officially in love.

"Nick, your mama is a mess," I whisper to my sweet baby as I gently rub the top of his head.

As we approach the end of Taylor's driveaway, I shift the sling a little and he stirs but doesn't wake. Thank goodness. The last thing I need when I already have anxiety over a date tonight is a newborn not getting his sleep. A date. Lord. When was the last time I had a first date? I was a lot younger than I am now and a whole hell of a lot smaller.

Oh my gosh! I have nothing to wear tonight. When I packed to come here, I was days post-delivery and limited my packing to leggings and tank tops. I did throw in a pair of my maternity shorts and a few T-shirts but definitely nothing that will work with these nursing boobs and my post baby body.

I pull my phone from my pocket and pull up Addy's name and send a S.O.S. text message.

```
Me: 911!

Addy: You have nothing to wear to-
night.

Me: You're clairvoyant now?

Addy: *shrugs* I remember the first
time Dickhead Dan took me out after
Mason was born. I wore a maternity
```

```
top with a belt because it *kind of*
passed for a dress.

Addy: DO NOT DO THAT! I've got you
covered. See you around 4:30.
```

I don't bother responding because what is there to say? Thanks for saving my ass even though I don't know how or what you're doing? Yeah, I'll pass. Walking up the long driveway, I see the garage door open and head that direction. Within a few steps of the door, I hear a "thwap thwap" sound and slow my walk and peek around the corner of my car, which has been pulled out into the driveway.

A shirtless and very sweaty Taylor is beating the hell out of his punching bag, and I'm not sure there's been anything hotter. I stand still for a few minutes and ogle him. The way his skin glistens with beads of sweat dripping onto the ground beneath him, I can't take my eyes off him. His shorts are slung low on his waist, that muscle at his hips shifting with each movement. The back and forth of his feet remind me of a complicated dance routine, and I'm lost in thought when the hitting sound stops.

Not wanting to be busted for staring, I quickly retrace my steps and head to the front door. As soon as I'm in the house, I take two deep breaths and laugh to myself. I am absolutely ridiculous. My hormones are in overdrive, and I'm acting like some love-sick teenager. I suppose I am a little love-sick, so maybe my behavior isn't as immature as I think it is.

Slowly, I move Nicholas from the sling to his portable bassinet in the living room. Since I didn't have a baby shower before he was born, I had very few items to bring with us when we came to stay with Taylor. This is a hand-me-down from Addy and absolutely adorable with little lions and elephants scattered all over it. Bending over, I check the tucks of my swaddle job from earlier and deem it sufficient.

As ridiculous as it sounds, I rub my finger across my teeth, fluff my hair and adjust my boobs inside my tank. Glancing at the clock, I note I have about forty minutes before Nicholas demands his next feeding. I could do a load of laundry or read a few chapters of my new book. *Or* I could snag another glimpse of Taylor.

Scurrying to the door off the kitchen leading to the garage, I slowly open it and am greeted by a sight far more amazing than the one I walked up on earlier. On the floor, Taylor is doing a routine of crunches and now I know how he earns those abs of his. I stand mesmerized for at least three counts of his intricate routine before he looks up and sees me. A slow smile creeps across his face, and I immediately follow suit.

"Whatcha doin', Red?" His voice is low, slightly gravelly, and absolutely not showing any signs he's out of breath. That's so unfair. Three regular sit-ups and I'd probably need oxygen.

"Uh . . . nothing. I was . . . just . . . umm . . .Yeah, I got nothing. I was just staring. You're really into ab work."

Laughing, he stops his movements and grabs his water bottle from the floor next to him, throwing his head back as he gulps down the water. I watch his throat bob with each swallow; who knew drinking from a tin water bottle would be hot? Not me.

He walks toward me, and leans forward like he's going to kiss me but stops. "I'm super sweaty. I should hit the shower."

"Oh, yeah. I'll just do laundry or something," I reply awkwardly.

Leaning around me, he pulls a towel from on top of the work bench and runs it down his face and across his chest. Tossing the towel aside, he takes another sip from his water bottle and sets it down with the discarded towel. Before I can blink, he's tugging me to him, lifting my feet off the ground, and I can't stop the squeal that escapes my lips. My arms wrap around his neck, and my eyes widen at the expression on his face. Smiling wide, he is only a few inches from my face, and because I finally found my words, I ruin the moment.

"You're much more affectionate than I thought."

"You thought about my level of affection?" he teases, his arms tightening around my waist.

"Stop it," I say, my smile widening as I smack his shoulder. "I'm just sayin'."

"I've never really thought about it but it's different. This . . . I can stop if you want. If it's too much. If you're uncomf—"

I cut him off with my lips on his. I am not uncomfortable, and the idea of him stopping hurts my soul a little. Instead, I give all I have to offer him in this kiss. Hoping to portray how okay with everything I am. He accepts it with each swipe of his tongue, and before I know it, his hands slide under my butt and he's lifting me up, my legs wrapping around his waist. He takes a step up into the house, never breaking our kiss until he runs me into a wall, and I start laughing.

My hand flies to my mouth to stifle the onslaught of hysterical laughter brewing inside me. We both glance to the living room where Nicholas sleeps and wait for him to wake, but he doesn't. Simultaneously, we exhale relief and look back at each other. Our lips meet again, the kisses more intense. The desire to move my body overwhelming.

He begins walking again, this time skirting all walls and other obstacles. When we make it to the bedroom, he lays me onto the bed, the coolness of the sheets send a chill up my back and I feel my nipples harden, begging for attention. Taylor's attention is elsewhere. Lifting the hem of my tank, he places tender kisses on my stomach beginning just above my belly button. Tensing at the thought of him seeing my stretch marks I suck in a breath but at the same time, he tugs open the button of my shorts and I lift my hips to help him slide them from my body.

Resuming his spot between my legs, I can't help the flood of wetness that covers my panties as he pulls the cotton to the side, exposing me to him. A low moan from deep in his throat is barely a whisper as his tongue makes contact with my skin. He must know how sensitive I am from last night because each swipe of his tongue is gentle to the touch but fills my body with nothing but pleasure.

Sucking, licking, and bringing me to the brink of orgasm, I lift my hips, unashamed of taking from him as much as he'll give. When he inserts a finger and curls it toward himself, I soar up and over the cliff of my orgasm. My breathing is labored, my arm flung over my eyes in exhaustion as I feel the bed shift, a quick moment of loss from his body touching mine.

It's only seconds but the loss is still there. Then, he's on me, the warmth of him covers me, I slowly open my eyes and stare back at his stormy grays with the brightest blue chips.

With one quick thrust, he fills me and my upper body lifts from the bed. Gripping his shoulders, I throw my head back and don't bother to hold in the sounds of passion that fall from my lips.

"Are you okay?"

Placing a hand on his cheek, I look deep in his eyes. "Yes. I'm not as fragile as you think. I just didn't expect it to feel this good. And for all that is holy, I need you to move and fuck me before I die."

Roaring with laughter, he leans down and kisses me while rotating his hips. Each movement hits me like a flick of a match. My skin is on fire, my heart is beating rapidly, and for the first time in a long time, I feel loved and wanted. It doesn't matter how much extra of me there is around the middle, or that I'm sure my boobs are on the verge of exploding; he makes me feel amazing.

Last night was slow and about two people getting to know each other's bodies. Connecting our hearts and minds with physical touch. This is different. It's more frantic and wilder. It's not an expression of love or emotions, it's pure sex.

Lifting my leg, he slings it over his arm, forcing himself deeper and in two thrusts, my orgasm explodes around us, my cries loud and without a care. He follows shortly after. Throwing himself off me, he lands with a small thud on the bed next to me, our rapid breaths filling the room.

I open my mouth to say something when Nicholas lets me know it's time for a little mama time. Lifting up on my elbows, I blow the hair from my eyes and turn to get up.

"I'll get him," he says, and I fall back, my head on the pillow and sigh in bliss.

Chapter 28

Taylor

After our morning romp, Scarlett and I took turns showering and spending time with Nicholas. It's amazing how quickly a baby grows. It feels like if you blink too many times, he'll have already doubled in size by the time your eyes come back into focus. As I watch him stare at the mobile over his bouncy seat, having his own conversation with the shapes hanging over his head, I smile. Maybe I need a vibrating seat that plays music to mesmerize me. I suppose that would be a massaging recliner for adults.

Being with Scarlett today, just hanging out and doing household chores was one of the best days I've had in a long time. I quickly realized that any time I spend with her, or them, are my best days. Since she's been here, I'm more relaxed, and although I'll never admit it to my sister, smiling more.

Speaking of my sister, she walked in my house like a hurricane and swooped Scarlett up and into the bedroom over thirty minutes ago. Rising from the couch, I bend over and pick up the baby, holding him in front of me, his eyes focusing on me before he blows a little bubble on his tiny lips then smiles.

"I wish you could talk so we could figure this out. Since you can't, I'll have to go with your expressions. I am taking your mama out for dinner tonight. A date. We're going on a date. I hope you don't mind that."

Smile still spread across his face, I continue, "I know I'm not your daddy, but I love you and will always be here for you both. The real question here is, *How long do we wait before we interrupt whatever it is they're doing back there?*"

The response from my little sidekick is a full diaper. "Thanks, dude." Laughing to myself, I grab the basket from the floor that is full of diapers and wipes as I shift him to my side. With all of the tools in my hand, I shift Nicholas to the couch and begin changing his diaper.

As I'm buttoning his little pajamas into place, I hear a clap and raise my eyes. Standing behind the couch with her hands pressed together in a prayer pose is my sister. Crying. "Oh my goodness. Taylor Cain, I never thought I would see the day. You're changing a diaper."

Rolling my eyes, I scoop Nicholas up and place him back in his seat before walking toward the kitchen. Tossing the diaper in the trash can, I move to the sink and lather up my hands.

"Seriously, little brother. I'm blown away. Seeing you with him. It was like . . . I wish Mom and Dad could see all of this. I know it's a little awkward, and you feel this obligation to Henry, but you're building a family here."

"First, you have to stop crying. It's a little over the top. Second, we've always been family. It just looks a little different because we've lost Henry. Now, you've eaten up at least thirty minutes of the three hours we have before that little dictator needs to be fed. Is my date ready?"

"Do not call my godson a dictator," she scolds.

I'm about to question her role as godmother when Nicholas begins whining. With a raised brow, I motion to the baby. Addy rolls her eyes and smacks me in the arm before attending to her charge.

I bark out a laugh but stop mid-bark when I see the beautiful woman standing across the room. Moving around the counter, I step toward Scarlett. Dressed in a long black and blue striped dress, she's a vision. Her long auburn hair is falling across her shoulders, but I see a sliver of skin through the tresses and move them to the side to expose it.

"You look beautiful."

"Thank you," she whispers.

"I should feed him a little before we go."

"Do you think that's—" Before I can finish my question, Scarlett gestures to her chest, and I nod in understanding. I watch as she walks around the couch and settles into her favorite spot in the corner, tucks her half donut pillow thing around her and reaches for Nicholas. Addy happily hands him off with a light blanket and takes a seat on the opposite side of the couch.

"I'm going to pull the truck out and give you some time," I say before leaving them alone. I can tell by the way my sister is staring at Scarlett, she's having some sort of maternal craving.

Heading to the garage, I take my time backing my truck out of the garage and into the driveway. I scroll through music options on my satellite radio, settling on a random country station. Resting my head back on the seat, I enjoy the quiet. I wouldn't call how I'm feeling nervous but it's something, that's for sure. Maybe it's a little excitement laced with . . . okay, it's nerves. I don't think I've been on an honest-to-God date in at least five years. It's been even longer since I've felt remotely close to a woman like I do to Scarlett.

Glancing at the clock, she's likely finishing up with Nicholas, so I leave the truck running and hop from the cab. As I enter the garage and move toward the door to the house, it opens. Standing in the doorway is my date. She's turned saying something to Addy so I quietly step up to the bottom step, but she takes that moment to turn. Jumping, she yelps, hands outstretched to push me.

Grabbing her wrists to steady myself, I say, "Shit, sorry. I didn't mean to startle you. I was coming in to see if you were ready."

"You scared the crap out of me. Hold on, I have to catch my breath."

Since I still have her wrists in my hands, I tug her toward me, causing her to spill into my arms. Perfect. Capturing her lips with mine, I relish in the way her body conforms to my embrace. Her mouth is sweet heaven. Slowing the kiss, she pulls back, a huge smile on her face.

"Do not think you are distracting me with your sexy kisses and rock-hard abs. I am starving and my boobs have at least two hours before I start complaining."

"Baby, you cannot use the words 'sexy' and 'boobs' in the same sentence. I'm only a man."

Laughing, she pushes at my shoulder and I mock stumble. Taking her hand in mine, I walk us out the door and to my truck. Everything about this feels right. And yet, guilt is knocking at my heart's door. She's still my best friend's wife. What am I doing to us?

Our drive through town is quiet. The soft sounds of Tim McGraw fill the cab as the sun continues to shine brightly. Reaching across the seat, I steal Scarlett's hand from her lap and lift it to my lips. Placing a quick kiss to her knuckles, I glance her way and watch as her body visibly relaxes and she rests her head back on the seat, staring out the passenger window. I guess I'm not the only one with a lot on my mind.

As I flip my blinker to turn into the parking lot of the small Italian bistro in town, Scarlett sits up straight in her seat and hums. Turning to me she says, "I love Italian."

"I know."

"You really do lo . . . I mean, thanks for bringing me here."

Shifting the truck in to park, I tug on her hand to get her attention. With her bottom lip tugged between her teeth, eyes wide, she looks at me. "You're welcome."

She releases a short breath and smiles. Her shoulders drop, and I know she's grateful I didn't ask her what she was about to say. We both know, but I don't think that's a conversation either of us want to have tonight.

I jump out of the truck, round the front, and open the passenger door. "Muh lady," I say holding my hand out. Giggling she takes my hand, and when she hops from the seat and her feet land on the ground, she drops into an over exaggerated curtsy.

Chuckling, I lead us into the restaurant. Since I made reservations, we don't have to wait to be seated. The hostess walks us to a small table for two in the back corner of the restaurant. Like the other tables in the restaurant, candles are lit in the middle of the table and a bottle of chianti nestles in a straw basket to the side with two small glasses.

I move around the hostess to pull Scarlett's chair out as she sits down. Looking up at me, she smirks. Returning the look, I wink before walking back to the other side of the table and taking my own seat. The hostess rattles off the specials and motions to the wine list before excusing herself.

We both open our menus, neither of us speaking. On occasion, we both look up at the same time and smile at each other but never speak. I have no idea why I'm looking at this menu, I'm going to get the same thing I do anytime I order from here. Although, I'm usually picking up takeout instead of sitting at one of the tables.

"Do you already know what you're having?"

"Yep."

"There are so many options, and everything sounds so decadent. I should get a salad. I won't lose this baby weight if I give in to my love of carbs."

"Hey," I implore. She looks up at me "You are beautiful always and less than two months ago you birthed a human. Be kind to yourself."

Nodding, she sniffles, but before I can ask if she's okay, the server approaches our table. I order a beer and Scarlett sticks to a Shirley Temple since she'll be nursing when we get home. We talk for a few minutes about the menu, and I finally convince her to order the carbonera she's mentioned three times in as many minutes. When the server returns with our drinks, we place our order and settle back into our seats.

"Does this feel awkward?" she asks.

"A little. Why do you think that is?"

"I don't know. I think I feel guilty."

"Because of—"

Her eyes widen and she shakes her head. "No. I don't feel guilty about what's happened with us. I feel guilty for not feeling guilty about that. Is that weird? It's weird, right?"

I suppose for some people it would be strange to feel guilt about not feeling guilty but in this circumstance, it makes sense. To me anyway, because I feel the same way. I've kept the boundaries defined with Scarlett, because I assumed if we crossed that line, it would make things difficult. Our friendship would be cast aside, and guilt would take its place. That hasn't happened. Here in Lexington, the only people who really know about Scarlett are my sister and Ashton. Outside of that, we can be two people out on a date. Nobody is looking at us like I'm a bastard moving in on his best friend's widow or at her like she's betraying a man she let go of long ago.

"I don't think so but then again, I'm kind of living it with you. At the end of the day, it's nobody's business but our own. I care about you, Red. I always have; that won't change. We've shifted things around a little but at the end of the day, we're just two single people who like each other. At least I think we do."

"We do," she says as she sips from her straw, a small smile playing on her lips. "Maybe too much." Her last words are a mumble, but I hear them.

Quirking a brow, I only smile in response and pull my beer bottle to my mouth. Instead of continuing our conversation, we table it as our salads are set in front of us. We spend the next hour getting to know one another as just Taylor and Scarlett; no ghosts to be found.

Chapter 29

Scarlett

Someone should give me a gold star for my behavior tonight. Not only have I allowed myself to enjoy the evening, I did not, in any fashion, throw myself at Taylor. I thought about it while we were in the truck but abstained. The moment I walked into the living room and saw him standing in the kitchen, my heart took flight and I don't know that it safely landed.

He's dressed in a dark gray button-up shirt with the sleeves cuffed to his strong forearms with a black matte watch on his wrist. It was the first thing I noticed and when I realized real-life watch-porn is an actual thing. I wanted to run my hand up his arm and back down to touch that watch. His dark wash jeans make his strong legs look long and lean. Since I know what lies beneath all the sexiness of his clothes, I had a hard time composing myself when he told me I looked beautiful. He's the perfect package of bad boy on the outside and southern gentleman on the inside. And, this girl has it bad for the bad boy and just may want it all from the southern gentleman.

I didn't mean to withdraw as we drove through town. When we left the house, I was excited and happy, but then "Live Like You Were Dying" by Tim McGraw started playing, and my thoughts drifted to Henry. He was a huge Tim McGraw fan and that was his favorite song. When we were dating, he would tell me that's how he wanted to live life. Live for every moment like it was his last. That was before he came back different. Before he was hurt and angry. Before he couldn't sleep and before our love wasn't enough.

Then I listened. I listened to the lyrics, and I knew that's what I needed to do. If I've learned anything since Henry's death, it's that there are no guarantees in life or love. I married Henry Gilbert with every intention of being with him for the rest of my life. Our love story ended early, the cards stacked against us, but it doesn't mean my story has to end.

I'm looking at my second chance now. As I watch Taylor sign his name on the credit card slip, I know this is what love the second time around is all about. Stolen glances, conversations about everything and nothing. Earth shattering sex and sweet kisses in the morning. A man who loves your child as if he's his own, not out obligation but because of who he is.

When I almost said the word "love" to him earlier, I stopped myself. It was in jest, but somehow, even saying it to him in a teasing fashion seemed disrespectful to how I feel. I know it's coming. I'm going to slip, and it will change things. How can I not? I have months of emotions and feelings bubbling inside me like a volcano and then he does something sweet like hold my hand and kiss my knuckles, and I want to word-vomit all of those emotions at his feet.

The twinges in my boobs tell me we need to head home

to Nicholas. I've been gone from him for less than two hours and my soul aches. I miss his little face and funny moans as he squirms and . . . shit I can't think of him or I'm going to start leaking. Thank goodness for nursing pads.

"Are you ready to go?" His voice pulls me from my thoughts.

"Yeah. I think it's about time for—" I'm cut short when his phone dings an incoming text message. "I'm sure that's Addy begging us to hurry home to a screaming baby."

He winks at me and smiles as he picks up the phone. His expression changes from one of happiness to . . . well, something I can't quite decipher. Anger? Frustration? It definitely isn't the happiness I've seen from him tonight. "It's Grant."

Grant. My heart races at the mention of his name. I know Grant cares about me like an older brother, but he loved Henry. I haven't told him about the status of our marriage. What will he say about this? My growing feelings for Taylor and about us being together. Are we even together?

"Is everything okay?" I ask as he taps the phone and stands.

"I'm sure it is. He wants me to call him. Let's get out of here, and I'll call once we're in the truck."

He slips the phone into his pocket and extends his hand to me as I rise. Smoothing my dress, I don't immediately take his hand. I know there's something about that text that has upset him. When I take his hand, he gives it a quick squeeze before interlinking our fingers and swooping in for a quick peck on the lips. Leading me from the restaurant, he doesn't say anything and only nods to the hostess as she wishes us a good night.

Once we've both settled into the cab of this truck and our seatbelts are buckled, he turns the ignition and the engine roars to life. He's tense, his shoulders high and posture stiff. I slowly move my hand toward him but think better of it when he throws the gear shift into reverse with a little more force than I've seen from him. The screen on the radio alerts the Bluetooth connection so he taps on his phone, the ringing of the call filling the cab. As we pull out of the parking lot onto the road, Grant's voice booms through the speakers.

"Sugar."

"Hey, Cap. Red and I just finished dinner and are headed back to the house. What's up?"

Snapping my head his direction, I look at him wide-eyed, but he's not paying attention. His focus is on the road in front of him. Was that his way of "outing" us to Grant or a warning to Grant that I can hear him?

"Hi, Grant," I say, never taking my eyes off Taylor. His attention never veers from the road in front of him.

"Ah Red, it's great to hear your voice. How're you feeling? How's the little man?"

Smiling at his sincerity, I smile as I respond. "We're both good. He's growing like a weed. I'll send you a new picture tomorrow."

"Looking forward to it. Sug, I'm following up to our conversation earlier. I have that stuff. Give me a call when you can."

"Ten four. Give me thirty."

Without a goodbye or another word, the line disconnects. Turning in my seat, I look at Taylor. When he doesn't look my way, I clear my throat. Still, nothing.

"What was that about? You two sounded very cryptic."

"It's nothing for you to worry about."

"Don't 'it's nothing' me, Taylor Cain. Is something wrong?"

Sighing, he runs a hand through his hair, and I realize he's gripping the wheel so tightly his knuckles are white. His profile is as handsome as always, but his jaw is tight, and I itch to touch him. For him to touch me. Touch is something important to Taylor and how he expresses his feelings. He's affectionate in even the smallest ways but now, it feels like there's a valley of distance between us. He's shut down and quiet, his gaze anywhere but toward me.

"You know what? Never . . ." I let out a groan of frustration, my hands fisted in my lap. My reaction is to let it go. To not stir the beast.

Then, I look at him. His handsome profile, the tense jaw, and death grip on the wheel sure indicators he's upset. He isn't Henry. I don't have to watch what I say. No need to tread lightly to not set him off. He isn't a live wire ready to explode at any moment. Taking a deep breath, I close my eyes and count to three.

Once I've calmed myself a little I say, "Not never mind. I know that conversation was about me. About the break-in. I will not sit here while you talk about my life like I'm not to be included." Looking out the window, I take in the beauty that surrounds us. Gorgeous shades of red and yellow swirl in the sky as the sun slowly makes its descent behind the hills.

"Scar—"

"I don't want excuses, Taylor. I want respect. I spent years tiptoeing around a man who would shut me out or would explode at the drop of a hat. Please don't send me back to that place. I'm finally finding myself again and I won't go back."

He doesn't try to explain further, he simply turns his attention back to driving. This time, I welcome the silence. Each of us are working through this. When he pulls into the garage and puts the truck in park, I don't wait for him to open the door. Instead, I let myself out and walk into the house. Addy is sitting on the couch watching television, her feet propped up on the table in front of her, with Nicholas nestled onto her chest. Taking a deep breath, I dampen down my frustrations and hurt and set my purse down before walking to Addy.

"How was dinner?"

"Decadent. I'm stuffed but also bursting here." Motioning to my chest, I can't help but smile at the look on her face.

"Oh, well he hasn't stirred once since you've been gone."

"Is that because you've held him the entire time?" She smiles sheepishly and I snort out a laugh. "I'm going to change really quick then I'll take him."

I hustle down the hall to our bedroom . . . *his* bedroom . . . to change my clothes. Stepping into the bathroom, I quickly throw my hair into a messy bun with a large claw clip and go about washing the makeup off my face before slipping into a pair of sleep shorts and nursing tank top.

I pad back to the living room. Addy has, surprisingly, placed Nicholas in the portable crib and is standing with her purse in her hand.

"Who's Tay talking to? He's going to wear a hole in the ground with the circle he's walking out there."

I look to where she's motioning and see Taylor in the backyard. The hand not holding his phone appears to be permanently attached to the back of his neck as he walks in a large circle in the yard. Obviously whatever Grant is telling him is upsetting.

"I think it's Grant," I reply, turning my attention back to my friend. "Thank you for watching Nick. It was nice to get out for a bit."

"Are you okay? You seem a little off."

Shaking my head, I try desperately to act casual, but part of me is so angry while the other is sad that I had to have that conversation in the truck. "I'm just tired. I need to go straight to bed after I feed him. Hopefully he'll give me a three hour stretch. That sounds heavenly."

"If you're sure."

Nodding, I walk with her to the door and give her a big hug before she steps onto the porch. Watching as she walks to her car, I wait until her headlights are on and she's moving from the driveway before I close the door and return to the living room.

Nicholas begins to stir so I grab myself a glass of water and pick him up before settling on a little one- on-one time with my number one guy. Trying to relax myself, I close my eyes and let my head fall back on the couch. I need to find my Zen. It's not good for the baby or me to be stressed and upset. I'm so damn annoyed.

I hate being dismissed or not included in what's happening around me. These men say they're trying to protect me, but what they don't understand is every time they talk around me and treat me like I wouldn't understand, it takes me back to the girl I used to be. The one who wished for attention from my parents only to be told I wouldn't understand. That conversation in the truck, the one they obviously didn't want to have in front of me, was one thing, but to ask what it was about to only be dismissed. That's too much.

As I close my eyes and embrace my little boy, I hear the clicking of the French doors and my eyes open. Lifting my head, I look at the man who has stolen my heart, and all the hurt I felt a few minutes ago disappears. He looks broken and sad. Furious and ready to maim someone. It's a plethora of emotions but they're all there, on his sleeve and in his eyes.

Chapter 30

Taylor

I'm so fucking pissed I can hardly see straight. I made myself stay outside a few minutes after my call with Grant ended, not wanting to take my frustrations out on Scarlett. My attitude in the truck sucked; I owe her an apology. The minute I saw his name on my phone, I knew Grant had pulled the pictures from the trail cam. I knew there was going to be a face of the person who scared all of us just weeks ago. The person who is responsible for sending her into labor early.

I just didn't expect it to be a blast from my past. Really, it shouldn't surprise me anymore. I'm just pissed I failed to connect the dots before now. I've been so consumed with this little bubble of a life we've been living in, I didn't want to think of how we got here. The reality is, we've locked ourselves away from the world, not facing the truths that are surrounding us. Now that I've seen the picture, it all makes sense. Birds of a feather and all that. There have been rumors, random messages on social media from high school friends, commenting on our old high school buddy and his life choices along with those of my best friend's parents.

It all comes back to money, but what I don't understand is why they didn't just ask for it. I'd die before I let Scarlett give them a damn penny, but this shit, the calls and the break-ins, that's a little more involved than I would have expected from them.

Why not ask or bully like the old days? Instead, scaring a pregnant woman was the path they chose. Joke's on them. All they've managed to do is enrage me and unleash the beast I locked down deep inside me.

"Hey," she says as I stare at her. She's beautiful and perfect. Her makeup is gone, and she's swept her hair on top of her head. Nicholas is nestled to her, having what amounts to his own dinner. Gone is the pain and hurt in her eyes from earlier, and is replaced with concern. For me. How ironic, since all I feel inside is concern for her. For them. My family.

The anger that so easily consumed me slowly lessens as I walk toward her. Leaning down, I kiss her gently on the lips. A soft sigh escaping as I pull back.

"I'm sorry I was a dick in the truck. I'm going to change, then we need to talk. Is he almost done?" I ask, motioning to the baby. Nodding her head, her brows furrow, but I don't give in and head to our bedroom to change.

Ours. That's what it's become. I've called it our bed a few times over the last few weeks, but neither of us has addressed that little elephant in the room. Now that I know who has been bothering her, and will be putting a stop to it, what does that mean for us? Will she move back to Fayhill? To her life. Or, will she want to stay here with me? To really make a go of this thing between us and build a life.

Unbuttoning my shirt, I toss it to the laundry as I take

in the room. The bed is made haphazardly following her short nap earlier. A few tops and a pair of jeans are tossed on the chair in the corner of the room. A package of diapers sits on the floor next to her side of the bed, and a pacifier on my nightstand. The scent is a mixture of my cologne and her body wash with a hint of baby powder. This is the room of a new family.

Quickly, I change into a pair of pajama pants and a T-shirt before returning to the living room. Nicholas is sleeping in his favorite seat with a smile on his face. Looking around, I don't see Scarlett immediately, but then she appears from the kitchen, a beer in one hand and very small glass of wine in her other.

"Wine?"

"I have a feeling I'm going to need it. It's barely two sips; I'm not worried."

Taking the offered beer, I turn to the couch and sit, patting the spot next to me. Sitting down so her back is to the side of the couch, her feet are pulled up onto the cushions, chin resting on her knees. The protectiveness of her stance does not go unnoticed. Gripping her calf with my hand, I squeeze it and shake her leg a little, hoping to relax her. It must work because she shifts so her feet rest on my thighs.

"When was the last time you spoke to Henry's parents?" I ask.

"His parents? I don't know, I've tried calling a few times but there's no answer. They sent me that card with the newspaper clipping months ago but other than that, not since the funeral."

Taking a pull from the beer, I contemplate how to word my next question. "And what about the payouts? From insurance and benefits. What did you do with those?"

"They're in the bank. Why? What's going on, Taylor?"

"Do you have the financial information for the bank accounts in your house?" I can tell my questions are confusing and irritating her. Hell, they're irritating me. It's none of my business. The money she received from Henry's passing is hers and not my business. We've never actually talked about money or if she's doing okay with her bills. I assumed if she was struggling, she would have said something.

"They're in a safety deposit box. Why are you asking me this? Did something else happen at the house? Oh my goodness. Was there another break-in?"

"There was, but I think I know why. You know we've had cameras up for a few weeks?" She nods in confirmation. "Grant and Connor have had to move them around to get the right angles. There have been some indicators that people were on the property, but nothing showed on the cameras. Until last night."

She lifts the wine glass to her lips and finishes the contents in just one swallow. She wasn't kidding it was only two sips. Taking the glass from her, I lean toward the table and set the empty glass and my bottle on the table. Shifting, I pull her onto my lap and kiss her temple as she rests her head on my shoulder, one arm behind my back and the other resting on my stomach.

"Grant went through the photos earlier tonight and found quite a few with pretty clear pictures. Did you know there is a family of squirrels living in your backyard?"

Her head bobs on my shoulder as she laughs. "Yeah I did."

"Well, in addition to the squirrel family, there are a few of a man. He's wearing a cap low on his head so you can't see his face. There are a few shots of him lurking around the house, peeking in windows. From what we can tell, he got inside again but didn't stay for long."

Sitting up, she looks at me, eyes wide and fearful, waiting for me to continue.

"It took me a few minutes to recognize him. Honestly, if it wasn't for the tattoo on his neck, I don't think I would have. It's been years, and they haven't been kind to him."

"I . . . I don't understand. You know the person?"

Her hand grips my T-shirt, and I tighten my hold on her. Her breathing increases, fearful eyes staring back at me. Cupping her cheek, I kiss her softly.

"You said it was a man. Why were you asking about Henry's parents?"

"Do you trust me?"

Lifting her hands to my cheeks, she holds my gaze and smiles. "With my life."

"I need you to trust me when I say I don't want to tell you until I have all the answers. This isn't like in the truck. I'm not keeping you in the dark for any reason other than I want to protect you. Will you give me a little time to work this out?"

She holds my gaze for seconds that feel like minutes before nodding.

"Thank you, baby. You trust me with your life?" I ask as she offers me a small smile and nods. "What about your heart?"

"Oh Taylor, I gave that to you months ago."

I follow her lead and cup her cheek as I pull her lips to mine. I pour every ounce of my love for this woman into this kiss. Expressing how much she means to me with each swipe of my tongue. Pulling out of the kiss, I peck her lips once then twice. I will put an end to the fear these people have instilled in her.

She may not know it, but while she was giving me her heart, she already owned mine. I may not be worthy of her or her son, but for the first time in my life I want to live my life with love and no regret.

"I love you, Scarlett."

Tears fill her eyes and she smiles. "I love you too."

"I know it's fast and you may not be ready, but I need you to know. This isn't just some casual friends with benefits thing for me. I am so fucking in love with you, it scares me. I never knew this was something I could feel, let alone have. You're my best friend, and I want you here with me. Both of you. I love that little boy like he's my own."

"Taylor, you are more than I deserve, but dammit if I don't want to have it all with you. I've never felt as safe and loved as I do with you. I'm sure that makes me a horrible person, and I'm going straight to hell, but it's true. I have to believe all of this, the pain and hurt, the loss and devastation of the last year has been for a reason. To bring us here, to each other. Fate."

"To love freely," I offer. Her tears are flowing fast and furiously now. A huge smile on her face as I kiss her.

"As much as I love this moment of declarations," she says between kisses. "I have a strong suspicion you're saying this now for a reason."

Sighing, I exhale long and look over to where Nicholas has fallen asleep. Knowing if the break-in had happened a few weeks earlier, there's a chance his birth wouldn't have gone smoothly makes my blood boil. Anger seeps into the spaces between the declarations we've just shared.

"Will you call Henry's parents? If my suspicions are

correct, they won't answer, but I want to make sure."

Shrugging her shoulders, she walks toward the kitchen and retrieves her phone. With a few taps, she brings it to her ear and after a few seconds ends the call and tosses it on the table.

"It's no longer in service."

"That's what I was afraid of. The man in the photos is Lyle."

When she doesn't respond to the name, I realize Henry never spoke of our childhood friend. Tapping my lap, she climbs back into her spot, and I continue, "Lyle grew up with Henry and me. He was our friend, but it was different with him. He was different. We all enlisted together but he didn't take to military life like we did. And he was bitter about it."

"Wolf was a hothead, but he didn't compare to Lyle. He was a straight-up bully with a chip on his shoulder. I lost track of him after a few years in, but rumors were rampant. Fighting, drugs, and a few other things I hate to even think of. Bottom line, he was a bad guy. He was dishonorably discharged and served a few years in the pen for possession. Rumors from high school classmates are he's back in the neighborhood and into some pretty heavy shit."

"Wow. He sounds lovely. Why would he break into our house? Did he not know about Henry?"

"Lyle is bad news, but he's not going to travel all this way just to break into a house of a former buddy. No, I'm going to guess he's working with someone. Honey, I think it's the money."

"Well first, I wouldn't have stacks of money laying around my house. Besides, I didn't keep it."

Confused I turn my head as if looking at her in a different direction will help me understand. Nick stirs in his seat and whimpers. Climbing off my lap, she moves to him and picks him up. Lifting him to her nose, she sniffs his bottom before settling in on the floor to change his diaper.

"What do you mean you didn't keep it?" I know for a fact she would have received quite the payout, and on top of any military benefits, Henry would have secured a life insurance policy for her and the baby.

"It wasn't my money. We were getting a divorce, so it wasn't mine to keep. He would have made Nicholas the primary beneficiary, and by all accounts that's his money, not mine. Don't get me wrong, I took enough money to pay off the debt we had and enough that I don't have to work for a few months. The rest went into a trust for this guy." She lifts the baby to her face and peppers him with kisses. His little legs are tucked up to his chest, so he's curled almost into a ball. She places him in the portable crib before gathering the dirty diaper and walking to the kitchen. I follow her and stand on the other side of the island while she washes her hands.

"Wait. You put it *all* in a trust for the baby and didn't keep any of it?"

Shrugging, she dries her hands and smiles. "It's not mine, Taylor. It was meant for Henry's family and we weren't going to be married any longer. I set up a trust and while I have access for major expenses for him, Nicholas will receive a portion for college, if that's the path he chooses, or full access at twenty-five."

"You're amazing. You know that, right?"

"Nah, I'm just not an asshole. So, why do you think this Lyle person broke into the house?"

Moving around the island, I wrap my hands around her waist and say, "I don't know, baby, but I'm going to find out. I'm heading to Austin in the morning."

Chapter 31

Taylor

*C*rawling out of a warm bed before dawn is the last thing, I want to do this morning but I'm driven by the need to kill Lyle. And the Gilberts. I knew they were up to something when they showed up at the funeral. They weren't there for bootcamp graduation, Henry and Scarlett's wedding, or a single other milestone in Henry's life. But, when he wasn't there to see them, they showed up. I don't buy it for a second.

What I can't figure out is how Lyle fits into this scam. Manipulation and guilt was their go-to when we were kids. Convincing people the next time would be different. They didn't mean to drive drunk. The bar fight was someone else's fault. If only Henry hadn't angered them, they wouldn't have to drink so much. One excuse and manipulation after another. It's who they were then, and I don't doubt it is who they are now. As much as she wants to believe it, they weren't there to share in Scarlett's loss; they are too selfish for that to be true.

Nicholas and I had a little man-to-man bonding this

morning as I made promises to come home and figure out our life with his mama. I confessed a lot to that little boy as the night turned to day. He's the ideal confidant since he can't respond and tell me I'm acting like a teenager with his first love.

When we left for dinner last night, I had no intention of laying it all out on the line for her. Declaring my feelings and making promises to her wasn't in my date night plan. I thought we'd come home from dinner, settle in for a movie, and crawl into bed together. The moment I saw that picture on my phone, I lost my mind. I thought of all the things that could have happened that night. What if she had come home earlier while Lyle was there? What if he was high? Would he have hurt her? So many questions and no answers.

Grant and Connor wanted to call the sheriff. Tell him who the man was and have him arrested. I wouldn't hear it. We argued but when they realized I wasn't going to back down, they conceded. With a little help of social media, Connor was able to track Lyle to a dive bar in Austin. The dangers of social media and its ability to stalk and find another person anywhere in the world normally anger me. I'm constantly harping on my nephew to limit tags and keep his location private. In this instance, I'm grateful for Lyle's refusal to do the same.

Austin is a large city, but since we know where he's been hanging out the last few nights, I have at least one place to start looking for him. I can't believe he's been only a few hours from Fayhill this entire time. I wouldn't be surprised to find Henry's parents holed up with him somewhere. The three of them plotting more ways to scare Scarlett. Just the thought of it sends my blood boiling.

The drive isn't too long, yet Scarlett has called a few times to check on me. Truthfully, I think she wants to make sure I'm not actually going to kill anyone. I suppose I could if I wanted, but I have too much to live for, too many promises to keep to her. But, to play it safe, Grant and Connor are meeting me in Austin. If anyone is going to keep me on this side of the law, it's those two.

Traffic is a bitch, but I make it to the hotel we booked with plenty of time for a shower and a beer at the bar before they're expected to arrive. As the front desk finalizes my check-in, I look over my shoulder hoping I don't accidently bump into the three people I'm hoping to surprise. I know they would never be in a place like this unless they had money and, if they had any, they wouldn't be harassing Scarlett.

Thanking the clerk, I take my key cards and head for the elevator. The ride to my floor is quick and, like she has some sort of ESP, my phone begins to ring with Scarlett's face appearing on my screen.

"Hey," I answer as I push the door open and toss my bag on the bed.

"Are you still driving?"

"Nope, I just walked into my room. What are you up to?"

Nicholas cries in the background, and I hear her telling me to hold on. Her voice is in the distance, so I assume she's put the phone down. I move around the room, opening the curtains and adjusting the air conditioner while I wait. She comes back to the phone, a little out of breath.

"Sorry about that."

"Everything okay?"

"Yeah, he's a little fussy so I just put him in the sling. I think I'll go sit in the back and get some fresh air. He always likes being outside, and we didn't get our walk in this morning."

"I know you think I'm being overly cautious but I'd rather you skip one walk and let me do this than take any chances. We don't know if they're high or what. If they've figured out you're in Lexington, there's no telling if they'd go there."

Kicking off my shoes, I pull my belt from the loops and toss it next to my bag as I settle onto the top of the opposite bed. I hear the tell-tale sound of the French doors opening at home and wait for her to say something.

"I understand the why, but I hate feeling like a prisoner. I also don't want you to do anything stupid. I want you to hurry home."

"I'm not going to lie. I get a little caveman thinking of you in our home waiting for me to come back."

"Dear lord," she scoffs and I can imagine her eyes rolling dramatically as she smiles. "You're ridiculous. Just don't get yourself hurt or arrested. We have a life to start."

"Deal. I'm going to shower off the drive before the guys get here. Remember if you need anything, call Addy and Landon."

Laughing she says, "Uh, they're coming over for dinner. Your sister tried to pretend it was casual, but she did mention that Landon is equipped to kick anyone's ass that may bother us, so I kind of figured she knew what was going on."

Thank goodness for my sister. "I'm not bummed you won't be alone. Have fun and kiss that little guy for me."

"Will do."

"I love you, Scarlett."

"I know and I you. Be safe. And smart."

We end the call and I head for the shower. As the steam fills the room, I strip off my clothes and step under the hot spray. The water thumps on my shoulders and I let it beat away some of the tension I've been holding. The rage I have for Lyle and what he's done is still there, but hearing Scarlett's voice and knowing I have a family waiting for me at home puts things in a little different perspective. Of course, it doesn't mean I won't still lay my hands on that motherfucker for what he's done.

Sitting at the hotel bar with a warm bottle of beer between my hands, I check my phone for the third time in twenty minutes. I'm about to call Grant and Connor when a big paw slaps me on the shoulder. My arm instinctively rises, but Connor's laugh pauses me before I can turn to swing.

"Save that for the bastard in the picture, man." I take Connor's extended hand and shake it while simultaneously glaring at Grant.

"Cap you can't walk up to a man and smack him like that and not put yourself in the path of a fist."

"Assess before acting. Did I not teach you anything in our years together? You were never the impulsive one, Sugar."

His eyes move to the beer, and he raises a brow in question. Drinking before I'm going to possibly beat the shit out of someone is not exactly the brightest idea. It's also why I've yet to take a sip from the bottle. As good as it sounded when I ordered it, knowing alcohol could alter my instincts, I haven't touched it.

"It's full and warm. I want a clear head for this. We're

still on the same page?"

"Yep," Grant says, motioning for a table away from the bar. I rise and throw a couple of bills on the bar next to my abandoned bottle and follow. We settle in and the waitress approaches almost immediately. We order soft drinks and burgers and the moment she walks away we revert back to our military ways.

Strategy is Grant's strong suit so he recaps how he thinks this should play out. "First, we'll go to the bar and ask around to see if we can find where Lyle lives. If we're lucky, someone will know where he's laying his head at night, and we can go straight there. Worst case, we have to wait it out and hope he shows for the third night in a row. My concern with confronting him at the bar is a brawl. We don't need that kind of heat."

Connor interrupts and says, "I think if we aren't able get a lead on where he's staying, I should hang out alone. I know what he looks like from the picture and his social media. That skull on his neck is pretty identifiable so I'm not worried. He won't know me, so there's no issue. I'll engage and see if I can get a feel for him."

"This sounds like some spy shit from a movie," I joke.

"Or, third option. We call the sheriff and let them handle this," Grant suggests.

"Nope. This is personal. After I'm done with him you can do what you want."

Nodding in agreement, we pause our conversation as the waitress appears with our burgers. Once she leaves our table, Grant clears his throat.

"Not that I don't fully trust you and know that this is all for Red and the baby, but do you want to explain to me who the fuck this prick is and why he's breaking into houses?"

Taking the mouth-watering burger in front of me as an opportunity to stall, I lift it to my mouth and take a bite. How do I explain Lyle? I'm not sure how much Henry shared with these guys about how he grew up. About the kind of people his parents are.

Grant watches me chew, patience his greatest virtue. "Lyle grew up with Wolf and me. He was kind of dick all through high school, running with a bad crowd half the time. He enlisted with us, thought it was his way of walking the straight and narrow. He didn't last long. Fast money, partying, and pushing people around were more his style than structure and service."

"Sounds like a gem."

I raise a brow to Connor in agreement. "When I saw Henry's parents at the funeral, I knew they were up to something. My best guess is they're somehow tied into this; I'm just not sure exactly how."

Without saying anything further, Grant digs into his food. The table is quiet for a few minutes, each of us deep in thought. I dip my last fry in the ketchup on my plate and pop it in my mouth just when Connor breaks the silence.

"So, Sugar—" He stops mid-sentence when I slowly turn my head to glare at him. Laughing he clears his throat, "*Taylor.* Geez, relax. Did you still have an opening for a bartender?"

"A few. You looking to relocate?"

Shrugging, he takes a drink from his glass before answering. "Maybe. There's not much for me in Fayhill." Grant scoffs and Connor laughs. "I love ya like a brother, man but I'm not staying there just for you. And I'm guessing since Taylor's on a mission to avenge Scarlett's honor, she's staying in Lexington."

I ignore his jab. "I assume you can mix a drink?"

"I do all right. Nothing a little practice won't fix."

"Job's yours if you want it," I offer.

As we finish our meals and settle the tab, the mood between us shifts. Connor excuses himself to the bathroom as we step out of the bar and into the lobby. Turning to Grant, I take a deep breath.

"Cap, I need to talk to you about something. Scarlett and Nicholas are going to be moving to Lexington. The last few weeks have changed things, and well, we're together. I know it's fast and you're probably thinking I'm a piece of shit friend to Henry but—"

"Do you love her?"

"I do."

"Then that's what matters. We've talked about this before and I want her and the baby to be happy."

Holding my hand out, I wait for him to take it. It's only a pause but enough that I question whether he's as accepting as he just stated. When he takes my hand, it's a strong grip. A lesser man would fall to his knees, but I won't be intimidated.

"You break her heart I will break your neck. Feel me?"

"Yes, sir. You're kind of scary, Cap."

Laughing, he pulls me into a hug, and when he releases me, I return his smile.

"Ready to whoop some dickhead ass?" Connor asks from behind me. Turning to face him, I look toward Grant, who nods in agreement.

Chapter 32

Taylor

The bar wasn't as bad as it looked on social media. Well, that's not completely true. It's still a shithole but fine for what it is. A dive bar with a few pool tables, more than enough beers on tap, and a slew of regulars positioned on their favorite stools at the bar. The bartender is a woman about ten years older than I am. Her top is cut low and her hair is teased high. She spots the three of us and a Cheshire cat grin slowly crosses her face.

"Well, hello there, gentlemen. What can I get for ya?"

"We're actually looking for a buddy of mine. I was supposed to meet him here last night, but didn't make it. He's about my height, shaved head, with a skull tattooed on his neck. Names Lyle."

"Oh yeah, I know who you're talking about. He's been here the last few nights. That guy loves his whiskey. Not the good stuff like I'm sure you guys would like."

I can read between the lines. Information isn't free and if I want to know more about Lyle, I'll need to drop some money. Nodding, I hold up three fingers. She turns and grabs a bottle of Pendleton from the shelf and lines up three glasses. While she's pouring, I pull a fifty from my wallet and set it on the bar. Connor coughs but the bartender smiles. Sliding the glasses across the bar to each of us, she pulls the bill from the table and puts it right in her pocket, surpassing the register.

"Thanks . . ." I say, waiting for her to provide me her name.

"Lana."

"It's a pleasure, Lana. Thanks for the drink."

"Your buddy was in here the last few nights. He's kind of an asshole once he gets a few drinks in him. Going on and on about some job he has."

Looking to Grant he gives me a brief head nod to keep Lana talking. "Do you happen to know where he's staying? Thought I'd drop in on him to catch up before we hit the town."

Squinting her eyes at me, clearly turning on her bullshit meter. I offer her the smile I use at my bar when one of the female customers is less than happy. It works just the same as it does at home because Lana motions toward the door.

"Up about two blocks there's a motel. That's where he was headed last night when I asked if he needed a ride-share."

"Thanks, Lana. You have a good night."

"You too, darlin'. Don't go gettin' yourselves arrested or anything. Y'all are a little too handsome to be wasted in a jail."

Connor turns on the charm, leaning across the bar and offering her his hand. When she takes it, he pulls it to his lips and places a kiss to the back like she's royalty. "Thanks again, Lana. Have yourself a good one."

Yeah, he's going to do just fine at Country Road. As we walk out of the bar and head the direction Lana suggested, I'm scanning the street. The last thing I want to do is encounter Lyle or the Gilberts on the street. People are milling about. Some have already been drinking by the way they're swaying. Others are loud and boisterous with their group of friends. Day has turned to night and we're well past the happy-hour crowd and quickly moving into the party scene.

The three of us don't speak until we've reached our destination. Stopping just shy of the door, I turn to my friends. "I will understand if you don't want to go in there. I'm not going to guarantee I'll keep my cool."

Instead of responding, Grant opens the door and ushers us inside. Then I realize we don't know what room he's in. This place isn't big, so I'm sure it won't be hard to find him. Like he can read my mind, Grant beelines it for the front desk. Unfortunately for us, the guy behind the counter isn't as easily swayed with compliments, but when Grant pulls a crisp hundred from his pocket the guys eyes light up, and he is happy to hand over the information.

It's a little disconcerting how easily we've managed to track Lyle down. I'd feel bad for his lack of privacy if it wasn't for the fact that he's a piece of shit. As we walk down the hallway toward room 137, I feel my phone vibrate in my pocket. Pulling it out, I pause at the picture. Scarlett is holding Nicholas in her lap with him dressed in his little footy pajamas that have fire trucks on them. The smile he wears after an epic nap is stretched across his face. The message says, "We miss you."

"What is it? Is something wrong?" Grant asks when I'm no longer following them.

Crossroads. This is another one of those crossroads my grandfather talked about. I can follow this hallway to the man who has harassed and frightened the woman I love, or I can let law enforcement handle it. Men like Lyle are weak. He'll crumble under the pressure and tell them everything and this will be over. Is that enough for me? Will handing this over to the sheriff be enough to bring peace to Scarlett?

"Cap, call the sheriff."

"What? You don't want to confront him?" Connor asks, clearly baffled.

"Oh, we're confronting him, but I'm not going to do anything other than speak to him. I have too much to lose."

"That's the good man I was talking about." Grant pulls his phone from his pocket and calls the sheriff. He's quick to tell him what we've discovered. After a few minutes, he confirms he'll contact local law enforcement. He also warned we should not do anything other than speak to Lyle.

Once he's hung up, we head toward the room. Standing before the door marked 137, I listen to the raised voices inside. We couldn't be lucky enough for the Gilberts to actually be here, could we?

With two raps on the door, I wait. The voices quiet, but the door isn't answered so I knock two more times, this time with more force. The dead bolt clicks, and the door slowly opens. Tabatha Gilbert is standing before me. She looks more like the woman I remember growing up than the version she presented at the funeral months ago. Just over her shoulder I see her husband. Acid burns in my stomach at the sight of them both.

The smell of cigarettes and cheap whiskey seeps from her pores, and it disgusts me that after all these years she hasn't changed. Not even after the death of her son could she be bothered to clean up her act.

"Taylor?" Her voice is a whisper.

"Let me in, Tabatha."

She doesn't hesitate and opens the door, stepping aside. Grant and Connor follow me into the room. Connor stays perched at the door, not allowing her to close it. Never lock yourself into a corner. Grant's reminder rings through my head as I look around the room. Discarded takeout boxes are strewn across the room. The beds are unmade and sitting at the small round table with a bottle of cheap whiskey next to him and a baggie of what I can only assume by its white powdery substance is cocaine, is my childhood friend.

"You can't just walk into my room, boy. Who do you think you are?"

I pull my attention from Lyle and direct it at Ed Gilbert. Not much taller than his wife, I have at least six inches on him and, by the way his dirty clothes hang off his body, a good fifty pounds.

"I think I'm the one about to ask the questions, Ed. Why don't you take a seat? You too, Tabatha."

Shuffling past me, Tabatha sits on one of the beds and tugs Ed to sit with her. Hands shaking, she pulls a cigarette from the pack and lifts it to her lips. I watch as she attempts to light the end, failing multiple times before giving up. I don't know if it's fear that has her shaking or something related to the drugs, but regardless, it's clear that Tabatha Gilbert is not a well woman. I look at Grant who nods his head, stepping to the side but closer to the bed. If these two make a play for me, he'll stop them. Although, I don't think it will take much from the looks of them. My concern is with Lyle and the drugs.

Leaning back in his chair, arms crossed over his chest, he clucks his tongue. "Well, well. If it isn't the golden boy. What's going on, Cain? Still a fucking altar boy?"

"Lyle. I see you haven't changed much."

"What's there to change? I'm living the dream, man."

Scoffing, I glance back to the Gilberts. Ed is staring at me, disgust all over his face.

"Oh yeah? What dream is that? A third strike waiting to happen?"

"Fuck you."

"Look. I don't have a lot of time, so I'm going to cut to the chase," I say as I rotate my shoulders back.

I'm trying hard not to kill this bastard, but I need to not only stall but also get what I came for. Turning my head to Connor, I see he's holding his cell phone in his hands with it pointed in my direction. Stepping to the side a little so he has a direct shot of Lyle and me before I get to the reason we're here.

"What were you after in Scarlett's house?"

"Don't know what you're talking about." He doesn't move his eyes from me. His arrogance never faltering.

"Cut the shit, Lyle. I know it was you. What did you want?"

He doesn't get an opportunity to answer because Ed speaks first.

"That is my son's house. That little skank doesn't deserve any of it."

His words hit me hard, and I swing my body around to face him. I see nothing but red and my hands flex at the thought of hitting this man. As I take a step forward, I hear Grant speak.

"Sugar." It's one word but stops me in my tracks. A warning and reminder all at once.

"Do. Not. Speak. Of. Her. Like. That," I grit out between clenched teeth.

"Oh, are you fucking her? She really is a skank like I said. Was my boy even in the ground before you took that from him too?"

I lunge for him, but Grant holds me back. "Let me go, Grant. I will kill the motherfucker."

"Ed, please stop this. Taylor, we just needed some money, and we know she has it. I loved my son. He was a good boy, and he would have wanted us to have something." Her voice is weak as tears fill her eyes. I relax at the sight. She's a broken woman, consumed by a life she'll never get out of.

"Why would you think you're entitled? You were never there for Henry from the time we were kids, and you think he'd leave you anything?"

She opens her mouth to speak, but I raise my hand to stop her. She complies, and her eyes divert to her lap once again.

"Tell me why the break-in and the calls? Were those necessary? You say you loved Henry, but did you love *his* son? You frightened her and sent her into early labor. Something could have happened to her or the baby. Did you think of that or were you too fucking selfish to think of anyone but yourself and your next fix?"

Tears stream down her face, and she begins shaking saying, "I'm sorry" over and over. Too little, too late. I return my attention to Lyle.

"And you? What's your fucking reason?"

Shrugging, he pours some of the white powder from

the baggie then says, "It was a job. Besides you and Wolf always thought you were better than me. I thought if there was a chance to prove you were both just as fucked up, I'd take it. Unfortunately for me, that chick was pregnant. I bet we could have had some fun. She's probably a wildcat in the sack."

That's it, I can't refrain myself and make it to him in two strides. I grab him by his neck and lift him from the chair, slamming him into the wall. His arm rises and he gets in one hit but instead of hurting, it only fuels the volcano inside me. My grip increases and his eyes widen.

"Do not ever speak of her again, or I will fucking end you, do you hear me?" My voice is calm, which should scare him. I could end him right now and not miss a wink of sleep. "Nod once for yes." He nods and I release him, his body folding into itself as he lands in a heap on the floor, gasping for air.

"You're all done," I say as I look at all three of them. Tabatha is sobbing, her eyes never leaving the ground. Ed only stares at me, likely wishing he was bigger, faster, and twenty years younger so he could kick my ass. "Do you hear me? No more calls. No more attempts to steal from Scarlett. You will leave them alone."

I take their silence as confirmation and turn to walk out the door. The soft sound of Tabatha's voice stops me. "How's the baby? My grandson. Is he okay?"

Looking over my shoulder, I reply, "None of your fucking business."

As we walk silently out of the room and down the hall, we pass two uniformed police officers and know exactly where they're headed. It may take a while to work through the facts that brought us here, but I know those three won't bother us again. When we step out into the lobby, I turn to

Connor.

"Got that?"

"Yep. I managed to stop before your little venture into assault land. Didn't need you getting arrested while we were here."

Laughing, I shake my head and follow him out of the building.

Chapter 33

Scarlett

A single text from Taylor letting me know he wasn't arrested but it was going to be a long night with the police is the only response to the dozen text messages and calls I've made to him. My nerves were shot most of the night while I waited to hear from him. Addy, her son, Mason, and boyfriend, Landon, were amazing and tried to keep me distracted through dinner and an intense game of Uno. When it was clear I wasn't the best company, they reluctantly left, and I spent a little one-on-one time with Nicholas.

He's currently lying next to me on the bed, squirming around like one does in the middle of the night when you're an infant and have next to no cares in the world. I, on the other hand, have nothing but cares and worries. I also know I need to get as much sleep as I can, so I pick him up and nestle him into my chest before walking around the room humming a lullaby until he calms and is asleep.

Once he's settled into his bassinet, I snuggle into the bed. When I can't get comfortable, I switch my pillow for

Taylor's and let his scent welcome me to sleep.

Stretching my arms over my head, I wiggle my toes and then fly up into a sitting position. Nicholas is wide-eyed and chattering to himself in the bassinet. The clock shows we just slept a solid three hours. Bright sunlight fills the room, and while it was only three hours, I slept hard and actually feel rested. Standing, I take the opportunity of his one-man conversation to handle my morning business in the bathroom before coming back into the room.

Scooping him into my arms, I grab my phone from the nightstand and light the screen to see if I missed a call or message from Taylor. When there are no new messages, I shift Nicholas in my arms before making my way to the living room and place him in his little chair. Kissing his head, I inhale his baby scent. I know the day will come that he smells of socks and testosterone. It's a long way off but the way Addy teased Mason last night, I'm going to dread the day.

Pulling up Taylor's name on my phone, I quickly press his number. When his voicemail picks up without a single ring, I don't leave a message. There's no point in leaving another message asking him to call me back. Instead, I plug the phone into the charger and attach it to the Bluetooth speaker in the kitchen. Once I'm connected, I cue up one of my favorite playlists and grind the decaffeinated coffee beans before setting the pot to brew.

I go about my new morning routine of starting a load of laundry and replenishing my diaper changing basket as needed. By the time Nicholas begins to whine that he's ready for breakfast, I'm ready to settle in with my glass of water and flip on the early morning news. Something I've learned since being in Lexington. Local news is sparse, not as sparse as Fayhill but close, and they really like their sports. The sports commentary is at least fifty percent of the show.

I think Nick likes the sounds of the morning show hosts because he nurses the fastest in the morning. Either that or he hates them and wants this feeding over quickly so I can change the channel. He gets his wish because as soon as he's done, I flip the television off and turn up my playlist. Now that he's fed and I've had a glass of water, I pour myself a cup of coffee and add a splash of creamer before pulling eggs and veggies from the fridge.

Turning up the music on the speaker, I sway my hips from side to side and sing along to the music as I chop and sauté. Lost in my own thoughts, I don't hear Taylor walk in the house. The moment I feel his hands wrap around my waist, I scream and kick him in the shins. My scream startles Nicholas, and he begins wailing. Taylor yelps and jumps back. Pivoting, I spin to see him rubbing his shin and let out a sigh of relief.

Leaving him in the kitchen, I rush to Nicholas and scoop him up. Holding him to my chest, I rock back and forth as he calms down. His wails turning to whimpers before he fully relaxes. I rush back to the stove and turn off the burners before turning my attention to my would-be assailant.

"You scared the shit out of me."

"I called your name twice. I assumed you heard me. Damn, girl, you've got one hell of a kick on you."

Proud, I smile and stand a little taller. Taylor strides up to me, capturing my lips with his. After a deep but too quick kiss, he pulls back and says, "I missed you." Then, before I can process what he said, he's taking Nicholas from my arms and kissing the top of his head and curling him into the crook of his neck. "Missed you too, buddy."

And I'm a goner. Seeing him with my son, holding him close to his heart with his eyes closed absorbing all the feelings of holding a precious baby in his arms triggers something in me. If I wasn't already one hundred percent in love with this man already, I would fall at his feet and beg him to let me love him.

"I'm going to put him down. Then we can talk, okay?"

"Yeah."

I give up on my attempt at a healthy breakfast and push the skillet aside before pulling a cup from the cupboard and filling it for Taylor. When he returns from the bedroom, he's changed into a pair of athletic shorts and a tank top. I hand him his cup of coffee, but he sets it on the counter and pulls me to him. Wrapping his arms around me, he envelops me into a hug of epic proportions. I hold on to him with all that I have, hoping to absolve some of his worries and stress. After a few minutes, he pulls back and brushes the hair from my face before kissing my forehead.

"God, I missed you. Thanks for the coffee, but do you think we can go lie down? I'm fucking exhausted, and I just want to hold you."

"Of course."

I let him lead me down the hall to the bedroom and we climb into bed. I scoot over to meet him in the middle, my head resting on my hands. He lifts up and pulls the sheet over us before settling his hand on my hip.

"I'm sorry I didn't call. It all seemed to happen quickly for us, but once the cops got there, everything slowed to a snail's pace. How about the quick version before a nap?"

Nodding, I stay quiet while he begins his story. To say I'm in shock would be an understatement. I believed with all my heart that Henry's parents were equally hurt and devastated by his death. I would never have believed they were faking their sadness in an effort to get money from me. To steal from their grandson. And this Lyle person . . . the idea of him being in my home and touching my things, it makes me sick.

"What happens now?" I ask.

"Connor turned over the video and the detective said he thought it was pretty cut and dry. Of course, it's up to the prosecutor. Worst case, they'll all get charged with the drugs. The Gilberts may get a slap on the wrist but Lyle had a laundry list of parole violations, so I don't think we have to worry about him anymore."

"Will there be a court hearing? Am I going to have to testify or anything?"

"I don't know. If you do, we'll all be there with you."

And just like that, it's all over. Or, just beginning. I suppose it's how you look at it all. As I lie here and look at the man staring back at me, I see the blue chips of promise and happiness in his eyes. A slow smile appears on his face, and he tugs me closer to him.

"What are you thinking?"

Placing my lips on his, I hum before wrapping my arms around him, crawling into his space so we're as close as possible. "I was thinking about beginnings. Thank you for doing this. For protecting us and saving me."

"You don't have to thank me. You're my family. I love you."

"Promise?"

"Promise.

Epilogue

Scarlett

Six weeks later . . .

Addison Sinclair does not listen to instructions. One request is all I had. No party games. Yet, here we sit in a circle watching her draw something on an easel of paper shouting out baby terms like our lives depend on it. Connor keeps shouting the word "binky" for everything drawn in Baby Pictionary and has yet to be right. He says it's the only baby thing he knows, and eventually he'll have the right answer.

"Why did we let her talk us into this?" Taylor asks as he leans in, Nicholas strapped to his chest in a baby carrier.

"Because we love your sister and she wanted to throw us a party."

"She called it a 'Sip and See.' Everyone has sipped all of our beer and have seen Nick. They can go now."

Laughing, I kiss my love then turn my attention back to the drawing. Everyone has quieted and when I see the picture I know why. It may not be an eggplant but that's exactly what it looks like. Then the buzzer sounds, and Addy hangs her head in defeat. Landon rushes to her rescue and whispers in her ear. When she mumbles something back, he barks out a laugh and turns to the crowd.

"It's a baby monitor. And, on that note I'm calling this game a draw—literally."

A chorus of laughter breaks out and Addy turns three shades of red before accepting the glass of wine Minnie hands her. I'm still blown away by how all of Taylor's friends have so easily accepted me into their group. Vera, Mercy, and Shane drove in from Fayhill I was thrilled to see them. I knew Mercy had worked for Taylor when she lived here, but it didn't register that she had also worked with Ashton. I was very surprised when I learned that Mercy was also acquainted with Ashton's fiancé, Jameson. That's a little triangle I quickly excused myself from. But I needn't worry because all three laughed it off, and Jameson thanked Mercy for pushing him and Ashton together in the first place.

Grant walks up to us with a beer in his hand and his eyes on my baby boy. When he pauses and rubs his hand over his little bald head, I take the opportunity to ask him a question I've been holding on to until the right time.

I slip my hand into Taylor's and squeeze as a request for him to do the actual asking.

"Grant, we wanted to ask if you would be Nick's godfather."

He looks at my son and then to us. Looking from Taylor and then to me, he says, "Are you sure, Red?"

"Positive. He has a daddy in heaven and a daddy in life," I pause to look at the man who will raise my son and back to Grant. "But he also needs a godfather."

"I would be honored."

Grant shakes Taylor's hand and then scoops me into a hug. He places a kiss on my cheek and whispers in my ear, "I'm happy for you, honey. Thank you for this gift."

Wiping the tears from my eyes, I smile. "This means you'll have to visit Lexington. With Connor moving here and working at Country Road you don't want him homing in on your uncle time."

"I was thinking about that," he says before taking a drink from his beer. "Know any realtors? It may be time for me to put down some roots."

"As a matter of fact, I do." Taylor looks around the yard and when he sees who he's looking for he says, "Hey, Dakota. Can you come here a minute?"

Dakota smiles and waves before finishing her conversation and walking across the lawn toward us. I watch as Grant follows her with his eyes. When she walks up to our small group, she smiles at us all.

"What's up?"

"Dakota Jennings, this is our good friend and Nick's godfather, Grant Ellison. Grant, Dakota." Grant offers Dakota his hand and she takes it saying hello. He's slow to release her hand which makes me smile.

"Grant is considering moving to Lexington and is looking for a realtor."

Eyes wide, Dakota turns her attention to Grant and smiles wider before reaching into her back pocket. When she pulls a small business card from the denim, she holds it up for him to take.

Laughing Grant says, "Wow, what else do you have in those pockets?"

"There may be a cookie or hair tie. You never really know."

"Ahh, beauty and wit. Tell me, are you always this prepared for prospective clients?"

"What? Oh! No, my sister just gave that to me. She designed it and brought it to me for approval. I actually just got my license, so you'd be my first."

Taylor and I look from Grant to Dakota and back as they banter. She's smiling a lot, and his hands aren't resting on his hips in the stance I'm used to.

"Well, I've never bought one, so you'd be my first too."

"We are still talking about houses, right guys?" Taylor asks but neither of them look away from the other as they say "yep" in unison.

I scrunch my eyes and look at Taylor, who is looking at Grant like he has two heads. We excuse ourselves and walk away, leaving the new realtor with her first-time client before we both break out in to hysterics.

"Was Grant just flirting?" I ask between gasps for air.

"I think he was."

By the time we compose ourselves, I have a side cramp and am bent over taking deep breaths. That's when I glance up to see Taylor eye-level with me. On one knee. Nicholas is still strapped to his front, but now a piece of paper is attached to the fabric of the baby carrier and reads: WILL YOU MARRY THIS GUY? With little arrows pointing up from the sides of the paper.

Gasping, I quickly stand, my hand covering my mouth as I look down at Taylor. A small velvet box is in his hand, and I couldn't stop the tears if I wanted.

"Scarlett Gilbert, you are the best gift I never knew I

wanted or deserved. Let's make this family official. Will you marry me?"

"Yes!" It's one word with so much meaning as I thrust my shaking hand toward him. Standing, he places the ring on my finger, and I step into his space, but before I kiss him, I look at my sweet boy and his gummy and slobbery grin. That's as good a blessing as I'm going to get, so I look up at my fiancé and smile.

Leaning down, he kisses me softly and public appropriate before whispering on my lips, "I love you."

A smile, the huge and toothy kind that only the happiest of women share, crosses my face. Tilting my head, I reach up, my hand cupping his cheek. "Why the 'this guy' part of the note?

"I love you and I love him. You are my family, but we've never talked about who I would be to him."

"You're his daddy. Henry is his father and will always be a part of who he is. We'll never keep him out of his life, but at the end of the day, you're the man who will sit up with him when he's running a fever, teach him to ride a bike, and have the important talks with him as he grows up. You are the one who will teach him to be a good man and what it means to have integrity and respect."

His eyes gloss over with tears as he leans down and places a soft kiss to my lips.

"You amaze me, Scarlett soon-to-be Cain. Thank you. We may have to discuss this fever thing, but I'm all in with the daddy part. Maybe we can talk about giving Nick a little sister."

"Whoa there, fella. Don't you know the saying 'first comes love then comes marriage'? We can pause the song right there. Besides, I'd love to get my ass back to how it was before this guy."

"I love this ass," he says as he lightly taps my butt with his hand, "and I love you."

"Promise?"

"Promise."

Acknowledgments

To say that this book challenged me would be an understatement. As authors, many of us share our goals to push our limits and step outside our comfort zone in our writing. This book is me doing just that. The phrase "blood, sweat, and tears" was my reality in writing this book and while it exhausted me, I am also very proud of every single word on these pages.

I'm a fairly open and transparent person (sorry Mr. J) and have been honest about my emotional struggles over the last few months. What I may not have fully expressed was how much of this book was written during a depression. I always say writing is my solace. My therapy. That was never more so than with *Promise Her.* There is so much stigma around depression and anxiety but what helps me through my journey is talking about it. So, here I am saying, *I wrote a book that pushed my writing and my emotional storytelling to new heights all while I struggled each day to find my personal bliss.*

This book would be sitting in draft 7 if not for the amazing people I surround myself with. I will forget someone here in this section because honestly, the list is too long. So, thank you for the messages, the cards, the texts, and the calls. The lunch dates and the hugs. Each one came at a moment it was needed and I thank you.

A heartfelt and special thank you to the men and women who serve our country *and* their families. Your sacrifice and commitment does not receive enough credit. Thank you for selflessly fighting for our freedoms.

Alyssa Garcia. I say it with each book but thank you. Thank you for being my cheerleader and my friend. Thank you for knowing me well enough to read between my awful visions for a book. I always know what I don't want, it's the what I do that's the mess. Your ability to take that mess and make it beautiful is a gift.

Karen L. – This is me sending you the biggest virtual hug. Your patience with me and this book is more than I deserve. Thank you for taking me on, making me a better writer, and for tolerating my misuse of the comma.

Megan – Team work really does make the dream work. I could not take this journey with out you. I am in awe of your drive and commitment to helping me find success. I will never be able to thank you enough.

Suzie – Just starting this makes me cry. I adore you and am so incredibly grateful for your support and friendship. Thank you for taking time out of your vacation (I'm still mad you did that) to help me with this synopsis. You are a true blessing and I wish I could hug you every day.

Andee, Chelle, Jennifer, and Kiersten – There would be no book without each of you. Thank you for your honesty, support, kicks in the ass, and friendship. I appreciate you all for your notes, texts, voice messages, and real talk when it comes to my writing.

Lynsey and Marisol – Thank you for taking the time to help me polish this book and make it ready for the world. Your friendship and willingness to pause life to help me polish this book means the world to me.

Debbie and Shannon – You are such an asset to the team! Thank you both for all you do!

Fiona, Karin, Becca, Kate, Lo, Kimberly, Adriane, Jodie, Hollis, Hazel, and Kathryn (yes, I searched all my PMs) thank you for the messages and check-ins. You'll never know how timely and perfect each message was. Thank you for your friendship, for making me laugh, and always knowing that sometimes I need to be reminded of the big picture and to love myself.

Bloggers and bookstagrammers – Thank you for supporting Indie authors. This life is hard some days but your support means the world.

Readers – You all inspire and challenge me. Thank you for loving a series about a bunch of friends who fall in love and the mysterious bartender who serves them. Without your fierce love of these characters, this book would not exist. Yes, Kathy, we know – you love Taylor.

To my husband – I took the extra time. I'll never admit it may have been what I needed but ya know … Thank you for loving me for 22 years and counting.

To my sons (and daughter in law to be) – Find your passion, fill your world with people who love you, and chase your dreams. Skies the limit!

About the Author

Andrea Johnston spent her childhood with her nose in a book and a pen to paper. An avid people watcher, her mind is full of stories that yearn to be told. A fan of angsty romance with a happy ending, super sexy erotica and a good mystery, Andrea can always be found with her Kindle nearby fully charged.

Andrea lives in Idaho with her family and two dogs. When she isn't spending time with her partner in crime aka her husband, she can be found binge watching all things Bravo and enjoying a cocktail. Nothing makes her happier than the laughter of her children, a good book, her feet in the water, and cocktail in hand all at the same time.

Connect with Andrea:

Facebook
http://bit.ly/AndreaJFB

Twitter
@AndreaJ1313

Instagram
@ Andrea_Johnston15

Or e-mail her at andreajohnstonauthor@gmail.com

Join Andrea's reader group – Andrea Johnston's Sassy Romantics
http://bit.ly/AJsSassy

Other books by Andrea Johnston

Country Road Series

Whiskey & Honey

Tequila & Tailgates

Martinis & Moonlight

Champagne & Forever

Bourbon & Bonfires

Standalones

Life Rewritten

The Break Series

I Don't: A Romantic Comedy

Small-Town Heart

Collaborations

Switch Stance

Ear Candy

Made in the USA
Columbia, SC
25 January 2020